EPIPHANY

EPIPHANY

(A FATHER JAKE AUSTIN MYSTERY)

by John A. Vanek

KENMORE, WA

A Coffeetown Press book published by Epicenter Press

Epicenter Press
6524 NE 181st St.
Suite 2
Kenmore, WA 98028.

For more information go to:
www.coffeetownpress.com
www.Camelpress.com
www.Epicenterpress.com

Author website: www.JohnVanekAuthor.com

ISBN: 9781684921195 (trade paper)
ISBN: 9781684921201 (ebook)

LOC: 2023936025

Printed in the United States of America

For the many fine authors who have guided me on my writing journey, and for friends, family, and the readers who have supported me throughout.

ACKNOWLEDGMENTS

It takes a village to write a book—or in my case, a small city. I am extremely grateful to my wife, Geni, for her advice and patience, and to Jessica & Randy Dublikar, Jen & Matt Vanek, Father Thomas Winkel, Sterling Watson, Laura Lippman, Les Standiford, Michael Koryta, and Dennis Lehane for their help and encouragement. Special thanks to Abe Spevack, Susan Adger, Barbara Schrefer, Sue Peck, and Richard Erlanger for their brutally honest critiques over the years. I am grateful for input and support from Marie Thomas, Kathy Kelly, Steve McCutchan, Guillermo Marquez-Sterling, Patti & Ron Poporad, Linda & Al Vanek, JoAnn & Jim Gavacs, Kathy & Emil Poporad, Mary Winter, the Pinellas Writers, and the Oberlin Heritage Center. I wish to thank Jennifer McCord and Phil Garrett at Coffeetown Press for guiding me through the morass of the publishing world. I also want to express my gratitude to all of the readers who have supported the first four novels in the series (*DEROS, Miracles, Absolution*, and *Bedeviled*) by recommending them to friends and posting kind reviews online.

The characters, settings, and all of the events in this mystery are fictional and the product of the author's imagination. If you enjoy the Father Jake Austin Mystery Series, please tell your friends. Word of mouth is the lifeblood of independent presses and their authors.

CHAPTER ONE

Easter Sunday, April 20, 2003, 2:00 p.m.

Spring had arrived in Ohio like a blessing after a long, harsh winter. On an unusually warm Easter Sunday, like many families we had gathered after church services for food and fellowship. Colleen, bless her Irish heart, had prepared a feast of baked ham with a brown-sugar glaze, panko-crusted green bean casserole, and then launched us into a food coma with her homemade soda bread pudding topped with whiskey caramel sauce and whipped cream.

The house smelled like heaven. I topped off the pinot noir in Emily and Colleen's glasses as they chatted in the kitchen. Emily's father, Irv, snored away in my recliner, rumbling like a freight train climbing a steep hill, completely oblivious to the local news show on the television.

I offered to help the ladies with the dishes, but Colleen mumbled something in Gaelic and shooed me out of the kitchen. My five-year-old nephew, RJ, was building a Lego skyscraper on the living room floor, so I joined him. It had only been about a year since I had assumed guardianship of RJ after my sister's death, but he had already become the bright light in my sometimes dreary world.

When my middle-aged body began to protest crawling on my hands and knees with RJ, I stood, muted the TV, and turned on the CD player softly. The room filled with golden oldies as my eyelids struggled against the relentless postprandial pull of gravity.

We could almost have passed for a Norman Rockwell family, *almost*—except we were in the Sacred Heart Church rectory and I was a Catholic priest. Emily was my best friend, and Colleen was my housekeeper, RJ's nanny, and my all-around Girl Friday. Our blended family was not exactly typical, but a family nonetheless. Unconventional yes, and not what most folks would consider normal, but how many families are truly *normal*?

Our symbiotic need for each other had super-glued us all together. For better or worse, most folks were stuck with the family they were born into. I was fortunate enough to have selected mine. God indeed worked in mysterious ways I would never understand, but I was grateful to be a part of this eclectic, ragtag crew. They were my *chosen* family.

Emily tapped her way over, folded up her red-and-white cane, and sat next to me on the couch. She and her father both had hereditary blindness. They managed the snack shop at St. Joseph's Hospital on behalf of the Society for the Blind and lived rent-free in the adjacent dormitories in return for serving as mentors and advisors to the interns and residents in training. The hospital offered them a safe and secure home as well as an income, and they had rebuilt their lives there after the loss of their vision.

She wore a floral dress belted at the waist with the small teardrop sapphire pendant necklace I had purchased for her by mowing lawns and shoveling snow when we were in high school. It brought out the bottomless blue of Emily's eyes—eyes that had once-upon-a-time left me breathless, and still did if I let my guard down.

"Mass was wonderful this morning, Jake." When she tilted her head, her short auburn hair caressed the side of her face. For an instant, I was back in high school again, that old longing for her a dull ache in the pit of my stomach. She lit up a smile. "Colleen told me the Easter lilies around the altar were gorgeous, and I loved their sweet fragrance. And what a turnout! You outdid yourself today."

"Thanks, Em. A lot of preparation went into it. Celebrating our Lord's resurrection is the high point of the church calendar. It's a bit like the Super Bowl for a priest."

"Super Bowl, huh? Your sermon did seem like a Hail Mary pass, or was it an end-run? Warning the congregation not to be judgmental was … what's the right word? Intriguing? Thought provoking? The Catholic Church does have a history of, shall we say, *inflexibility* on certain topics such as contraception, divorce, and the LGBT community." She gave me a conspiratorial wink. "If I didn't know better, Father, it almost sounded as if you were encouraging tolerance toward such things."

"You're not wrong, Em, but don't tell my bishop. I'll let God judge. I'm here to serve. Besides, Easter is about new beginnings."

"Like women in the priesthood?" She lobbed a wry grin at me. "Or married priests?"

I volleyed with a laugh. "From your lips to God's ears. I'm obliged to follow the church edicts, but that doesn't mean I agree with all of them."

Emily filled me in on the latest gossip from the hospital where I also worked. I had been a physician before entering the seminary, and the Church allowed me to work there part-time, caring for the indigent and infirm. We were happily cocooned in light conversation when Sheriff Tremont Macon appeared on the television screen.

"Wait Em." I turned up the volume. "They're interviewing Tree on the news."

Tree Macon was the only member of our blended family not present at supper. Emily and I had attended high school with him and we'd remained close friends.

Tree stood on the runway at the county airport, the afternoon sunlight glistening on his shaved scalp. He adjusted the microphone and looked directly into the camera. His expression hardened. "Since the recent confrontation at the airport, we have arrested twelve more individuals involved with the local human trafficking ring." Photographs of a dozen people, men and women, filled the screen. "I'm happy to announce that their organization is now out of business."

Tree began to relate the details of the investigation and subsequent arrests, but I turned off the TV. Emily and I didn't need to hear any more. We had both been involved in the case and didn't want to relive one moment of it.

Since returning to town, I had faced more than my fair share of chaos and danger. Death threats from a gangster had compelled me to install a security alarm system at the rectory for our protection. While helping Tree with the human trafficking case, I'd also been involved in a serious car crash that had nearly cost me my spleen. I wanted nothing more than to resume my mundane parish duties in peace.

Lost in our own thoughts, we sat in a comfortable silence that old friends earn over time. After a few minutes, Emily turned to me. "Well, that explains why Tree couldn't join us for supper today. He works harder than anyone I know. I don't think the big guy even has an *off button*."

Emily often referred to the two most important people in my life as the big guy and the little guy—the Sheriff and my nephew.

"True. If you were to look up 'civil servant' in the dictionary, you'd probably find Tree's photograph there. His boss wanted him to go on the tube and put a happy spin on the whole sordid affair."

"Let's hope the folks in the county appreciate him." Emily took a sip of wine, then frowned. "I hate to ask, Jake, but Dad and I could use your help."

"Sure. What's going on?"

"Don't laugh. I know you're the Sultan of Skepticism, but we think the hospital snack shop may be … haunted."

I tried not to, but chuckled anyway. She punched me gently on the arm.

"Sorry, Em, it's just that I grew up hearing scary stories about ghosts at St. Joe's. It's been around for over a hundred years and thousands of patients have died there. Bump-in-the-night tales are inevitable. Strange sounds and patient moans, yes. But ghosts, not likely. Darkened hospital hallways are inherently spooky, as I'm reminded every time I work there after midnight."

"How about in a well-lit snack shop on sunny afternoons?" She shook her head. "I'm serious. Dad and I have been having … serious problems. And we're not the only ones affected. Some of our customers have complained too. Four years ago, paranormal researchers found evidence of unnatural events in the obstetrical unit, but the administration buried their report under a pile of promises and red tape."

"Paranormal investigation isn't exactly a legitimate science, Em."

"Well, whatever's been happening in the snack shop is creepy as hell and definitely unnatural. Dad and I are freaked out."

I hesitated.

"Come on, Jake, you know me. We sherlocked together on the bleeding Virgin Mary statue investigation, and I helped Tree with the human trafficking case. I'm no flake!"

"Okay, okay. So tell me what's been going on."

"It's weird. Things'll be fine for months at a time, then suddenly for no reason I'm overwhelmed with waves of fear and dizziness. The room feels as if it's spinning. When it happens, Dad gets the same symptoms. This started several years ago. Problem is, these occurrences are random and unpredictable. Nothing happened over the past six months, so Dad and I thought that was the end of it. But at shift change yesterday, it hit us both again. I was so anxious I could barely breathe, and so lightheaded I nearly passed out."

I reverted to my medical training. "Did your heartbeat become fast or irregular?"

She considered this. "No, not that I noticed."

What she had described sounded similar to mass hysteria, but I continued my line of questioning. "Now don't get mad, Em, but I have to ask. Have you seen an ENT doctor? This could be an inner ear problem."

The wattage behind her eyes amped up, and their usual gentle blue glow burst into flame. "In *both of us* at the same time? Damn it, Jake, this doesn't happen to me anywhere else in the hospital. Dad and I are at our wit's end. If we didn't love working at the snack shop, we'd quit!"

"Sorry, Em, I hear you. How can I help?"

"We need to get to the bottom of this, but the hospital administration's not taking our complaints seriously. They might listen to you. Next time it occurs, I'll call and you can see for yourself."

The whole story sounded like a Halloween prank or an April Fools' joke, completely out of place on Easter. I wanted to scoff, but I read pleading in her eyes.

"Sure, Em. Call me any time and I'll come over."

CHAPTER TWO

Monday, April 21, 9:00 a.m.

In what had become our usual routine, I got RJ dressed in jeans and his favorite GI Joe t-shirt, then hurried from the rectory to offer morning Mass, while Colleen fed him breakfast and drove him to preschool. Sacred Heart Church had a small but devoted group of parishioners who regularly attended morning services, and I gave them my full attention.

After Mass, I removed my vestments in the sacristy, put on slacks and a shirt and tie, and stepped into a pleasant spring morning. The eastern sky glowed crimson and the sun poured down liquid honey, a welcome benediction after a brutal winter. Typical Ohio weather—from one extreme to the other. The week prior we'd had snow flurries; this week, a heat wave.

When I arrived at St. Joseph's Hospital for my shift, I slipped on a white coat and draped a stethoscope around my neck. Several times per week, I morphed like some comic book character from a mild-mannered priest into Captain Healthcare, a hard-charging healer fighting disease. Such was my life.

I was a member of the Order of St. Camillus and had taken a fourth vow to care for the sick, in addition to my priestly vows of poverty, chastity, and obedience. Having been an internist before entering the seminary, I was a perfect fit for the Camillians. Back in the 16th century, our founder, St. Camillus, had encouraged his followers to love the sick as deeply and unconditionally as a mother loves her ailing child. That's what I tried to do every day.

St. Joseph's Hospital was located in the inner city and treated the majority of the county's poor. When I walked into Urgent Care for my shift, the waiting room was filled to capacity. I was greeted by sour expressions, coughing and sneezing, bloody bandages, and screaming children—a typical day at the office. Fortunately, a competent resident had been assigned to assist me.

We worked our way through the backlog, but all afternoon patients poured in. By the end of my shift, we had completely emptied the waiting room and I was finishing the chart on my last patient when my cellphone chimed. The 414 area code appeared on the screen: Milwaukee. I knew the phone number well: Demarco.

"Jacob, my son, do you have a moment to talk?"

I always had a moment for the Very Reverend Father Stefano Demarco. He was the Superior General of my Camillian Order and had recently promoted me to be his personal consultant and troubleshooter.

"Of course. What can I do for you?"

"I just read the report of your involvement in the human trafficking case. I didn't realize you'd been injured. You're in my prayers. How're you feeling?"

"Much better, thanks. Nearly healed. In fact, this is my first day back at the hospital."

"Glad to hear it." Demarco paused. "When we last spoke, I told you about the possible theft of funds at a church west of New Orleans. Since then, I've made some inquiries and things are worse than I'd suspected. The priest under suspicion is a member of our order, and the local bishop has accused him of being either incompetent or a crook. I need you to fly down and investigate. How soon can you travel?"

"My doctor's asked me to take it easy for at least one more week. Reduced hours, no physical labor, lots of rest."

"That will work. I'll have my secretary call you and set a travel date. He can buy your plane ticket and arrange your accommodations."

"I'm only working part-time at the hospital now, so getting coverage when I'm out of town isn't a major issue, but there is one other problem. Bishop Lucci still hasn't assigned an associate pastor at Sacred Heart. I can't leave the church uncovered while I'm in Louisiana."

"Lucci's dragging his feet, is he? I instructed him to appoint someone, but he can at times be … difficult. His Excellency is quick to ask for my help with the Vatican when he needs something, however, so let not your heart be troubled. Rest assured, he'll be my next call and you *will* have an assistant this week!" He scoffed. "Lucci and I have … a clear understanding of our roles. I must be going now, Jacob, but my secretary will be in touch. Go with God, my son."

It was my first assignment for Demarco as his investigator. Both excited and somewhat apprehensive, I dropped off my white coat and stethoscope at my locker in the doctor's lounge and headed for my car. I was looking forward to spending time with my nephew at the rectory when Emily called.

"Jake, the haunting! It's happening again." The fear in her voice gave me chills. "Can you come to the snack shop now?"

"On my way."

CHAPTER THREE

Monday, April 21, 5:15 p.m.

As I hurried to the snack shop, I passed a plaque in the hallway honoring Father Bihn who founded St. Joseph's Hospital in 1892 to care for sick children. The snack shop was located in the oldest part of the building. The remainder of the structure, including Urgent Care, had been erected much later.

I raced out of an emergency exit into blistering heat and sunshine that felt more like midsummer than spring, then crossed the large courtyard. Tulips, crocuses, and daffodils were poking their heads up. The air was filled with birdsong and the aroma of newly mowed lawn, and the trees were budding. The courtyard was a pleasant oasis at our inner city hospital where Emily and I often spent our free time, but I was on a mission and couldn't stop to admire God's magnificent handiwork.

When I entered the snack shop, Emily's father was standing behind the counter drumming his fingers impatiently, head down. The years had not been kind to Irv Beale. He was hunched over, balding, and wore sunglasses because his eyes had become sensitive to light after the loss of his vision. Emily was pacing on the far side of the room.

"What's going on?" I asked.

Emily tapped her cane over to me and, to my surprise, gave me a hug. "Thank God you're here, Jake. I was afraid it would stop before you arrived. Do you feel it?"

The room was warm, and an oscillating fan hummed away in the corner stirring the sultry air, but otherwise I sensed nothing.

"Sorry, Em. I don't feel anything unusual."

Her expression cratered and she plopped down onto a chair near the window. "Then I guess Dad and I must *both* be crazy."

Irv Beale removed his sunglasses, revealing his rheumy eyes. "Then do you hear or *see* anything, Jake?" He tapped the sunglasses and added sarcastically, "Our vision's not so good, you know. Emily thought she might have heard the voices of two young boys."

There were no customers in the room. Sunlight from the window electrified the highlights in Emily's auburn hair and cast a yellow-orange rhombus onto the tile floor, warming the room. Nothing seemed abnormal or out of place.

"No, I don't see or hear a thing. Sorry. What boys?"

They sighed in unison. Irv buried his face in his hands.

"Talk to me, Em. What happened here?"

"I had the daytime shift and everything was routine. The morning was busy but the afternoon slowed down, so I was reading." She tapped the cover of a Julia Spencer-Fleming novel in braille. "About an hour ago, I heard a rustling sound near the counter and kids whispering. I called out, but no one answered. I didn't think much of it since children occasionally sneak in and swipe a candy bar. No big deal, just part of the cost of doing business when you're blind." She drew a deep breath. "Then I began to feel dizzy, a little sick to my stomach, and an eerie sensation washed over me. A sense of foreboding … of overwhelming dread. It's hard to describe."

Irv walked over. "Emily called, told me what had happened, and asked me to relieve her early. We were going through our usual shift change routine when the same damn thing happened to me. First, the dizzy-woozys hit me. Queasy and shaky, you know, like I was punch-drunk. Then I got real anxious, as if somethin' awful was happening."

Emily ran a hand down her face and frowned. "It was déjà vu, Jake, an exact replay of what happened to Dad and me on and off all last summer. Wooziness, then fear and dread and confusion, accompanied by a tightness in the chest. We hadn't been bothered for months and assumed that was the end of it, but…."

Irv sat at the table next to her. "I think it's the ghosts of those two kids, the six-year-old boys who drowned at the docks in the 1920s. The night janitor has spotted them in the hospital halls a bunch of times, but whenever he gets near them, they disappear. Last week he chased the two of 'em into a vacant patient room on the fourth floor but when he entered, they were gone—even though there was no other exit from the room. *Spooked*, that's what he was. The poor man got so scared he quit his job." Irv tilted his head to the side and thought for a moment. "Or maybe we had a visit from that nurse killed in a car accident years ago, the one who sometimes roams the halls after dark."

I had heard many stories about ghosts in the hospital and knew the legends of the "Dock Boys" and the "Night Nurse." However, I was trained in the sciences and believed in rational explanations, and as Emily often pointed out, I was also the Sultan of Skepticism.

I walked to the candy counter looking for an indication of childish mischief, but found none. Not knowing what else to do, I circled the room hoping to stumble upon evidence of something, anything.

"We've written the administration several times asking for help," Emily said, "but they aren't interested in *our* problem."

Irv stood. "To hell with them! I'm gonna call that local paranormal investigation team. They'll look into whatever the heck is happening here. Doesn't matter what the hospital honchos say, the snack shop is a hazardous workplace."

"I doubt the administration will permit that, Irv. And even if they do, it's unlikely they'll pay for it."

"I don't care! I'll foot the bill myself, Jake. I'm serious. We can't put up with this crap any longer. Will you speak to Harvey Winer for us? You're the administration's fair-haired boy. Ask him to look the other way till we figure this out."

I checked the wall clock. "I'm sure Winer's gone home by now. I'll phone him tonight or drop by his office tomorrow, but no promises."

Emily unplugged the coffee maker and walked to the door. "Unless you want to stay, Dad, I'm closing shop and going home. I've had enough for one day."

"Me too. Let's stop in the cafeteria for dinner on our way." Irv switched off the fan, flipped the sign on the door to CLOSED, and turned to me. "Thanks for coming, Jake. Go home and play with RJ, and let us know what Winer says."

As I walked out of the room, I had to admit that I felt … a touch queasy and a bit lightheaded. Odd. I stopped in the doorway, looked back into the snack shop, but still didn't see or hear anything. *Spooked at my age?* I thought. How embarrassing. My blood sugar was probably just a little low because I'd skipped lunch. That made more sense than ghosts.

CHAPTER FOUR

Monday, April 21, 6:30 p.m.

When I arrived at the rectory, Colleen was in the kitchen stirring a pot on the stovetop with a wooden spoon older than she was. Without looking over her shoulder, she said, "Is it yourself at last, Father? Running late again, are we? Your cellphone must be broken, I take it."

"Sorry, I should have called. Mea culpa."

Colleen was my own personal leprechaun, straight from the Aran Islands off the west coast of Ireland. A devout Catholic and my senior, she always treated me with deference, but never failed to chastise me if I strayed in any way from her version of the straight and narrow. Over time, Colleen had learned how to push all my buttons and could occasionally be frustrating, but she was the glue that held my fragile, unconventional family together. She was our housekeeper, my nephew's nanny and his surrogate grandmother, the best darn cook in town, and my conscience when I needed one. With my dual roles at the church and the hospital, there was no way that I could have cared for my nephew without her. She was definitely an acquired taste, but one I had learned to savor.

"Any problems with RJ today?"

She removed her apron and ran a hand through her short-cropped white hair. "No, a fine young lad he's been, and a joy to be with. After I fetched him from school, he picked out a book and we worked on his reading. I rewarded him with some time at the telly."

"Glad to hear it. Would you care to join us for dinner tonight, Colleen?"

"I cannot, Father. I've a Legion of Mary meeting and need to go home and make myself presentable. There's a tuna casserole warming in the oven and a pot of homemade tomato-basil soup on the stove for your supper. I'll see you in the morning."

And with that, my very own Mary Poppins in gold-rimmed spectacles vanished out the door and flew away from the rectory.

I entered the living room and found my five-year-old nephew sprawled on the living room carpet. RJ's red curls had crept over the top of his ears, and I made a mental note to take him to a barber. His eyes were laser-focused on the television as Casper the Friendly Ghost appeared on the screen.

Et tu, RJ? Just what I needed today, another ghost story. I hadn't seen an old Casper cartoon in years, and wondered if God was having a little fun messing with my head.

I dropped to my knees. "Hi, buddy. I'm home."

My nephew jumped up and ran to me, all skin and bone and freckles and grins. He screamed, "Daddy," and jumped into my open arms.

And there it was; Daddy. RJ had begun calling me "Daddy" a few months after my sister died. His biological father had abandoned him, and we had no other relatives. I didn't want him to be warehoused in the foster care system and had volunteered to be his guardian.

I had tried several times to convince him to call me Uncle Jake, however I'd relented one day when he gazed up at me with those sad, silver-blue eyes and said, "It's not fair! *All the kids* at school have mommies and daddies."

Hearing him call me Daddy was always both heartwarming and a little painful. The word was not only ironic for a Catholic priest, it was also an uncomfortable reminder that I could never completely fill the cavernous void my dear departed sister had left in RJ's life. I had stepped into a role I'd never even imagined. Yet truth be told, he'd become the center of my universe, and I'd come to think of him as my son.

I swallowed the lump in my throat, reluctantly relinquished my hug, and stood. "Time for dinner, Sport. Come and tell me all about your day."

And he did—on and on and on. After my human chatterbox had filled me in on the minutest details of school life, we built Lincoln Log cabins until it was time for his bath. Afterward, I tucked him under the covers and read him *Goodnight Moon*. The little bunny's antics and the rhythmic rhyme quickly guided my boy into dreamland.

Downstairs, I poured a bottle of Molson Golden into a frosted mug, leaned back in my recliner, and phoned Harvey Winer's office to request an appointment to speak with him in the morning. I had expected to get his voicemail and was surprised when he answered.

"Harvey, it's Jake Austin. What in the heck are you doing at the hospital this time of night?"

"Board meeting. And after two hours of nitpicking and squabbling, believe me, I'm now thoroughly bored. What can I do for you, Jake?"

I filled him in on what was happening in the snack shop. "Irv and Emily want to bring in a paranormal investigator to get to the bottom of these … occurrences."

"The hospital doesn't have money to waste on nonsense, Jake."

"I understand, but they're willing to pay the expense themselves and simply want your permission. I know it's a lot to ask, but they're really frustrated. I'd hate to see them quit their jobs over this."

"I must admit, I didn't see that request coming. Things are never boring when you're involved, Father." Winer released a deep sigh. "They're *spooked*, huh? I sure don't want to lose either of them … then again, ghosts and goblins? Ridiculous! I allowed a similar investigation several years ago, and the hospital board and church diocese were not happy about it. I got an earful. You think they'd actually quit their jobs?"

"It's possible. They're very upset."

Another sigh. "Okay, I'll approve this, but only if you're involved too. Put on your pragmatic physician hat to eliminate any mumbo jumbo, Jake, and be there when these so-called *experts* arrive. What I don't need in my life are charlatans conjuring up a fictitious ghost scare to promote their paranormal business. Don't make me regret this."

"Not to worry. I'll keep an eye on things. Thanks, Harvey."

After I hung up, I phoned Emily, gave her the go-ahead, and let her know that the investigation needed to happen before I left town next week. She seemed relieved. I was not.

CHAPTER FIVE

Tuesday, April 22, 11:00 a.m.

The unseasonable heatwave subsided on Tuesday and temperatures dropped to a more normal seventy degrees. Urgent Care was unusually quiet, which always made me nervous. My resident and I were cruising along until I entered room two and found a pale, sickly-looking young man whom I vaguely recognized as a hospital employee.

I checked the name on the chart. "What's going on, Mr. Porter?"

"Beats the hell outta me, Doc. Think I got the flu. I'm dizzy, and this damn headache never goes away. And I'm tired all the time. Never felt like this before I started working here. I was so worn-out today I damn near fell asleep standing up. My hands were shaking and I was havin' trouble remembering stuff. My supervisor told me to get looked at, then head home and go to bed."

I performed a physical exam. He had no fever or evidence of the swollen lymph nodes commonly found with the flu.

"Do you have any muscle aches or GI symptoms, like diarrhea or vomiting?"

"No. I'm a bit sick to my stomach but nothin' else. Well, a little short of breath too, and I can't keep my eyelids up."

I picked up a tongue depressor and asked him to open his mouth. The color of his lips caught my attention. Although his skin was pale, his lips were red—cherry red. Alarm bells clanged in my head. I ran a finger across them to be certain I wasn't being fooled by lip balm or lipstick.

Not wanting to delay his workup by sending him to the lab or waiting for a phlebotomist, I drew his blood myself. Our transporter was sitting at the nurses' station and I asked him to take the tubes immediately to the lab. In addition to routine blood tests, I ordered stat blood gasses and carboxyhemoglobin levels.

I reentered the exam room and clipped a pulse oximeter on Mr. Porter's finger. It registered at the lower limits of normal, but just to be safe, I placed an oxygen mask on his face and continued taking a history.

"Where do you work, sir?"

"In the hospital laundry," he replied. Mist wafted from the oxygen mask with every word. "Down in the basement, near the boiler room."

"What exactly do you do there?"

"Normally, I'm in charge of washing the patient gowns and surgical scrubs. But the guy who runs the dryers went home sick with the flu last week, so my supervisor sent me to take over till he comes back to work."

"Tell me about the dryers."

"They're humongous. Each one holds up to 450 pounds. I don't need no gym membership, loading wet clothes all day long. They weigh a ton. And man-oh-man, the noise!"

"Are they gas or electric?"

"Gas. It'd take forever to dry all that laundry with electricity."

Everything seemed to fit. Symptoms mimicking the flu but no fever, a coworker with the same problem, and cherry-red lips—a definitive sign. Mr. Porter appeared to have a classic case, right out of the textbook.

Although the pulse oximeter on his finger continued to indicate borderline normal blood oxygen levels, I suspected that the reading was falsely elevated, which sometimes happened. Rather than pace the halls waiting for the results of his blood tests, I increased the oxygen delivered through his mask, asked a nurse to keep an eye on him, and saw my next two patients. By the time I had finished, Mr. Porter's lab results were available.

Carbon monoxide poisoning! The odorless, colorless "silent killer," and the reason people are unaware of the danger unless they have a CO detector. Mr. Porter's levels were high enough to cause severe symptoms, but not yet sufficient to cause permanent brain or heart damage, coma, and death.

I called Harvey Winer in administration, explained the situation, and suggested he clear the laundry area and have the maintenance department or a qualified heating contractor check for the presence of carbon monoxide.

When I reentered the examination room, Mr. Porter said, "I'm feeling better, Doc. What the heck is going on?"

"I suspect there may be a problem with the clothes dryers. Maintenance is looking into it. You'll be your old self in a day or so, but I'm glad you stopped here on your way home." On oxygen, more than half of the carbon monoxide would be out of his system by the end of my shift, so I added, "We can keep you here on the oxygen mask for a few hours and see how you feel, or I can admit you to the hospital for observation. Your choice."

"Overnight? Not what I had in mind, Doc. My girlfriend's having me over for dinner tonight, so try to get me outta here in time." He tapped the oxygen mask. "I'm doing pretty good already."

The rest of my morning was uneventful, and I was on my way to see my next patient when Harvey Winer called.

"We found the problem with the gas dryer, Jake. Great pickup. How's Mr. Porter doing?"

"He'll be okay, but you better check on the coworker who went home sick a week ago, as well as any other folks working in the vicinity. Darn it, Harvey, don't they have CO detectors in the laundry?"

"They do, however they're battery operated and the batteries probably haven't been replaced since the Reagan administration. That'll never happen again on my watch. Soon as they put in the new batteries, the detectors started screaming. Simple solution to a nasty problem. Thanks for your help. I owe you one, Jake."

It's always good to have the head honcho in your debt.

Quite pleased with myself, I was on my way to see the last patient of the morning when I remembered what had happened to Emily and Irv. The proverbial light bulb lit up. Crap! They had both complained of dizziness, nausea, weakness, anxiety and confusion. Carbon monoxide? Why hadn't I thought of it sooner?

I asked Nurse Ochs and my resident to hold the fort, grabbed the CO detector from the wall socket in Urgent Care, and hurried to the snack shop.

Emily was working behind the counter. Sure enough, there was no carbon monoxide sensor in the room. I plugged in the detector and told her about the similarity between Mr. Porter's symptoms and what had been happening at the snack shop. Emily gasped, wilted onto a chair, and we waited for the detector's alarm to sound.

We waited and we waited.

Nothing happened—not a single peep, no evidence of carbon monoxide.

Damn it! Back to ghosts and goblins in the snack shop.

CHAPTER SIX

Tuesday, April 22, 12:15 p.m.

It was a teacher conference day and my nephew didn't have school. I'd asked for the afternoon off and was looking forward to relieving Colleen and spending some quality time with RJ. I had entered the hospital parking garage and was opening my car door when Colleen called.

"Why'd you not warn me that we were expecting company at the rectory, Father?"

"I didn't know we were. What're you talking about?"

"Phineas Snapp just arrived, and he's moving all his things into the guest bedroom, including his pet bird."

"Who the heck is Phineas Snapp?"

"I was hoping you could tell me. He says he's a priest and Bishop Lucci assigned him here. Didn't his Excellency send you any notice?"

"He did not." This was no surprise, given the tension between the bishop and me.

"The thing is, Father," Colleen lowered her voice, "there's nothing priestly about the man. He's tall and thin as a post, and in his flowing black robes he looks like an overgrown bat. Reminds me a bit of the character Lurch from those old Addams Family telly shows. No, more like the monster in Frankenstein. A strange one he is, let there be no doubt about that, and silent as a tomb. He makes me … uncomfortable. And RJ took one look at him, scurried up to his room, and slammed the door. Think it's best you come home soon."

I hopped into my car. "I'm on my way."

I suspected His Excellency's lack of warning about Father Snapp's arrival was a passive-aggressive swipe at me. Lucci was a petty bureaucrat who ran his fiefdom with an iron fist, and since my arrival he'd kept me under his iron thumb. When my Superior General, Father Stefano Demarco, became my champion and elevated me to his personal consultant and right-hand-man, I knew Lucci had felt devalued. And although the two men were friends, when the bishop tried to undermine me, Demarco had become angry, chastised him, and required him to provide an assistant for me at Sacred Heart Church. Then, to add fuel to the diocesan wildfire, Demarco had replaced my old second-hand Ford with a much nicer car than Lucci drove.

But it was more than jealousy on Lucci's part. When I'd promised my dying sister that I would care for my nephew, he had demanded that I place RJ up for adoption. I'd refused and become his legal guardian. Although the Vatican had permitted priests to adopt on rare occasions and there was church precedence, His Excellency believed it was unseemly for a priest to raise a child. Worse than that, I'd been honest with Lucci and confessed that I still harbored strong feelings for Emily. He'd demanded that I break off our friendship, something I was unable and unwilling to do. Ever since then, it had been clear he wanted me out of his diocese and out of the priesthood. The unexpected arrival of Father Snapp appeared to be an act of retaliation by His Deviousness.

I arrived at home to find a peculiar vehicle parked near the front door. It looked like a cross between a hearse and a van. When I entered the rectory and saw Phineas Snapp for the first time, the reason for RJ's behavior and Colleen's concern became clear. Snapp wore a flowing ebony-colored robe with a hood that was definitely not standard Church issue, and when he entered the room he almost hit his head on the doorframe. The man had to be nearly seven feet tall. Shoulder-length, greasy black hair framed a skeletal face with cold, dark eyes, sallow skin, and a thin-lipped mouth. His appearance was striking … and macabre.

I walked over. "Father Snapp, I presume. Welcome. I'm Jake Austin, the pastor here."

I reached out a hand. He considered taking it for a long time with a deadpan expression, grunted, then shook it with a hand so heavily scarred I had to force myself to look away.

"Yes, I'm aware," he replied in a deep sonorous voice. "The bishop told me *all* about you."

The atmosphere in the room seemed to curdle.

Snapp reached into a pocket in his robe, removed an envelope, and handed it to me. "My letter of introduction." He turned and started to walk away. "I've one last thing to move in. Come with me."

This was not exactly the meet and greet I was hoping for.

I followed him to his battered van. He had an awkward, uneven gait and wore thick-soled, lace-up hiking boots, an odd choice with his robes.

He slid the side door of the van open. The interior had been customized, with a couch and small refrigerator located in the back. A large wooden steamer trunk secured by thick leather straps and two separate locks rested near the side door. It looked to be a hundred years old.

"Tools of the trade," he said, taking hold of one handle. "It's heavy. Grab the other end."

We hefted it out of the van and wrestled the monstrosity upstairs into the guest room. RJ's bedroom door was cracked open. He peeked out as we passed by, fear in his eyes.

By the time we set the old wooden chest on the floor in his room, Snapp and I were both breathing hard. It had several hand-carved symbols on the front I didn't recognize. I pointed to it. "Impressive. The carvings are beautiful. Is it a family heirloom?"

"Family business." His lips nearly reached a smile, revealing uneven yellow teeth beneath a hooked nose. "My great-uncle, Thomas Snapp, designed it in the 1800's."

I was asking about the significance of the carved symbols when I heard a hissing sound behind me, then a high-pitched shriek. "Intruder!"

I whirled around. A large gray bird with black-tipped wings and red tail feathers tilted its head and eyed me from its cage in the far corner of the room, then screamed again, "Be gone!"

Snapp walked over and opened the cage. The bird hopped onto his hand and he stroked it gently. He turned his gaze to me. "A gift from a grateful Romanian boyar."

"A what?"

"Boyar. One step below a prince. I've moved around a lot, but Moarte has been at my side for twenty years."

Reassigned often—it was not hard to see why. One could only hope.

"Her speech is amazing. What kind is she?"

"*He*. An African grey, though his previous owner said he might be part raven."

Snapp whispered something to the bird. Moarte hopped onto Snapp's shoulder and said softly, "Stranger."

The bird eyed me again and shrieked, "Be gone!"

I must have looked stunned.

"Sorry. Moarte's very protective. He may warm up to you in time." Snapp glanced around the room. "Well, it appears we're done here. You may go."

I may go? In my own home?

I'd had enough nonsense for one day. "Supper's at 6:30, Phineas."

Snapp merely turned away and grunted.

CHAPTER SEVEN

Tuesday, April 22, 2:00 p.m.

After my first encounter with Phineas Snapp, I understood completely why RJ had hidden in his room. Since Snapp was my new assistant and part of our life at the rectory, however, I needed to comfort my boy and reassure him that he had nothing to fear.

I knocked softly on RJ's door and entered. He was lying on his bed engrossed in a Dr. Seuss book. Seuss was the other doctor in his life. He slid his finger from word to word, reading each one out loud.

"Hey, buddy, I don't have to work this afternoon. How about we have some fun? What'd you want to do?"

"Don't know."

"Want to play catch?"

He shrugged.

"Is something bothering you, sport?"

He looked up at me. "I don't like that man. He *scares* me."

"Father Snapp? I know he looks different, but that doesn't mean he's a bad guy, RJ. We should get to know him. He might turn out to be cool." Personally, I had my doubts. "He even has a talking bird."

"It *hissed* at me, Daddy! Like a snake." He sat on the edge of the bed. "And he looks like that mean teacher in the Harry Potter movie."

I'd thought so too. *Severus Snape*. Even their names were similar. I had made the mistake of taking my five-year-old nephew to see *Harry Potter and the Sorcerer's Stone*. He loved watching Harry and the other children fly, but I'd paid dearly when the violent scenes caused RJ nightmares. Now we had a Severus look-alike living in the rectory, complicating our already complicated life.

"Well, Father Snapp is a guest in our home and we need to be nice to him. Okay? Promise me you'll try." He nodded. "Now, it's a beautiful day. How about we go to the park?"

RJ smiled, hopped out of bed, and put on his sneakers.

"Bathroom first. I'll meet you downstairs."

While I waited for him, I opened Snapp's letter of introduction from Bishop Lucci.

Per your request, I have assigned Father Phineas Snapp as associate pastor at Sacred Heart Church. I think he will be an interesting addition. He also has some special duties, which may take him away from time to time, but I'm sure you both will reach an understanding and arrange your schedules to the benefit of the parish.

Yours, The Most Reverend Antonio Lucci.

An interesting addition? *A complete disaster*, more likely—and vindictive. Lucci knew damn well that Snapp would rattle my nephew. He had intentionally thrown a monkey wrench into the well-oiled machine that my life at the rectory had become.

Well so be it, Your Underhandedness. I accept the challenge!

RJ and I walked to the park past trees flush with new growth and a field ablaze with spring flowers. After he wore out all the equipment, we strolled downtown to the library and checked out three storybooks. With Colleen off for the afternoon, I decided to toss a salad, fire up the grill, and make hamburgers for dinner. We were on our way home when she phoned.

"I thought we should have a special meal tonight in honor of our new guest. I popped over to the rectory and I'm making honey garlic chicken with au gratin potatoes. I'm free this evening, Father, and I'd be happy to join you for supper, if that's all right with yourself."

"Great idea, Colleen" … and a wily one too. Living in the rectory under her watchful eye was like living in a fish bowl. Queen Busybody not only intended to snoop on Snapp, but was dying to see how he and I would interact—a little like going to a NASCAR race hoping to see a six car pileup.

"RJ and I will be home around 6:15. Will that work for you?"

"Fine by me, Father. See you soon."

When we arrived at the rectory, Colleen was removing dinner from the oven. The dining room table was set with china, crystal, and cloth napkins. I hoped Father Snapp wouldn't expect to dine like this every night.

I sent RJ to wash his hands, then climbed the stairs, walked to the guest room, and said, "Phineas, Colleen is serving dinner."

"Fine. Be down in five minutes." To my surprise, Snapp was kneeling by the open door to his room, a screwdriver in his hand. "Just changing the lock," he added, as if every visitor to the rectory changed the lock.

Shaking my head, I returned to the dining room. When Snapp arrived at the table, I said grace and Colleen began to serve. RJ and I had worked up an appetite at the park and we dug in with enthusiasm. Snapp took only a small serving of au gratin potatoes and green beans.

I noticed my nephew staring at the scars on Snapp's hands and distracted him with questions about his friends at school.

When the conversation died, Colleen asked, "Do you not care for chicken, Father Snapp?"

"I don't eat the flesh of animals." He looked directly at my nephew. "I love all of God's creatures, especially those with feathers."

RJ's jaw dropped. He glanced from Snapp to me, then pushed his chicken aside. Apparently I would need to have another talk with my nephew this evening. Raising a five year old was hard enough without this man undermining me.

Snapp's comment again put a halt to the dinner conversation. He continued to focus on his meal, although he ate very little. Finally Colleen asked him, "Where were you assigned before this, Father?"

"All over. I'm not long in any one place."

As far as I was concerned, not long *here* would suit me fine.

Colleen persisted. "And where was your last parish, Father Snapp?"

"Montenegro. Before that, Atlanta and Madrid."

Colleen continued her interrogation. "What's Montenegro like? I've never journeyed to that part of the world."

"Mountainous and medieval," Snapp replied gruffly, then stood. "Excuse me. I must meditate and pray now."

Frustrated, Colleen turned toward me pleadingly for help.

"Care for some dessert, Phineas?" I asked. "Colleen made a German chocolate cake especially for you."

He headed into the kitchen. "No. I'll just grab some fruit. Moarte and I will share."

Colleen leaned toward me and whispered, "They're quite a pair, him and his feathered friend. The man even eats like a bird!"

Snapp peeked into the room and waved a banana. "Sleep well."

And with that, he disappeared as if by magic.

CHAPTER EIGHT

Wednesday, April 23, 9:30 a.m.

After getting RJ off to school and offering morning Mass at Sacred Heart, I settled into the routine in Urgent Care. My day was uneventful until Maya Ruiz, the talented senior resident assisting me, intercepted me in the hallway between patients, a scowl on her face.

"I need you to evaluate my patient, Dr. Austin."

Dr. Ruiz was a gifted young physician who'd nearly completed her residency. She seldom asked for or needed help.

"What seems to be the problem, Maya?"

"My patient is an elderly woman complaining of pharyngitis but … I may be wrong, but I think there's more going on. I'm worried about her general welfare."

I had watched this young woman blossom from a bumbling trainee into a fine physician. She had exceptional potential, and I looked forward to mentoring her whenever I had the opportunity. She was a hard worker with a keen intellect but more importantly, she had *uncommon* common sense and was a critical thinker.

"Mrs. Barr is in room three, Dr. Austin. Please look in on her. I don't want to bias you with my concerns, but let me know what you think of her condition … and her grandson." She took the chart from my hand. "I'll take care of your next patient."

"Sure. No problem."

I entered room three and introduced myself to Mrs. Vera Barr, an extremely thin eighty-year-old woman. It was immediately apparent that both she and her clothing were in desperate need of soap and water.

She'd been complaining of a sore throat and difficulty swallowing, so her twenty-something grandson had driven her to the hospital. My physical examination confirmed swollen tonsils, as well as yellowed teeth stippled with decay. As I took her history, it was obvious that Vera was suffering from dementia.

I turned to her grandson, who sat in a chair texting on his cellphone. He wore a pricey lambskin bomber jacket over what appeared to be a silk shirt. Gold chains hung from his neck, numerous and hefty enough to drown him if he happened to fall into a lake.

"Does your grandmother live in a nursing home?"

"Nah, I take care of her," he managed to reply before returning to his phone.

"We have several good facilities in the county you might consider."

He finished his text and looked up at me. "I've tried. Nana refuses to leave her home."

"That must be hard on you."

"Yeah, it is. I also got a job." He sighed, silenced his phone, and slipped it into his pocket. "But I do the best I can."

"Have you thought about hiring a home health aide, to take some of the burden off of you? You know, help with bathing and meals and such."

"Nah. Too damn expensive. She's poor."

I examined Vera's emaciated abdomen, then listened to her heart and lungs. Her body odor was overpowering. I studied her gaunt face and bony hands.

"How's your grandmother's appetite?" I asked.

"She don't eat much. Kind'a plays with her food, shoves it around her plate. But I give her as much as she wants." He stood and glared at me. "Look, Doc, we came in for her sore throat. Can you help her or not? I got stuff to do, places to be."

I helped Vera down from the exam table, wrote a prescription for antibiotics, and handed it to her grandson. "Make sure she finishes all the medication, and bring her back if she's not better in a few days. She should also see a dentist."

He gazed at the prescription and frowned. "Is this stuff covered by Medicare?"

"It is, but the medication alone isn't enough. It's also important that you keep her well hydrated and—"

Before I could finish the sentence, he'd led Vera from the room. Apparently the *stuff* he had to do was quite urgent.

I walked out of the exam room and caught up with Dr. Ruiz in the hall.

"Nice catch, Maya. You were right to be concerned."

"Neglect?"

"Looks like it. Not to worry, I'll take it from here."

I slumped onto a chair at the nurses' station and mulled over what I'd seen, then called Kiara Robinson, one of my parishioners who worked at Adult Protective Services. No one was nearby to overhear the conversation, so I told her the story, gave her Vera's name and address, and asked her to evaluate the situation.

"How soon do you think you can stop by? I'm really concerned."

She chuckled. "You asking for special favors, Father?"

"I guess I am. Sorry. Can you help?"

"Turns out I'll be in that neck of the woods this afternoon. I suppose I can stop in on my break. I'll let you know what I find."

At noon, I joined Emily in the cafeteria. She appeared distressed.

"What's up, Em? More problems at the snack shop?"

"No, nothing since Monday, thank God. But that's why I wanted to get together over lunch. Dad called the Tri-City Ghost Hunters. They're the largest group in the state and have been doing investigations for years. The problem is, they're heavily booked and the only opening they have before you leave town is Friday night. I know it's short notice, but can you come? Otherwise the administration won't give us the go-ahead."

"I'll check with Colleen. If she can stay with RJ, I'll be there."

"Thanks, Jake."

"What time?"

"Their team of investigators will arrive with their equipment at seven. Dad and I really need to know if there's a logical explanation for what's been going on in the snack shop or if we're dealing with paranormal activity."

She fiddled with a button on her dress, then massaged the back of her neck.

"Is something else bothering you, Em."

"Everett's condition has been deteriorating." She dragged a hand through her hair. "His doctors aren't hopeful." A tear ran down her cheek.

Everett McDermott was Emily's ex-husband. He had been shot in the head a year earlier and had never recovered physically or mentally.

"I'm so sorry, Em," I lied.

The truth was, I detested the guy. As a young man, I'd loved Emily and had hoped to marry her after my stint in the Army, but Everett had wined and dined her in my absence, and swept her off her feet. They'd wed while I was in a bloody war overseas. Everett, however, was an alcoholic who had abused Emily during the short time they'd been married. Although I absolved sinners for a living, I'd never been able to forgive him for what he'd done to her.

As I watched Emily shed more tears for this drunken lout, it became clear that she was a much better Christian than I was.

"Please say a prayer for him, Jake."

"Of course." My beeper went off. I checked the number and pushed away from the table. "Sorry, I have to go. As soon as I hear from Colleen about Friday, I'll let you know."

Back in Urgent Care, I guided Maya Ruiz through the management of an elderly man's leg ulcer, then I phoned Colleen, explained the situation, and asked for her help.

"Yes, I'm free Friday evening and don't mind looking after RJ, but …."

"But what?"

"It's just that I'm not sure I want to be alone in the rectory with Father Snapp at night. There's a darkness about him that makes me … uncomfortable. I think I'd sooner shake the Devil by the tail than spend time with that man."

Snapp gave me the willies too. His mere presence at the rectory was already upending our routine.

"I wouldn't ask if it wasn't important, Colleen. Emily and her father have begged me for help."

"Well then, what I might do," she paused for a second, "is pick up RJ after school for a sleepover at my apartment and make the evening into a grand adventure, if that's alright with yourself, Father."

"Good idea. RJ will love it. He had a great time at your place last month."

I called Emily and told her I would be available to join her in the snack shop when the paranormal investigators arrived. I'd just hung up when Kiara Robinson phoned from Adult Protective Services.

"Got a problem, Father. When I arrived at Vera Barr's house, the grandson refused to allow me inside. He was holding a kitchen knife, said he was making lunch, but … he waved it in my direction. I told him I could return later, but he just shook his head and pointed to my car with the knife. Felt a lot like a threat. I'll be honest with you, he's a pretty creepy guy." She sighed. "Without evidence of imminent danger, my hands are tied for today. My boss will want me to attempt entry one more time before asking for an inspection warrant. It may take some time, but I'll do what I can."

I thanked Kiara and hung up. By the look of things, *time* did not appear to be on Vera's side. I thought about how helpless and totally dependent she was on her knife-wielding grandson, and it pissed me off. I called the Sheriff's Department and asked to speak with Tree Macon.

"Hey Tree. Would you be willing to put on your righteous crusader cape and help me protect a vulnerable old lady?" I explained the situation. "I want to do a welfare check at her home and wouldn't mind some company. There might be a six-pack of Guinness in it for you."

"Protect and serve, that's what I do, buddy. And I do love both Guinness and grandmas a lot. You really think the woman may be in danger?"

"She certainly looks neglected. I want to make sure she's not being abused."

"Sounds like reasonable grounds for an intervention. As a healthcare provider, you are legally mandated to report abuse or neglect to the authorities—*and I*, as the Grand Poobah of Justice, am empowered to bust heads whenever necessary. I've been sitting at my desk for so long I'm getting calluses on my behind and need an excuse to get out of the office. How soon can you meet me at the woman's home?"

"I'll get coverage for Urgent Care and meet you there in an hour." I gave him Vera's address.

"Let's play bad cop, good cop—I mean good doc, bad cop. Wear your white coat and your best caring bedside manner. I'll bring the attitude and muscle."

I called in a favor with an internist willing to cover the remainder of my shift, and I was in my car and on my way in thirty minutes.

CHAPTER NINE

Wednesday, April 23, 4:00 p.m.

Vera Barr's home was literally in the middle of nowhere—a rundown double-wide trailer set deep in a pine grove, barely visible from the street. I parked off the road near the long gravel driveway and waited. Tree Macon arrived a few minutes later. When he extricated his six-and-a-half foot, two hundred and fifty pound frame from the cruiser, it looked as if he'd arrived in a child's toy police car.

I joined him and he pointed at the mailbox, which had a confederate flag stenciled on it. "I'm already looking forward to meeting this punk." Tree ran his hand over his shaved scalp and his expression hardened to black granite. "As a descendant of cotton pickers forcibly relocated from Africa, for me those Stars and Bars are like waving a red cape in front of a bull—but they also give me a glimpse inside the owner's head."

"Reverse racial profiling, Sheriff?"

He gave me a hard look. "Just considering all available information."

Tree lifted the lids of two metal trash cans.

I raised an eyebrow. "Dumpster diving? Is that even legal?"

"Oh, it's legal. Curbside trash is in the public domain." He shrugged. "I always want to know what I'm getting into. An ounce of prevention, Jake, is better than taking a serious pounding." He kicked a clod of dirt off the driveway. "Once upon a time, back in the days when I had use for a comb, I checked out some trash cans and found dozens of cold and allergy medicine packages, so I knew the homeowners were smurfing."

"What's smurfing?"

"Hopping from pharmacy to pharmacy, buying allergy meds at each one, squirrelling away enough pseudoephedrine to cook meth—you know, like the little blue cartoon smurfs gathering roots and berries for Papa Smurf's cooking pot. Same idea. I also found rubber gloves and a bunch of plastic soda bottles in their rubbish that are used in the shake and bake method." He grinned. "That trash put *them* in the can for seven years."

"Find anything here, Tree?"

"Nah, nothing obvious." He put the lids on the rubbish cans and we started walking toward the trailer. "Let's go check out Vera's grandson. Hopefully he'll be taking good care of grandma, and I won't have to assign some poor rookie the nasty job of digging through his garbage."

As we approached the trailer, Tree said, "You ring the doorbell and ask to see Vera. I want to see how the grandson reacts. I'd like to stay out of this if he lets you in. But Jake, stay on your toes. Domestic calls are among the most dangerous. Don't worry, though." He tapped his nightstick. "I got your back."

There was no doorbell. I knocked, but got no answer. Tree stepped a few yards to my left, out of sight. I heard movement inside and knocked harder.

The grandson answered. It took a couple of seconds before his eyes widened. "What do *you* want, Doc? Nana took her pills and she's doing fine. Her throat's better already."

"I'm following up on her condition. It won't take long." I heard moaning inside and rummaged through my mind for an excuse to enter the trailer. "Sometimes patients have severe reactions to that antibiotic. I need to check her pulse and breathing, make sure she's okay."

I tried to sound convincing. Although severe reactions can occur with almost all medications, this one was no more dangerous than any other. I needed to get a look at Vera's living conditions.

"Now ain't a good time." His cold stare nearly gave me frostbite. "My grandma's okay, and I'm busy makin' their dinner."

Their?

Another groan. "Sounds like she may be suffering. I hear moaning. Please let me help her."

His voice became a growl and his hands fisted. "This is my home, and I said no!"

He tried to close the door, but Tree stepped out of the shadows and blocked it with his size thirteen boot.

"County sheriff's department. What's your name, son?"

"Uh, Zach Barr," he stuttered. "Whatcha want?"

"I want you to let this doctor in, so he can do his job." Tree placed his hand on the butt of his holstered weapon and took a step forward. "The Department of Social Services is concerned about Vera Barr's welfare. You got nothing to hide, right? So open the door please."

Barr's initial shocked expression gave way to a nasty scowl. "This here's my house, and you're gonna hafta show me a warrant first."

"Wrong … on both counts. The property is titled to Vera Barr, and I don't need a warrant to perform a welfare check."

I didn't know if Tree was bluffing or if he'd done his homework, but it had the same effect. Zack Barr took a step backward.

Tree swung the door open and entered the trailer, his frame filling the doorway. I followed as he edged cautiously inside.

The interior of the double-wide looked and smelled like a cross between a landfill and the aftermath of a drunken bash. Old newspapers, empty pizza boxes, and crushed beer cans were scattered everywhere. Filthy clothes littered the floor and furniture.

Vera lay on a couch, partially covered by a ratty blanket, mumbling incoherently. An even older woman sat hunched over in a wheelchair next to her, half-asleep. I hurried over and Vera's eyes grew wide with fear, so I quietly explained that I was a physician before I began to examine her.

Tree walked to the small kitchen area and picked up an open can of dog food next to a paper plate. A dozen more cans were piled on the counter. A peek inside of the refrigerator revealed a six-pack of Budweiser and little else.

"Making them dinner, huh?" Tree glanced around. "I don't see a dog here, Zachary. You got an invisible one? Who the hell are you feeding this to? You best show me your dog right now!"

Zach Barr's eyes widened. He grabbed a stack of mail off a table and bolted out the door. Tree was two steps behind him. My money was on the sheriff.

I resumed my examination of the two women. The older one was in worse shape than Vera. Emaciated, anemic, and covered in pressure sores. I phoned for EMS, then contacted Kiara Robinson at A.P.S. and filled her in. By the time I hung up, Zack Barr staggered through the door, his hands cuffed behind his back. He was covered in dirt and grass clippings and had a bloody nose and a nasty scrape on his forehead. All defiance was gone. His eyes were filled with panic.

"This ain't right! You got no grounds to arrest me. I ain't done nothing."

"Let's start with assaulting an officer and resisting arrest, Mr. Barr, and we'll go from there. Maybe kidnapping and elder abuse, who knows? Let's see what I can think of. I can be very creative." Tree waved the letters the grandson had grabbed. "Guess what came in the mail, Jake. Social security checks for Vera and her sister. Bet you a six-pack of Guinness there's a paper trail of these checks leading right to Mr. Barr's bank account."

"I stopped betting against you a long time ago, Tree." I pointed to Zach Barr. "Does this, ah … *gentleman* require medical attention?"

"Nah, we'll see to all his needs at the station house. You gonna be all right here?"

"Sure. I'll wait until EMS arrives."

After I filled in the paramedics on the situation and the two women were safely in ambulances, I walked down the driveway to my car. Strangely, the mailbox with the confederate flag lay on the ground. It appeared as if it had been accidentally knocked over by a passing car … or possibly an enraged bull … or the descendent of reluctant cotton pickers.

CHAPTER TEN

Thursday, April 24, 3:00 p.m.

Although I had reduced my hours at the hospital so I could spend more time with RJ, I still had the occasional overnight on-call duty supervising the interns and residents, and Thursday was my night. If my advice over the phone was not enough, I sometimes needed to drive to the hospital to assist a young doctor with a procedure.

Normally, Colleen spent the evening in the guest room at the rectory, so my nephew wouldn't be alone if I was called into the hospital. But Father Snapp was now living in that room and she was uncomfortable in his presence, so she'd decided to extend my nephew's sleepover at her apartment for one more night. As RJ's de facto grandmother, Colleen had purchased a few games and toys he'd been longing for, and he was thrilled at the prospect.

I'd had an uneventful morning in Urgent Care when Tree called me mid-afternoon.

"Got some follow-up for you, Jake. Zach Barr has lawyered up and is claiming Vera gave him all her money voluntarily and he did nothing wrong."

"The poor woman is severely demented and not competent to make financial decisions. Please tell me he hasn't drawn a get-out-of-jail-free card."

"Nah. The paper trail leads right to Zach's savings account, and the district attorney is going for the maximum fine and jail time, but we may need to go to court. Just a heads-up, buddy. One of my deputies will contact you to take your statement."

"That's paperwork I won't mind doing. I'm happy to help in any way I can."

"Great. I'll be in touch. Talk soon."

As the clock ticked toward the end of my shift, I was smiling and looking forward to supper with my boy, grateful to have had a quiet day in Urgent Care before the usual mayhem of night call began.

Kiara phoned me shortly after four o'clock from Adult Protective Services to say that Vera and her sister had been released from the hospital, and she had been able to place them at an excellent nursing home. With proper care and a better diet, I hoped their later years would be more pleasant. Knowing Tree Macon, I was certain that what was in store for Vera's grandson would be anything but pleasant.

My next patient was a seventeen-year-old girl who was sitting on the exam table, dressed in street clothes when I entered the room, the patient gown hanging on the door hook.

"What seems to be the problem?" I opened her chart and skimmed the nurse's note. "It says here you can't sleep, Brittany. What's going on?"

"I like need your help, Doctor." She swept her long blond hair behind one ear. "Can you like write me a prescription so I can be homeschooled? Like for my mental health? Classes start way too early in the morning and it's messing with my head. I'm always *soooo* tired, and it's like I'm walkin' around in a fog."

Patients occasionally requested a note to explain their temporary absence from work or school due to illness, but this was a first.

"What time do you go to bed, Brittany?"

"Oh, that's not the problem." She pointed to her abdomen, and I saw the hint of a baby bump. "I'm pregnant, and it's like really hard to get up in the morning."

Many women experience some degree of sleep disturbance during pregnancy. I opened Brittany's chart and reviewed her recent visit with her obstetrician and the results of her blood work. She was not anemic, her physical examination had been normal, and she'd shown no evidence of underlying depression. Her OB doctor had noted a similar request for homeschooling—denied—with an addendum that read: *The difference between motivation and laziness is that motivation has its limits.*

And my good mood flew right out the window, along with the last of my patience.

I wanted to ask her how in the heck she was going to get out of bed at three in the morning when her baby needed to be fed. Instead I said, "A note from me won't matter to anyone. I'm sorry, but the decision about homeschooling is between you and your parents."

"But they said *no*! I thought they'd listen to a doctor and—"

I held up my hand to stop her. There was no magic cure in my little black bag for what ailed her. I sure as hell was not going to prescribe a sleeping pill for a pregnant teen, which would only make getting up in the morning harder for her—and I refused to be one of those physicians who sees a pill as the solution to every problem. She had needlessly tied up overworked hospital personnel and resources *twice* with this nonsense, and I'd had enough.

I tried to mask my frustration. "Remember to take your prenatal vitamins every day, Brittany, and try going to sleep a bit earlier at night."

She jumped down from the exam table and marched to the door. Before she slammed it shut, she shouted, "You doctors are all like soooo heartless!"

One does have to toughen up to do this job on a daily basis, but heartless? No. Sadly, sometimes life *is* heartless, and some predicaments have no easy answers. I chalked up my encounter with Brittany as preparation for RJ's future turbulent teenage years, then went to see my last patient of the day.

Dinner with my nephew at Colleen's apartment that evening resurrected my good mood and rejuvenated me. Saint Luke the Evangelist, the patron saint of physicians, must have been smiling down on me because things remained quiet at the hospital long enough to allow me to finish supper with RJ, then shave and shower at the rectory. I was even able to watch the Cavaliers victory over the Dallas Mavericks and get three hours of sleep before being called in at two a.m. to help treat victims of a horrendous seven-car pileup.

When I arrived in the ER, Maya Ruiz was examining a comatose patient in room one. An oxygen mask was in place, but the patient's complexion appeared dusky gray. A nurse was recording vital signs.

"What's the situation, Maya?" I asked.

"Thirty-year-old driver with head trauma. CT scan of his brain's been ordered and a neurology resident is on his way." She wrapped her stethoscope around her neck. "The steering wheel hit him in the chest. He was moving air on the left when he arrived but I couldn't hear any breath sounds on the right side. Just got the chest x-ray back. Complete pneumothorax." She pointed to the film hanging on the view box, which showed three broken ribs on the right and collapse of the adjacent lung. "I was about to call a surgeon to place a chest tube."

A teachable moment.

"No need, Maya. There's no evidence of hemorrhage or fluid on the x-ray, so we don't need to subject the patient to a thumb-sized drainage tube when a small catheter will work just as well. Ever inserted a Heimlich valve chest tube?" She shook her head. "Well, we'll do it together. Glove up. Prep and drape his chest, while I get the equipment."

When I returned, I said, "Numb up his skin and make a tiny incision. Good, now slip the needle through that small rubber tube with multiple side holes and attach the Heimlich valve to the tube."

"This? The plastic cylinder with the small rubber flapper inside?"

"That little device has saved a lot of lives on battlefields and in emergency rooms. It's a portable one-way flutter valve. The pressure of the patient's expiration expands the valve's rubber lips and drives out excess air from the chest cavity, but the flapper closes on inspiration and won't allow any to reenter."

She assembled the device.

"Now with the needle leading the tube, Maya, insert them as a unit into the incision and through the chest wall until all the side holes are inside the patient's chest, then remove the needle, leaving the tube and valve in place."

When she did, air gushed out of the valve, which then sealed again with each inspiration. The patient's dusky skin color soon took on a pinkish hue, and Maya sighed with relief. She was cool under pressure, and I was proud of her.

"Good job. As the patient's breathing drives more air out of his chest cavity, the lung will re-expand completely."

I showed her how to affix the tube and valve to the patient.

As the neurologist entered the room, my beeper went off. "Finish up, Maya. I have to go."

I headed out to see who else needed help. It was nearly two hours before we finally got all the accident victims stabilized and admitted.

Before leaving the hospital, I went up to Pediatrics on the fifth floor to teach an intern how to perform a lumbar puncture on a baby suspected of having meningitis.

By the time I left Peds, I was feeling every one of my forty-eight years and my eyelids were losing the battle against gravity, so I decided to drive home to catch some sleep. Walking toward the elevator through a poorly lit corridor under flickering fluorescent lights reminded me of the story Irv Beale had told me about the night janitor. The poor man had been so frightened after his alleged encounter with the illusive dead "Dock Boys" that he'd quit his job. Anyone who works the night shift at a hospital or has been an inpatient knows how eerie the halls can be amid the shadows, night sounds, and occasional patient moans. When you're completely exhausted, it's not hard to imagine how you might hear voices or see apparitions.

I was softly humming the classic rock song "Spooky" as I stepped into the elevator. When I heard footsteps coming toward me, I held the door open. A young nurse entered and nodded a thank you. I was immediately assaulted by the stench of stale cigarette smoke on her clothing. I wondered if she was from another hospital because her nursing uniform seemed oddly old-fashioned for a young woman.

I pushed the elevator button for the lobby and asked her which floor she wanted. She smiled and raised two fingers, and I hit the button for the second floor. When the doors opened on two, she removed a pack of cigarettes from her pocket and lit one.

I was stunned. "Excuse me. Smoking's not permitted in the hospital."

She ignored my protest, stepped from the elevator, and disappeared across the hall.

I was too tired to chase after her and I had no desire for a confrontation. My day had been too long as it was, so I let the incident go and walked toward the parking garage. As I passed the security office, the night guard said, "Hey, Doc, what the heck was that on the second floor?"

I stuck my head into his office. "What was what?"

He pointed to one of the monitors on the wall. "The strange glow floating out of the elevator."

"Just a nurse going for a smoking break."

"What nurse? You were alone. I was watching. And smoking ain't been allowed in the hospital for over a decade."

"Of course there was a nurse. A young one. I saw her. She got on the elevator with me on the fifth floor and got off on two for a smoke."

"Where'd she go then? The light disappeared across the hallway."

"Through a fire escape exit door, I assume."

"I'm not buying it, Doc. I been working this night shift for years and I know what I saw." He motioned me closer. "Fifth floor, you say?"

He flipped a couple levers and an image of me entering the elevator came into view. A few seconds passed, but no one else got in and the doors closed. He flipped more levers and the screen marked FLOOR TWO showed a light floating through the open elevator doors and vanishing across the hall.

A glowing light, like the tip of a lit cigarette—but no nurse.

"There's no fire escape door across from the elevators, Doc, and the emergency stairwell exits are nowhere near there. So what the heck was that strange light, and where did it go?" He stared at me. "You don't look so good. You feelin' okay?"

I'm not sure what I was feeling, but it was definitely *not* okay. I mumbled a thank you to the guard and headed to the parking garage. By the time I reached my car, I had almost convinced myself that what had happened was simply my exhausted mind playing tricks on me.

Almost.

CHAPTER ELEVEN

Friday, April 25, 7:00 a.m.

I had the next day off after my night on-call at the hospital. I slept for a couple hours, showered and shaved, then walked to Father Snapp's bedroom door. I heard an odd, guttural singing coming from inside, something that sounded like an off-key Gregorian chant in a language I didn't recognize. I knocked. The music stopped and I heard a loud thud, as if the lid of his trunk had been slammed shut. When he finally unlocked his door, his window was wide open and I smelled a strange aroma. Not marijuana, but unlike anything I'd encountered.

"Good morning, Phineas. Sorry to bother you. As it's the Feast of St. Mark the Evangelist today, I require your assistance with morning Mass."

He gazed down at me over his hooked nose for a moment. "I'm in the middle of something. Some other time perhaps."

The man had lived at the rectory for three days, and had done nothing but eat our food, scare RJ and Colleen, and seclude himself in his room. He had been sent here to assist me and I needed to begin assigning his duties, but I also wanted to introduce him to the congregation and see how he handled himself in church. It was time to put on my big-boy pastor pants.

"Sorry if it's inconvenient but I need you there this morning."

"I much prefer to celebrate Mass privately in the side chapel of the church."

Personally, I'd prefer to be thirty years old again, marry Emily, and remain a priest … but if wishes were houses, we'd all live in mansions. I had tiptoed around Snapp far too long already.

"And I'd prefer not to have to pull rank, Phineas. Eight o'clock sharp."

We exchanged glares and I walked to the sacristy to prepare for Mass.

Much to my surprise, Snapp proved adept at the altar, and with his wild mane combed, he looked quite presentable. My parishioners appeared intrigued by the new priest and to my relief, no one ran screaming from the church. I spoke with him after the service, and we divvied up the parish workload, agreeing to be flexible when necessary.

When the last of the congregation had departed, I removed the spent votive candles and replaced them with new ones, then updated the sign in front of the church to read: CHURCH PARKING ONLY. VIOLATORS WILL BE BAPTISED. When it came to advertising, Madison Avenue had nothing on me.

Afterward, I attacked the growing mountain of church-related paperwork on my desk: bills, baptismal and first communion certificates, and the quarterly financial statements. When the mountain was down to a small mound, I returned phone calls I'd received from parishioners.

I had a pastoral counseling session in the afternoon with Mrs. Irene Blake, whose forty-year-old husband was dying of stage four cancer. Having recently dealt with my sister's passing from leukemia, I sympathized with her and was able to offer her some practical advice regarding financial arrangements and end-of-life care. Finding concrete answers to age-old questions about why terrible things happen to wonderful people, and providing spiritual reassurances, however, was much harder to do. I gave her the best that I had, but suspected our next conversation would include a discussion of when to end life support and how to make funeral arrangements.

Thinking about my sister's death and Mrs. Blake's anguish brought my own spirits low, but picking up my nephew after school helped raise them again. He had my sister's silver-blue eyes, red hair, and quirky sense of humor. Spending time with him was like having her back in my life.

I had a few hours to bask in my boy's sunny world before the paranormal investigators would arrive at the hospital, so we walked downtown and browsed the MindFair Bookstore for a while. Afterward, we picked up the DVD of Disney's *Return to Never Land* from the library, and I let RJ talk me into a Happy Meal at McDonald's for dinner. Because I didn't know how late the investigation would go, I bathed him at the rectory and drove him to Colleen's apartment. There, I loaded the DVD into the player, settled RJ in with Peter Pan and Wendy's daughter for another sleepover at Colleen's, and headed to the hospital.

When I arrived at the snack shop at seven fifteen, the sign on the door read CLOSED, but the inside was a flurry of activity. The door was unlocked and I entered. Emily was standing near a window and her father was seated behind the counter. Several people scurried around the room.

I walked over to Emily and greeted her. "Wow, I'm surprised. I didn't expect this many people would be involved."

"These folks are serious, Jake. They have technical and audio specialists, and even a medium and spiritualist. I'm excited."

"How are you feeling? Have you or your dad had any more dizziness, nausea, or other problems since Monday?"

"No, nothing, but these attacks come and go. I spoke with Dixie Curry about our symptoms. She runs Tri-City Ghost Hunters. She told me that the eerie sense of a *presence* is a common occurrence with hauntings and often causes confusion, but she says it's rare to experience our other symptoms. Let me introduce you to her. I think you'll find her … interesting."

I'm not sure what I expected a paranormal investigator to look like—perhaps a twenty-something with spiked neon-blue hair and a nose ring, dressed in a bright red muumuu decorated with stars and moons. I couldn't have been more wrong.

Dixie Curry had caramel-colored skin, and with her white hair pulled back in a tight bun, she appeared old enough to be my grandmother. She wore a black pantsuit with an American flag pin on one lapel, and a Phi Beta Kappa key on the other.

"Ms. Curry, I'd like you to meet Dr. Jake Austin," Emily said. "He has a science background and is our resident skeptic."

I extended a hand and Curry met it with a firm shake.

"Delighted to make your acquaintance, sir. Please call me Dixie," she said in a drawl born somewhere south of the Mason-Dixon Line. "And y'all are not the only skeptic. I have a doctorate in chemistry from Tulane, and I'm trained to follow the empirical evidence, but … some *personal* experiences in my life have forced me to reevaluate my opinions and beliefs. You may find, Dr. Austin, that we are more alike than you may think. Allow me to show you our equipment."

Dixie Curry was well-named, an interesting blend of a Southern belle charm seasoned with a touch of cumin and cayenne pepper.

She led us to a table in the corner. "You may recognize this, Dr. Austin. It's an Infrared Thermometer." She picked up a handheld device, pointed it at a window, squeezed the trigger, and read the temperature on the screen. "Y'all have heard the expression, 'cold as a grave'? Well, an unexplained cold spot in a room can indicate the presence of an invisible spirit. But this handy-dandy tool can also rule out rational explanations such as a drafty window." Curry set the Infrared Thermometer on the table. "That's why I took the liberty, Emily, of unplugging the oscillating fan on the counter to avoid any man-made anomalies."

Curry picked up a black device with orange buttons.

"This is an EMF Meter, the kind used by electricians. It helps me exclude conventional items, such as household appliances, as a source of electromagnetic fluctuations. If we detect a large amount of electromagnetic radiation without evidence of a cause, however, that's highly indicative of the supernatural, as ghosts are believed to emit EM radiation or disturb the existing magnetic fields in a room. My assistant is disabling electrical equipment in the snack shop, and we'll be collecting all cellphones before we start."

This sounded a bit extreme to me but rather than challenge her, I pointed to a rectangular box with an antenna on the far side of the table that looked like an old-fashioned portable radio from the sixties. It was emitting a hissing sound, so I asked, "What's this?"

"It's a radio frequency scanner, commonly called a Ghost Box or Spirit Box. It sweeps AM and FM frequencies and produces white noise, clearing the air for spirits to come through and send a message. The idea is that a spirit can use that white noise to communicate," she added, picking up another device, "in a way that we can document on this electronic voice phenomena recorder. It detects all manner of sound, from unexplained footsteps when no one is present in the room to the occasional communicating spirit."

I groaned. "A Ghost Box? Really?"

She chuckled. "Come now. Not everything can be explained with science or logic."

A bearded man across the room hollered, "We're ready to begin, Dr. Curry."

She nodded at him, then turned to me. "That's the basics. After we finish our investigation this evening, we'll set up these other devices to monitor the empty snack shop overnight." She gestured around the table. "Geophones and motion sensors to detect vibration and unexplained movement, motion-activated cameras with night vision, along with digital voice recorders and the Ghost Box." She gestured toward the door. "We'd prefer to perform our investigation without spectators in order to avoid contamination of data. When we're finished collecting and evaluating all the information, we will provide you, Emily, with a complete report of our findings."

Emily's jaw dropped, her frustration evident. "But Dad and I were hoping to be present."

"Sorry. That's our policy."

Every good cop needs a bad cop. Emily was too gentle a soul to put up a fight, so I jumped in. "Sorry, Dr. Curry, but we *will* be staying," I said. "That is the only way the hospital administration will permit this investigation."

Curry glared at me. "Fine, fine. Stand by the door and try not to interfere."

Emily, Irv, and I silenced our cellphones and relinquished them, then huddled by the door as the Tri-City Ghost Hunters hurried around the room, fine-tuning their equipment and recording measurements. Dixie Curry stood in the center of the snack shop like a ringmaster, barking out commands and logging data on a clipboard.

I glanced at the large Tri-City team and all their equipment, lowered my voice, and asked Emily, "How much is this traveling circus charging you and your father? I hope they're not ripping you off."

"Not as much as you'd think." She smiled at Irv. "Dad can be a fierce negotiator when money is involved, and Dr. Curry wanted an excuse to further investigate paranormal activity at the hospital." She lowered her voice. "It's not as if Dad and I could tolerate what's been going on here much longer. It was either this or quit our jobs, which we love. These folks are professionals and have the equipment and the experience to get to the bottom of things. Dad and I did our research. We chose the Tri-City investigators because Dr. Curry is first and foremost a scientist."

"Hope you're right. Her explanation sounded like unadulterated mumbo jumbo to me. A *Spirit Box*? Come on. More like a high-tech Magic 8 Ball."

"You really are the Sultan of Cynicism, Jake. EMF sensors, infrared thermometers, and EVP recorders? Sounds very scientific to me! Give Dr. Curry the benefit of the doubt."

"Ghost voices picked up through the hissing static?" I scoffed. "That's merely pareidolia."

"What's that?" Irv asked. "And don't bury me under a pile of scientific gobbledygook."

"Pareidolia is the tendency of people to interpret random occurrences, such as electronic static, as something they're familiar with, like words. It's similar to seeing the shapes of animals in the clouds. It may *look* like an elephant, but you know darn well none are flying overhead."

Several team members became animated and called Dr. Curry over to the candy counter. They took a flurry of measurements and heatedly discussed the findings. The bearded man gestured excitedly, but Curry pointed to the microwave, unplugged it, and they began retaking the readings.

I explained to Emily and her dad what was happening, then added, "It looks as if Dr. Curry thinks her team detected an electrical anomaly rather than a spirit."

"I'm rooting for Curry," Irv whispered. "I'd be much happier if we've been dealing with faulty wiring instead of ghosts. Let's hope they find a logical explanation."

"Me too," I replied. My mind drifted to the *illogical* cigarette floating from the elevator the previous night. I drew a deep breath and gave them a detailed account of what I had witnessed: a nurse who was invisible on the security video walking out of the elevator and through an exit door that did not exist.

"Taking a smoke break outside by going through a second floor window?" Irv snickered. "That's a great way to be admitted as a patient or take a one-way trip to the morgue. What'd she look like, Jake?"

"Tall and thin, large green eyes, and butterscotch-colored hair. Maybe twenty-five years old, with a small, oval café au lait spot the size of a dime on her cheek near the corner of her mouth."

"Was she wearing a name tag?"

"Not that I noticed."

Emily stepped closer. "You said you didn't recognize her nursing uniform. Can you describe it?"

"Unlike any I've ever seen before. Blue blouse with a white apron and collar, and an unusually long white skirt extending well below her knees. Traditional white cap, but with a thick blue stripe."

"A real long skirt?" Irv shook his head. "Huh. Sounds more like a uniform from the fifties. I think you met the Night Nurse, Jake, the one killed in a car accident. We should send the ghost hunters to check out the elevator and second floor when they're done here."

"Dad's right. Nurses haven't worn those kinds of dresses for decades. I've heard there are photographs in the hospital library of every nursing class trained here. You should check it out."

Dr. Curry flicked the lights off and on, then shouted, "That's enough noise from you three! Either remain silent or leave the snack shop." When we didn't move, she added, "All right, then. Not a word from y'all and don't move." She and her assistants put on goggles. "We're going to night vision," she added, and the room went dark—as dark as my thoughts.

CHAPTER TWELVE

Saturday, April 26, 7:30 a.m.

The whole paranormal fiasco on Friday evening cost me a decent night's sleep. Tri-City Ghost Hunters finished their investigation after eleven p.m., set up their overnight monitoring equipment, and then locked the snack shop door. After I told Dixie Curry about my bizarre encounter in the elevator, she and her team went to examine the area, and I headed home.

A powerful spring storm blew in as I left the hospital, filling the night sky with daggers of lightening. Diagonal sheets of rain blurred the streetlights on my drive to the rectory. Halfway there, my headlight flashed in the eyes of a deer, and I had to swerve to avoid hitting the poor creature.

Arriving after midnight, I scampered from my car to the back door, punched RJ's birthday into the security system to silence it, and entered the kitchen, then changed out of my wet clothes. Too edgy to sleep, I tossed in bed for twenty minute before reading a Michael Koryta novel into the wee hours. Fatigue finally dragged my eyelids down, but my dreams were filled with shadowy apparitions. I awoke as tired as I'd been the night before.

I was scheduled to work the morning shift on Saturday at the hospital, so I'd assigned Mass at Sacred Heart Church to Father Snapp. Busybody that she was, Colleen had taken RJ to church and attended Snapp's first solo performance. She phoned me after the service and grudgingly admitted that she approved, although she added that it was a little like having a ghoulish Rasputin place the Blessed Eucharist on your tongue. She also noted that he had seemed easily distracted by any commotion from the children at the service.

When I arrived at the hospital, I grabbed a doughnut from the doctors' lounge and threw on my white coat. The waiting room was nearly empty and my *resident du jour* proved competent and motivated. It was the kind of shift you hope for when you're overtired.

My only interesting patient of the morning was a giant of a man, a biker who'd come to Urgent Care on his Harley. If I'd happened upon him outside the hospital after dark, I would have crossed to the other side of the street to avoid him. His new employer had required a TB skin test, a tiny subcutaneous pinprick injection. The instant he saw the needle, he looked away, turned ghostly pale, and shook violently. I thought he was going to pass out—and I almost burst out laughing because his neck and arms were covered in tattoos—ironic. He was a textbook example of the Pin-Prick Paradox, which states that "for some patients, the fear of needles is directly proportional to the number of their tattoos." I suspected that he had self-medicated heavily before the tattoo artist used him as a canvas.

That's the incredible thing about practicing medicine; patients never fail to surprise.

The memory of my encounter with the nurse in the elevator had plagued me all morning long. When I finished my shift, I walked to the medical library. As Emily had predicted, photographs of every hospital nursing class lined the library walls. Some graduates were nuns wearing traditional habits, wimples, and veils. I started with the 1940s classes. Color photographs began with the class of 1959, and the blue blouses with white collars were introduced in 1961. Nursing caps with matching blue stripes were added to the uniform in 1963 and the next year, there she was—the nurse I'd met in the elevator—dressed in the uniform I'd seen, with the same green eyes, rich butterscotch hair, and small café au lait spot near the corner of her mouth. No doubt about it, the same young woman. The name under her photo was Dorothy Margaret Clay.

I booted up a library computer and searched for her name in local newspapers but found no reference to her. Although the online obituaries only dated back to the mid-1970s, she was not mentioned in them. It was possible she had married and changed her name or moved away from the county. Any attempt to look into her background would now involve a long, tedious microfilm or microfiche search through obituaries, so I abandoned the hunt and opted instead to spend the afternoon with my nephew.

As I walked from my car toward the rectory, my cellphone chimed and Emily's number appeared on the screen.

"Oh, Jake, something terrible has happened." She sobbed. "Everett died this morning."

Given her ex-husband's severe brain injury and deteriorating condition, from a medical point of view the news was hardly surprising.

"I'm so sorry, Em. I know how much you cared for him. Is there anything I can do to help?"

"I was hoping you'd offer a funeral Mass for him. That's why I called. Could you, Jake? Please, for me."

Everett had been one of the most *unchristian* people I'd ever met. He may have attended church a few times during his miserable life, but that didn't make him a Christian any more than standing in a garage made him a car. But as much as I had despised her ex for the terrible way he had treated her, I cared too much for Emily to deny her anything.

"Of course, Em. I'll make the arrangement here at the church."

"Thanks, Jake. I'll call you with the details. Talk to you soon. Bye."

I was opening the rectory door when the full implication of Everett's death hit me. I froze. It changed everything. The woman I had loved since high school, the woman who also cared deeply for me, who had previously been unavailable, was now *available*.

I staggered into the rectory in a daze. As I headed for my study, Father Snapp brushed past me without a word and walked out the door. With an hour before I needed to pick up RJ from school, I plopped onto my desk chair in the study and pondered what Everett's death meant.

Emily and I had loved each other as long as I could remember and we had once talked of marriage. I'd seriously contemplated leaving the priesthood so we could marry, but the Church had refused her petition for an annulment. I'd even considered becoming an Episcopalian priest, but neither of us was willing to leave our faith, so the possibility of marriage had been taken off the table—until now. With Everett's death, Emily was not a *divorcee* and unavailable in the eyes of the Church. She was a *widow*, making a church wedding again possible, except … I was still a priest—a priest with a sacred obligation. A tsunami of roiled emotions—hope, angst, frustration, and uncertainty—surged over me.

With my thoughts more muddled than when I'd entered, I walked out of my study past the open guest room door. Curiosity got the best of me. With Snapp away, I peeked in for a closer look at the wooden steamer trunk belonging to the strange man who had invaded my once tranquil home. It was secured with thick leather straps and two locks. I recognized some of the symbols carved into the sides of the trunk: a human skull, a long-handled scythe with a curved blade, and the ancient Chinese Yin-Yang. I was unfamiliar with most of the other symbols except for a large shamrock on the top of the trunk. Unlike the images on the sides, the shamrock was raised a quarter of an inch and painted a faded green color.

Stepping into the room, I ran a finger over the carvings, but startled when I heard, "Intruder!" The creature in the cage flapped its wings and eyed me. "Be gone!"

As if by magic, Snapp appeared at my side. Away from the altar, he seemed a lot more like the darker Yin than the brighter Yang.

"Snooping, Father Jake? Tsk, tsk. How disappointing. Guess I'll have to remember to lock my door." He walked to the cage, opened it, and the bird hopped onto his shoulder. "Moarte is very … protective. Be careful, he's been known to bite." He whispered something to the bird, then turned at me. "What can I help you with?"

"Sorry Phineas, I didn't mean to intrude. I'm just fascinated by the symbols on your trunk. Did you say it was made in the 1800s?"

"Thomas Snapp, a great-uncle of mine, carved it from the trunk of an African Blackwood tree. He was a missionary there in the nineteenth century."

I touched the shamrock. "He was Irish, I gather?"

"On his mother's side. We Snapps are mongrels, with ancestors from all over the world. The three leaves of the shamrock represent the Holy Trinity. Father, Son, and Holy Spirit. The Celts believed it had mystical power, protecting the bearer from evil."

This was the first time Snapp had said more than a few words to me since he'd arrived. I had no idea who he really was and wanted to keep him talking. "And the other symbols?"

He walked over to the steamer trunk and pointed to what looked like a simple cross. "The Ailm is the first letter of the Ogham alphabet." He moved his finger to the left. "The Celtic Spiral signifies fate's unpredictability. Life is not linear, and everyone's journey through this world takes unexpected turns."

I certainly knew that to be true. My path had taken me from Army medic, to physician, and finally to the priesthood. My life was a splendid example of God's incomprehensible plan.

Snapp took a step closer and gestured to a triangle formed by three interlacing arcs. "The triquetra has many meanings. Past, Present, Future. Spirit, Mind, Body. Creator, Destroyer, Sustainer. Life, Death, Afterworld."

He glanced at Moarte and said, "Domum." The bird jumped from his shoulder and flew back into his cage.

Domum; it was the Latin word for *home*. In the twenty-first century, I suspected only priests and African grey parrots spoke classical Latin.

Snapp must have read my surprise. "Moarte's extremely bright and knows many words." He sighed as if he had tired of our conversation. "The other symbols you can probably figure out. The Celtic Cross protects the bearer from dark forces and gives him wisdom. The ancients believed the snake to be the source of magic and healing. Vultures literally *eat* death, and the raven represents the Devil."

Snapp caught me staring at the scars on his hands.

"My burns? Are they what interest you, Father?" He sighed again and began walking toward his desk. "In my vocation, my calling, I sometimes ... touch evil. Literally. Now if you'll excuse me, I must return to my studies."

I'd had enough. We had danced around the truth far too long already. I needed to know who this man was and why Bishop Lucci had assigned him here.

"Tell me about your work for Mother Church, Phineas?"

"Perhaps someday. It would take too long and I'm busy." He opened a leather-bound book that appeared older than the trunk. "Suffice it to say that our jobs are not dissimilar. I've been known to delve into the murky waters of the unfamiliar and solve a mystery or two myself."

"Is that so?" I thought for a moment. "Then maybe you can help me with one of mine."

That piqued his interest. I told him about my encounter with the Night Nurse. "She graduated from nursing school in 1964 and her name is Dorothy Margaret Clay, but I can't find anything about her on Google or in the local newspapers."

He stared at me for what must have been a full minute, then closed his book, booted up his computer, logged into Ancestry.com, entered his password, and searched for her.

"Nothing mysterious about her whereabouts, Father. She died in an accident in 1965. Her car went off a cliff and burst into flames. In those days, most cars didn't even have seatbelts. The poor woman never stood a chance." He pointed to the computer screen. "Here's a photo of the burned-out remnants of her car."

So sad. She'd died only a year after graduating. All that promise had been snuffed out in the blink of an eye.

Snapp swiveled his desk chair around and fixed me with his dark eyes. "What is interesting to me is why her spirit lingers at the hospital, and why she showed herself to you. I'll do some research and let you know what I find." He swiveled away from me again. "See you at supper."

And just like that, I was dismissed.

With the few minutes remaining before I picked up RJ at school, I reentered my study and searched for Phineas Snapp's name online. I suspected he was a rogue priest who quickly wore out his welcome, and Bishop Lucci needed a parish in which to warehouse him. Annoying me was simply a bonus for Lucci.

Having recently arrived in town, Snapp wasn't listed in the Clergy Directory published by the Cleveland Diocese, so I searched for him in the official national Catholic directory. Under "Location" it listed Snapp at Podgorica, Montenegro. His "Current Assignment" read "pending." The only photograph I found of him must have been taken many years earlier when he had been a seminarian, well before his long hair, sallow complexion, and skeletal frame. But even then, his dark piercing eyes seemed to look through you.

Frustrated, I Googled "talking birds." African greys were regarded as the most vocal. They were highly intelligent and lived for up to sixty years. Some amassed vocabularies of hundreds of words and were capable of having simple conversations.

Then I searched the name Moarte. Besides being an uncommon surname, it was the Romanian and Aromanian word for "death." I wondered what Snapp could have possibly done for a Romanian nobleman to be rewarded with a bird whose name meant death.

My search efforts only proved that four days after Snapp's arrival, I knew more about his bird than I did about the man sharing the rectory with RJ and me. Cloaked in a heavy shroud of unease, I drove to pick up my nephew from school.

CHAPTER THIRTEEN

Sunday, April 27, 11:00 a.m.

Emily and her father came to Mass regularly at Sacred Heart on Sundays. They always kept RJ company in the Quiet Room, the soundproof seating area at the back of the church intended for babies and young children.

As I walked to the altar, my boy looked up, grinned, and waved. I returned RJ's smile and nodded, but it took all my self-control not to laugh out loud and wave back at him—what a kid!

Father Snapp, who was celebrating Mass with me, was not at all amused by our display of affection. He cast a scowl in my direction and shook his head.

I offered a greeting to my parishioners and set about the joyous task of celebrating our Savior and the glory of God. I treasured my time with the Lord. As a young man, my world had imploded and it was faith that had cemented the pieces back together—and I was not about to allow Snapp to diminish the wonder and majesty I found in Mass.

After the service, Snapp removed his vestments and left the sacristy without a word. I wasn't sure what had upset him and frankly, I didn't care. Emily and her dad were joining us for supper, and two of the best cooks I knew, Colleen and Sonya Macon, were creating a culinary masterpiece at the rectory. Spending time with my chosen family ran a close second to the joy of offering Mass, and I nearly jogged across the church parking lot to the rectory. When I entered, I found my favorite Baptist heretic, Tree Macon, lounging in my recliner in the living room, completing our unconventional family unit.

He greeted me, then added, "You shouldn't leave the door unlocked, Jake. I'm afraid my unexpected presence here scared the daylights out of the tall, skinny dude. He said he was your new associate and scampered up the stairs. Good thing I wasn't in uniform. I think he might have had a stroke."

"Ah, so you met Father Phineas Snapp." I lowered my voice. "He's an acquired taste." I glanced around the room. "Where's your lovely wife?"

"Sonya's in the kitchen putting the finishing touches on her Bouillon soup."

Tree and I set the dining room table, then Emily and I spoke briefly about Everett's funeral arrangements. Her tears again flowed and I wanted to hug away her sorrow, but doing so would have been motivated more by my desire to hold her in my arms again rather than comfort her, so I resisted the urge. What I really wanted to discuss was what his death meant for the two of us. I couldn't, of course, because she had once loved the man and needed time to mourn his loss. Even broaching the subject this soon after his passing would have been crude and insensitive.

When Irv, Sonya, and RJ joined us, and Colleen began serving, I went up to Snapp's room, knocked, and peeked in.

"Supper's ready, Phineas."

"Not hungry," he growled, then opened the book on his desk. Moarte eyed me from his cage and hissed.

I stepped into the room. "Is something bothering you?"

He pushed his desk chair back, stood, and turned toward me.

"For one thing, I value my privacy and don't like to find strangers wandering around the rectory."

I'd already had my weekly quota of B.S. from this man. "Emily, her father, Tree Macon, and his wife, Sonya, are my friends. They often visit, so get used to it. Come down and I'll introduce you."

His eyes grew cold and dark. Moarte growled and hopped wildly around inside his cage.

"Something else, Phineas?"

"Darn right there is. I'm tired of that Irish woman always spying on me. And it's unseemly and *irreverent* for a priest to be raising a child. We both took a vow to serve the Lord, forsaking all others. Offering an undivided heart is central to our commitment. 'Celibate' was also intended to mean *childless*. Let me be clear, I want nothing to do with the boy."

We stepped toward each other and were nose to nose. I had no idea who I was messing with or how volatile he was—but then again, neither did Snapp. We were two loose cannons at point-blank range. My hands fisted. I didn't know where this was going but I'd had enough!

"Now I'll tell you what's bothering *me*, Phineas. You're scaring RJ, and that ends today. I'm pastor of this church and you're my assistant. I'll give you as much space and independence as I can, but you will treat everyone here civilly. Are we clear? Now come to supper."

Snapp's eyebrows drifted up and his expression changed from fury to something akin to amusement. A smirk danced across his lips. "Sure, *boss*. Anything you say."

"And for the love of God, Phineas, clean that damn bird cage. It stinks in here."

Without a word, he pushed past me and headed downstairs.

When I entered the dining room, I introduced Snapp to everyone and he took a seat between Sonya and Colleen, as far from me as possible. I offered everyone a glass of merlot, sat, then said grace.

Having already discussed Everett's funeral arrangements, we moved on to lighter conversations. The food was delicious, so I said to Sonya, "I've never tasted anything quite like this. What is it?"

"Bouillon. It's a favorite dish in Haiti, Jake, where my mother's from," she replied in a Caribbean lilt as gentle as a summer breeze. "It's made from beef, yams, kelp, cabbage, plantains, peppers, and celery." Each word from her lips was an exotic spice. With her large burnt-almond eyes, lovely cinnamon-colored skin, and keen intellect, she was without a doubt Tree's *better* half.

Emily and Colleen made several attempts to engage Snapp in the discussion. He replied with few words and displayed no interest, so the ladies gave up. He ate the broccoli salad and pushed the rest of his food around his plate. RJ, who was usually a chatterbox, also ate little, staring quietly at the scars on Snapp's hands, fear in his eyes. I attempted unsuccessfully to distract him by asking about school and his best friend. Snapp responded by glaring at my nephew until RJ shifted his gaze to the floor. It was all I could do to refrain from jumping to my feet and telling him to pick on someone his own size.

Emily filled Tree and Sonya in on the problems at the snack shop, and I told them about my bizarre encounter with the nurse in the elevator. Colleen hung on every word, and Snapp's interest level appeared to rise.

Tree said, "The nurse died in a single car accident in 1965? Driving off a cliff sounds like a suicide or possibly a DUI to me." He paused. "I could find out if there's a case file on her death, if that would help."

"Thanks. I'd appreciate that." I topped off my wine. "Any word from the Tri-City Ghost Hunters, Em?"

"Dixie Curry dropped off the report yesterday. It wasn't what dad and I had hoped. Inconclusive. No convincing evidence of paranormal activity in the snack shop. We wanted a definitive answer."

Snapp finished the last of his wine, cleared his throat, and said, "There are many things beyond our comprehension." All heads swiveled in his direction. "That doesn't mean they don't exist. Our senses are sometimes more sensitive than scientific instruments," he added and poured himself another glass of merlot.

Irv turned to me. "The Tri-City team may not have found anything definite in the snack shop, Jake, but there was nothing inconclusive about the second floor hallway. Dixie said the area was teeming with activity, especially by the elevator. Her Ghost Box thing went nuts, right Em?"

"Yes, and her voice recorder picked up one word—'glub.' Dixie said it was repeated over and over again. Glub, glub, glub. The kind of sound a fish might make in a cartoon. Very weird. It also recorded the sound of footsteps at the same time the night vision cameras filmed a strange red-orange light floating down the hall."

Like the tip of a lit cigarette in the hand of an invisible nurse, I thought.

Colleen poured coffee for everyone. Emily took a sip and continued. "Apparently, the electromagnetic radiation fluctuations were off the charts at that end of the second floor hall that used to be part of the original hospital."

"Yeah," her dad added. "Dixie said it was also *cold as a grave* near one patient's room there. Unfortunately, that doesn't help us with our problem in the snack shop. We never know when the next episode will happen. Any thoughts, Jake?"

"I have some ideas but need to do more research this week—that is if I don't have to fly out of town. My Superior General wants me to investigate the theft of funds at a church near New Orleans."

"Ah Louisiana, the land of voodoo," Sonya said. "Some of my Haitian relatives still practice it, and black magic remains strong among some of the Cajun and Creole communities." She looked from Emily to me and chuckled. "Beware of the voodoo *love spell*. It's strong juju."

Snapp waved Sonya's comments away. "Forget voodoo. Steer clear of the town of Reeves, west of the Big Easy. I almost died there a few years ago on an assignment. I should have expected trouble when I saw their area code was 666—the *mark of the beast* in Revelation 13."

The room fell silent. Snapp glanced at me, then addressed Emily and Irv. "If Father Austin is unavailable, I'd be happy to assist you. I've done considerable research into the occult. I'd also like to see the area on the second floor where the unexplained readings were taken."

Snapp volunteering? That was a first. I didn't know what to make of it. Was he really offering his help or was this personal, an opportunity to outshine me?

"Drop in at the snack shop anytime," Irv replied. "I'll even throw in a free cup of coffee for any insight you can offer."

RJ tossed his napkin on the table. "I'm done eating, Daddy. Can I go watch TV?"

"Sure, sport."

At the word *Daddy*, Snapp glared at me and stood. "Sorry to leave, but I must meditate and study. Thanks for the interesting conversation."

He nodded, and my personal nightmare disappeared like a puff of smoke.

CHAPTER FOURTEEN

Monday, April 28, 11:30 a.m.

I had arranged my schedule so that I only had to work until three o'clock on Monday, which gave me enough time to return to the church and offer a funeral Mass for Emily's ex-husband.

It was a slow day in Urgent Care and I was in a good mood and feeling relaxed—and that's when I made the cardinal mistake. I ordered two large pizzas for the staff. Susan Ochs, the head nurse and majordomo, overheard the phone order, asked me if I'd lost my mind, and stomped away.

Our receptionist must have read my confusion. "Do you know what you've done, Doctor? You violated Ochs' Law!"

"What the heck is that?"

"Never order pizza on a quiet day."

"Why?"

She shook her head. "You'll see."

Everything became clear the moment the food arrived and the aroma of melted cheese and hot pepperoni drifted through the department. As if the deliveryman had opened the floodgates, our waiting room instantly filled with patients, standing room only; sick patients, angry patients, impatient patients.

Our quiet day went to hell on wheels, and we spent the next three hours darting around the department like a bunch of lunatics on roller skates. When my replacement finally arrived at 3:00 p.m., I was staring mournfully at the two cold, unopened pizza boxes.

Nurse Ochs appeared at my side.

"Sorry, Susan," I said. "I just heard about Ochs' Law today. I won't ever forget it."

"There's a corollary to my law, Doctor: To eat hot pizza at the hospital, you need to retire. Now go home, Jonah, before a giant whale swallows up Urgent Care. You've done more than enough for one day."

No need to tell me twice—before she could fire another salvo at me, I was out the door and on my way to the second floor to visit Steve McCutchan, one of my parishioners. He had been part of the horrendous seven-car pileup early Friday morning, and I'd helped treat him in the emergency room.

The door to room 232 was open and I knocked on the doorframe. McCutchan lay in bed with his forearm encased in a fiberglass cast. His left leg was in traction, the skeletal fixation pin protruding through the skin below his knee. It made me wince. The airbag had pummeled his face, leaving multiple cuts and bruises, and he looked much older than he had when I'd last seen him in church.

"How are you feeling, Steve?" A stupid question.

"Better than I did when the ambulance brought me in, though that may be due to the morphine." He closed his eyes. "No offense, but I'd rather see you at Mass than in the hospital."

"None taken. Anything I can do for you before I go home?"

He thought about it. "Yeah, can I have a sleeping pill this evening? I can't get any rest here with that nurse waking me up all night long."

"I'll request a sedative from your surgeon, but the nurses need to take vital signs every so often and check on you."

"No, I get that. But there's one nurse who comes in and just gazes around the room, as if she's looking for something. Never says a word. Doesn't even respond when I talk to her. It's like she's in a trance."

"Do you know her name?"

"No. No name tag, but she's a heavy smoker, I can tell you that. Smells like a damn chimney in here whenever she walks in. It's enough to make me gag. Even lit one up once as she was leaving. Please ask them to send someone else at night."

I suspected I knew exactly who Mr. McCutchan was talking about. I walked to the nursing station and asked the head nurse if any of her team smoked. She denied it, so I relayed the bizarre story he'd told me.

"Guess I'm not surprised, Dr. Austin. That room is a perpetual pain in my behind. But I know how to solve the problem. We discharged a patient down the hall this morning. As soon as housekeeping finishes cleaning the room, I'll move Mr. McCutchan into it. I'm sure he won't have any more problems."

"Why? What's with room 232?"

"No idea. Wish I knew. Patients have all kinds of problems in that room. I only use it when we're filled to capacity. Sometimes we find the water running in the bathroom sink or the call button in there goes off at all hours of the night, even when the room is unoccupied. I've had maintenance come a dozen times, but they never find an electrical short or any other explanation."

My thoughts turned to Mr. McCutchan's safety, and to any possible danger Emily and her dad might face from a spiritual presence.

"Have any patients been injured in 232?"

"No, thank God. Not physically anyway. But one poor lady was convinced we were having an earthquake because the bathroom door and nightstand drawers kept opening and closing all night. She was so terrified I had her moved to another room at four a.m."

I thanked the head nurse, headed to the elevator, then stopped and focused on the vulnerability of Emily and Irv in the snack shop. Being sightless was challenging enough without inanimate objects moving around the room. I called Dixie Curry.

"Where exactly did you find paranormal activity on the second floor, Ms. Curry?"

"That whole hallway, but especially the south end, past the nurses' station. In all my years of investigating, I've never detected temperatures that cold or electromagnetic readings as distorted as in that area. Our psychic felt a presence and heard moaning from one of the rooms. When I rushed in with a nurse, the patient was sound asleep, but the hot water in the shower was turned on full blast and … there was a *baby's footprint* on the steamed-up bathroom mirror. Damnedest thing I've ever encountered. Unfortunately, the ruckus we caused woke the poor man up. His leg was in traction and he'd just fallen asleep. I felt terrible."

"Did he have a cast on his arm?"

"Yes, but how could you possibly…?"

No doubt about it. Steve McCutchan had met the Night Nurse in room 232.

"He's a patient of mine, Dixie. Tell me about the word the electronic recorder picked up in the second floor hallway. Was it *glub*? Think. It could be important."

"Sounded like it, though there was a lot of static and it was muffled, so we're not entirely certain. My audio expert is trying to remove background noise and clean up the recording. I'll contact you and Emily if we come up with anything definitive."

I thanked her for her help and was walking to my car in the parking garage when my Superior General's secretary called.

"Father Demarco is worried about theft at Blessed Savior Church outside of New Orleans, and he wants you to review the finances there. They'll be expecting you at the rectory. I've purchased your airline ticket and arranged your rental car. You should receive the ticket and confirmation information in the mail tomorrow. The package will also contain a letter of introduction from Father Demarco, which should open doors and provide you with any assistance you may need. You fly out on Wednesday. Have a blessed day, Father Austin. Goodbye."

And just like in my Army days, I had my marching orders from my Superior General.

CHAPTER FIFTEEN

Monday, April 28, 4:00 p.m.

I arrived at the church in time to change into my vestments and meet the processional as the pallbearers carried in the closed casket. Besides Emily and her father, there were only a handful of mourners present, which was no surprise, given that Emily's ex-husband had not been a nice person.

Father Snapp had been called to a meeting with Bishop Lucci, so Deacon Pat Lyons had volunteered to assist me. He had worked at St. Joseph's Hospital for several years and we had become friends. In some ways, I envied him.

Priests assist the ministry of the bishop and the pope, whereas deacons are servants of the church and the priests. Besides assisting at Mass, a deacon served the Church in many other ways. Although he couldn't hear confessions, give absolution, or anoint the sick, as an ordained deacon Pat could baptize babies, counsel families, visit shut-ins, and preach homilies—many of the duties I loved about the priesthood. What he *could* do that I couldn't was … marry. Deacon Pat had a wife and two lovely daughters … hence, my envy.

I blessed the casket with Holy water, then draped it with the pall, a cloth symbolizing Everett's baptism into the church—although I suspected this was the first time he'd been in church since his wedding.

The service went smoothly. For Emily's sake, I set aside my personal feelings about her ex. In my homily, I told the congregation that God would guide them through their mourning just as He had been at Everett's side during his last days. I reminded them that the resurrection of Jesus taught us that the end of this life is just a beginning, and that God, not Death, has the final word.

As I spoke, I read sadness in Emily's eyes and wondered if mine revealed my loathing for the man. After Communion, Emily read a lovely poem she had written praising her ex, which reaffirmed for me what an incredibly kind and forgiving person she was.

When the service ended, I incensed the casket again, blessed it with holy water, and the pallbearers lead the recessional from the Church. Because Everett had requested to be cremated, the actual burial would take place in a few days. That posed a problem. I explained the situation to Deacon Lyons.

"Could you officiate at the burial on Thursday, Pat? I'll be out of town on assignment at a church in New Orleans."

"Of course. I'd be glad to." He looked at his watch. "Sorry to run, Jake, but it's my daughter's birthday. My house is about to be invaded by a couple dozen screaming, sugar-crazed kids, and my dear wife will need some adult reinforcements."

I greeted the mourners as they filed out of the church. Emily was the last to leave. She wore a touch of makeup and a simple black dress that accentuated her figure. Showered in stained-glass light, her beauty made it hard for me to breathe. She thanked me for offering the funeral Mass and as she walked away, I would have liked nothing more than to share the sugar-crazed chaos of RJ's next birthday party, and every birthday to come, with her at my side.

There could be no doubt, I still desperately loved her. My head was losing the battle with my heart. I stood there for a long moment in my sacred vestments watching her leave, wondering if I even deserved to wear them.

Colleen was waiting for me inside the rectory. She handed me an envelope.

"Sheriff Macon sent this for you by courier, Father."

It was sealed and stamped CONFIDENTIAL. The case file on Dorothy Margaret Clay's death that Tree had promised. Colleen bit her lip and gazed at me, no doubt hoping I'd elaborate and provide some juicy gossip. I didn't oblige. Instead, I asked about her day.

"RJ was a delight, but that towering mute came back and has been shambling around the house, complaining about every little thing and getting on my nerves."

"Sorry. I'll speak with him. Would you care to join us for dinner, Colleen?"

"Kind of you, but I've seen enough of that man for one day, thank you very much. I'll be taking my leave. Meatloaf is warming in the oven, and there's a salad in the refrigerator."

A mischievous smile danced across her lips.

"I have some … interesting information for you, Father," she whispered. Her eyes pinballed around the room like Mata Hari searching for an enemy agent. "I don't know what Father Snapp did in Montenegro, but I asked a friend in Atlanta to do some research. She spoke with a local pastor who told her that …." Colleen leaned in and lowered her voice even more. "Snapp performed an *exorcism* on a young woman there. It didn't go well. A window was shattered and there was quite a to-do. The commotion disturbed the neighbors and drew the attention of the media. Thought you should know."

The interstate gossip grapevine had been hard at work, and the Queen Busybody couldn't wait to pass on the latest report to me. It appeared she was more titillated than appalled. No need for an internet search engine when I had Colleen around; she could put Google out of business.

Given Snapp's steamer trunk with the ancient symbols, his secretive behavior and self-imposed isolation, and the menacing way he lurked around the rectory, however, a clearer picture of the man began to form. Rumor maybe, but it rang true.

When I didn't react, Colleen scowled and asked, "Were you already aware of this?"

"No, but I had my suspicions. Thanks for the information."

"Should we not evict him from the rectory or report him to Bishop Lucci? Or at least do *something*?"

"I'm sure the bishop knew Snapp's history before he assigned him here." I understood that the Church sanctioned exorcisms on rare occasions, but it was Snapp's mental state and judgment I was concerned about. "I would love to evict him for a number of reasons, not the least of which is the disdainful way he treats you and RJ. Unfortunately, that's not my prerogative but … let me see what I can do."

Colleen heaved a woeful sigh and her shoulders slumped as she left the rectory, clearly disappointed there would be no public flogging.

I was, however, more concerned than I'd let on about the man living in the rectory with RJ and me. There is a fine line between eccentric and unhinged. I joined RJ in the living room and after a pleasant evening together, I tucked him into bed and knocked on Snapp's door.

"Yes?"

Without waiting for an invitation, I marched in. Phineas was seated at his desk, the ancient leather-bound book open in his lap. Moarte greeted me from his cage with, "Be gone!"

"So Phineas, exorcism? Really? I realize it's occasionally practiced, but—"

"That's not *all* I do for Mother Church." He rose from his chair to his full, lofty height and peered down at me. "Though occasionally, driving out demons is the only option left for some unfortunate souls. And it's necessary more often than you might think."

"Were you ever planning to tell me?"

"My assignments are on a need to know basis … and you didn't need to know. The details of my duties are well above your pay grade, Austin, so keep your nose out of my business."

He picked up an apple from the desktop and took a bite, then unfolded a jackknife, cut off a slice, and fed it to Moarte through the bars of the cage.

Snapp pointed the steel blade in my direction. "Don't act so outraged and righteous with me. The bishop told me that you're the chief hooligan for the Camillian Order and filled me in on your other unsavory activities."

"So Lucci sent you here to *spy* on me, did he?"

A grin creased Snapp's lips for a second, then vanished.

"You're missing the point, Austin. You're in no position to judge me. We both have jobs that at times may be … shall we say, unpleasant. You solve mysteries of this realm; I deal with the unearthly variety."

"But what you do has no basis in science and can cause irreparable harm."

"No, it's based on *centuries* of experience, much of it achieved by my ancestors. There are many problems that your science has no solution for, many questions it cannot answer. At times, members of your medical profession fail and cause their patients permanent psychological, physical, and emotional damage." He waved the knife in my face, and I stepped back. "Hell, I heard you damn near got yourself and the Sheriff killed on one of your assignments. Don't talk to me about causing harm!" He gazed down at the jackknife, hesitated, then closed it and slipped it into his pocket. "There are risks involved in *both* of our jobs."

Snapp opened Moarte's cage and the bird hopped onto his shoulder. "So don't get all high and mighty with me, Austin, and don't even *think* about comparing our ministries for Mother Church. You hold the hands of a bunch of guilt-ridden sinners." He raised a heavily scarred hand and made a fist. "I'm in mortal combat with demons!"

"No, I minister to *real* people, Snapp, flesh and blood, with life-altering problems and physical diseases."

"Real? Are you denying the presence of the supernatural in our world, of the very existence of Satan? Perhaps your invisible nurse at the hospital will teach you otherwise. The Devil's cleverest trick is making people think he doesn't exist. Perhaps he's fooled you too."

He stepped toward me and raised his hands.

"Behold my battle scars! I've grappled with the Beast, Austin, looked into his blood-red eyes, touched his searing flesh, felt his fury. Believe me, he exists!"

Moarte fluttered his coal-black wings and screamed, "Sinner be gone!" then flew wildly around the room. I closed the door so he couldn't escape and frighten RJ.

"Can't you silence that infernal bird, Snapp? Was that … that *creature* your payment for an exorcism?"

No reply. He grinned again as he watched my blood pressure rise, then reached an arm out in front of him. Moarte landed on his forearm. He stroked it as if comforting a petulant child.

"No, Moarte was a gift from a Romanian nobleman—out of *gratitude* for saving his child from a living Hell." He shook his head. "Does my bird frighten you?" A smirk slithered across his lips. "Perhaps Moarte's choice of words strikes too close to the truth? I am many things, but I'm no fool. I've seen you and Emily Beale together, seen the sexual tension, the smoldering connection—and your united effort to raise that child down the hall. Is he yours? Are you a *sinner*, Father?"

"How dare you! RJ's my *nephew*, and I'm his legal guardian. My sister begged me to care for him from her deathbed and by God, that's exactly what I'm going to do!"

We stared at each other until Snapp whirled around and put Moarte back in his cage.

"That doesn't mean you're not a sinner, Austin. Evil has many forms, and is ever-changing and eternal. I could tell you tales that would keep you awake for days." He fed the bird a grape. "Battling Satan is like fighting the mythological Hydra—you cut off one of Lucifer's heads and another grows back. I get little rest, so if you'll excuse me, I have *important* work to do."

I stared at him for a long time. Snapp was probably the kid in school that no one wanted to have lunch with, and he definitely was the house guest everyone hoped would never arrive. He'd frightened RJ and Colleen, and had unsettled our fragile household in a matter of days. I made a decision.

"Listen Snapp, I fly out of town on Wednesday, and I won't have you alone in the rectory with RJ and Colleen in my absence. I don't care where you go, I want you and your bird gone until I get home. And just so you know, I'll be calling Bishop Lucci tomorrow and requesting your transfer."

"Fine by me, Austin. You think I want to be here? Nothing would please me more than to spend time away from that meddlesome Irish woman and your brat. My van is fully equipped. Believe me, I've lived in worse places."

"And God help me, you'll be in charge of the parish while I'm gone, Snapp. Try not to reduce it to rubble in a week!"

I opened the door to his room and found RJ crying softly in the hall. His eyes were wide as he gazed up at me, tears running down his freckled cheeks.

"Daddy, I can't sleep. I … heard yelling. I'm scared."

"It's okay, RJ. Everything's fine. There's nothing to fear." I wrapped an arm around him and we started down the hall. "Let's get you to bed, and I'll tuck you in for the night."

As we passed Snapp's room, his lip curled and he slammed the door. He could slam all the doors he wanted, but we weren't done settling our differences. I had a few more choice words for that bastard and I wanted him out of the rectory permanently—but at that moment, my only concern was comforting my boy.

CHAPTER SIXTEEN

Tuesday, April 29, 7:00 a.m.

Before leaving for work in the morning, I asked for Colleen's help.

"I need to fly to New Orleans on Wednesday. Will you be okay caring for RJ alone for about a week? I'm grateful for all you do, and sorry to add to you burden."

"The lad is a joy, Father, no burden at all. I'll be fine, but … what about our resident ghoul upstairs?"

"I've asked Father Snapp to find other lodgings while I'm away."

She hesitated. "Pardon my concern, Father, but the man still has a house key and knows the security alarm code. I've no desire to deal with him in your absence, not without a shillelagh at the ready. How certain are you he'll not wander back in while you're gone?"

Given our last contentious squabble, I suspected it would be a while before Snapp returned to the rectory, but I wasn't positive. "I'm fairly confident he won't. I hate to disrupt RJ's routine any more than necessary, Colleen, but if you have any concern, take him to your apartment."

"Okay then, Father, if you say so."

I thanked her and left for the hospital. As soon as we cleared the Urgent Care waiting room of patients that morning, I made some telephone calls to enlist the assistance of my "village" in caring for RJ while I was away. Emily volunteered to pitch in whenever Colleen needed help or relief. Unfortunately, they both had conflicts on the same day. I crossed my fingers, called Tree's wife, and asked Sonya for her help.

"I've raised three daughters to womanhood," she answered in a sweet Jamaican lilt, "and I'm nearly done raising my husband. RJ is already better behaved than Tree. Caring for one small boy will be no problem."

I then informed Nurse Ochs of my trip, and phoned Harvey Winer in administration to arrange for coverage of the Urgent Care Department while I was gone. I was only scheduled to work until noon, so when my shift ended I drove to the rectory, grabbed a ham sandwich, and opened the envelope Tree Macon had sent. It contained Dorothy Margaret Clay's police file from 1965.

The folder was thin. Little time and attention had been given to her death. A picture taken from the top of one of the shale cliffs carved by the Vermilion River showed a small black blotch on the rocks below. There were two close-up photographs of her burned-out 1959 Volkswagen Beetle in the ravine below, black smoke rising from the wreckage. The investigator reported that a blood alcohol level could not be obtained and the victim couldn't be visually identified because the body was too badly burned. Dorothy had been identified from her dental records.

The coroner ruled her death an accident, but couldn't entirely exclude the possibility of suicide. His report also noted that Dorothy had multiple skull and extremity fractures consistent with trauma from the one hundred foot plunge from the cliff, but found nothing else. Not much evidence had survived the fire. The metal head of her stethoscope was found in the front seat. The car's trunk contained a tire iron and jack, the rim of a spare tire, and a two-inch metal tube attached to a four-by-two-inch ribbed steel wedge of uncertain purpose. Everything combustible had been incinerated. Except for several short interviews with her coworkers, there was little information about Dorothy Margaret Clay's life or the circumstances of her death—and absolutely no indication of why her spirit might be roaming the hospital at night.

Dorothy's parents were dead, but I noticed that she had a sibling. A few clicks on the computer revealed that her younger sister, Sybil, lived in town at her parents' old address. I had a few hours before I picked up RJ from school, so I dialed her number. When I explained that I worked at St. Joseph's Hospital and wanted to speak with her about her sister, she hesitated. Only after I told her I was a priest did she agree to meet with me.

I slipped on a clerical shirt and Roman collar, drove across town, and Sybil invited me into her home. A crucifix hung over the doorway. She led me into her living room, a museum of 1950s furnishings, fads, and fashions. Sybil was short and thin, sheathed in a flowered dress, and wore her gray hair in a pixie cut that hugged her narrow face.

She offered me a cup of tea with a small, delicate hand before picking up her own cup and settling on the couch across from me.

She took a sip. "So, Father, you want to know about Dorothy?"

How to begin? I certainly didn't want to mention my encounter with her dead sister in the elevator. I needed to open the conversation with something nonthreatening and make a personal connection.

"I heard the story of Dorothy's tragic accident. It was such a terrible loss to our hospital family."

Sybil's eyes narrowed to slits. "That was a long time ago, Father." She sat rigidly on the couch, lips pursed, skeptical. "Why now?"

I wanted to alleviate her suspicion and engage her in the conversation. "Honestly, I can't explain why I feel such a strong connection to her, but I do." I resorted to the truth. "Maybe it's because I was very close to my mother and lost her unexpectedly in a house fire."

She relaxed and leaned forward.

"I wanted to learn more about Dorothy's life in happier times, Sybil. That's how I try to remember my mother, when she was in high spirits and joking around. I hope you don't mind my asking." Glancing around the room, I saw a couple of photographs of the two sisters as teenagers, but none of a husband or children. "Were you and your sister close?"

"Oh yes, Father. Like the proverbial peas in a pod, especially after our parents died. She was such a pretty thing and so kind. And smart as a whip. I miss her to this day. I wanted to be just like her. That's why I became a nurse. Best decision I ever made. My patients *are* my family."

"Did Dorothy enjoy working at St. Joseph's Hospital?"

"Absolutely. She loved caring for people and enjoyed her time there. Caring and joyful. That's who she was in a nutshell, Father. Always laughing. Our dad used to call her Little Miss Sunshine. She was in love with life, especially after she met someone special at the hospital, someone she cared deeply about."

"Oh, who was that? Anyone I might have met?"

"I don't know really. One of her friends introduced them. When I would ask Dorothy, she'd tease me, calling him her *mystery man*. Someone quite important at the hospital, I gather from what she said. Every time she spoke about the guy, her eyes would sparkle and she'd giggle like a school girl, but she would never tell me who he was. After her accident, I forgot all about him. Didn't seem to matter anymore."

"I understand." I'd been looking for links to the hospital that might cause Dorothy's spirit to linger there and needed to keep Sybil talking. "Who was the friend that introduced them?"

"It's been so many years, Father, I can't recall. One of her classmates. A nun."

That gave me two connections between Dorothy and the hospital. Her boyfriend who worked there, and a nun who introduced them. I wanted more.

"What did Dorothy do for fun? Did she have any hobbies?"

"Neither of us was athletic. We enjoyed long drives together in her VW Bug and loved to sew and crochet." Sybil tapped an intricately designed, orange and yellow afghan comforter next to her on the couch. "This is one of Dorothy's creations. It warms me on cool evenings—well, the combination of the afghan and her memory." She stared off into the distance for a while, as if lost in a reverie. "Although Dorothy did become interested in golf just before she … left us. Said her beau was teaching her." Sybil blushed. "Said he was helping her learn to *swing*."

I didn't dare ask if she thought her sister committed suicide, so I said, "I couldn't help but wonder why she was driving along the cliff road. Did you go there with her when you took car rides together?"

"No, never. We preferred the gentle rolling hills of the countryside. I can't imagine why she drove up there that day." Her brow wrinkled and her look of suspicion returned. She checked her wristwatch and picked up the tray and the teapot. "Now if you'll excuse me, Father, I'm working tonight and need to get ready."

I thanked her, drove to the hospital, and stopped briefly in the medical library to look again at the graduation photographs hung on the walls. The 1964 nursing class picture showed only two women wearing nuns' habits. I didn't know if one of them was the friend who'd introduced Dorothy to her boyfriend, but it was a place to start. I wrote down their names, then picked up my nephew from school.

When we got home, Colleen was removing dinner from the oven. I undertook the unpleasant task of explaining to RJ that I had to leave town for a while. It would be the first time we were apart for any length of time since his mother died. My nephew stomped his foot and began to cry, but when I told him that Colleen was moving into the rectory to stay with him, she somehow spun the news into an enchanted adventure. Forget Mary Poppins and her spoon full of sugar. I preferred the magical mistress of Irish blarney to sweeten my five-year-old sourpuss.

After RJ was asleep, I Google-searched for the two nuns who had graduated with Dorothy Margaret Clay. One had passed away, but the other was alive and working in a Catholic nursing home in Nashville, Tennessee. It was too late to telephone, so I wrote down her contact information and packed a suitcase for my trip to New Orleans.

As I finished, Keri Novak phoned me. She was an FBI agent I had worked with to bring down Big Angie Giordano, the head of a large drug ring. She was also my only connection to my father, who had testified against the mob boss in order to take the heat off of RJ and me. Dad was now in WITSEC—the federal Witness Security Program. I hadn't spoken with him since the trial. Only the U.S. Marshals Service knew exactly where he was located, and direct communication with anyone from his past was forbidden.

My dad and I had been estranged for years, but when he risked his own life to protect my boy and me, I had forgiven past transgressions and begun rebuilding our relationship. Novak occasionally called me with briefings on his activities, and kept him up-to-date on ours.

"How's my dad doing, Keri? Is he staying out of trouble?"

"Yeah, with a little help from his federal friends."

"Is he still playing with that jazz band and drinking too much whiskey?"

"Drinking yes, but his jammin' days are over for a while. That's why I called. Some guy's been sniffing around town, asking too many questions. The Marshalls Service got nervous and decided to move him to a new location, so you won't be hearing from me until he's safe and settled in."

I snapped the suitcase closed and sank down onto the bed. "You think Giordano's thugs are after him?"

"We're not positive, but we're not gonna wait around to find out." She went quiet for a while. "*You* haven't had any recent problems have you, Father Austin? Nobody snooping around town askin' questions or acting suspicious, right?"

"Hold on, Keri." I massaged the back of my neck. "Are you saying my nephew and I are in danger?"

"No, no. I'm not saying that at all. Relax, Father. Let's not jump to conclusions. We don't even know if your father's in jeopardy. I'm just covering my bases, but give me a call if you notice anything hinkey. I'll be in touch. Gotta run. Good night."

The instant she hung up the phone, my pleasant evening went swirling down the toilet.

CHAPTER SEVENTEEN

Wednesday, April 30, 10:30 a.m.

My flight to New Orleans was a bone-jarring roller-coaster ride, and I hoped that wasn't an omen of things to come. Much to my surprise, the Camillian Order had rented a Buick Park Avenue for me, a full-size luxury car, far nicer than my car at home. My new gig for Father Demarco appeared to come with perks.

An hour west of the Big Easy, I arrived at Blessed Savior Church, a lovely brick edifice with ornate stained-glass windows. The roof, however, was covered in a blue tarp. Ladders and shingles were stacked in front of the building, and a dumpster filled with broken terra cotta roofing tiles was parked along one side.

Wanting to get the lay of the land before revealing why I'd been sent, I knocked at the rectory door and was greeted by Charlotte Trumble, who introduced herself as the administrative assistant for the church. She looked to be in her early fifties and wore her russet hair pulled back into a tight bun. A tall, imposing woman, she was dressed in a gray pantsuit with padded shoulders, which gave her the appearance of an aging bodybuilder.

"Father Austin, I presume." She raised an eyebrow. "Father Demarco's secretary notified us of your arrival but gave us no details about your stay."

"I'm on vacation for a couple of weeks, Ms. Trumble, and looking forward to sightseeing, quiet reflection, and a taste of the local cuisine."

"Oh, please call me Lottie. Everyone does." She smiled. "It's lovely here this time of year, Father, though a touch warm and humid. Just beware of the alligators. They're aggressive during mating season. Hopefully, the bellowing of bull gators from the nearby bayou won't interfere with your meditation." She held the door open and we stepped inside. "Let me show you to the guest room. We're having lunch in an hour. Please join us."

I followed her upstairs. As expected for a rectory, my quarters were modest but pleasant. I unpacked my bags, changed into shorts and a Polo shirt, then entered the dining room and introduced myself to a young man seated at the table.

He stood and extended a hand. "Welcome, Father Austin. I heard you were coming. I'm Father Wronka. Please call me Edwin."

I shook his hand. "And I'm Jake."

His collared shirt and slacks were starched and pressed, and he looked to be in his thirties. He couldn't have been much more than five feet tall with flaming red hair, large ears, and a pear-shaped body, which his belt strained mightily to contain. Elfin features highlighted a moon-shaped face with a scruffy, almost-beard, and a complexion as pale as egg whites.

Ms. Trumble joined us and we sat at the table and feasted on red bean and sausage jambalaya.

I took a bite. "This is delicious. Did you make it, Lottie?"

"No, I did," Wronka replied. "Cooking is my hobby. Next to offering Mass, it's my greatest passion."

"How long have you been here, Edwin?"

"I was sent here on temporary assignment to help out while the pastor underwent cancer treatment. Unfortunately, he hasn't responded as hoped, so I've been here over a year." His gestures were an effete symphony of movement and he spoke in a soft, breathy voice. He shrugged. "Like you, Jake, I'm a member of the Camillian Order with a background in medicine. I'm a physical therapist and normally work at a rehab facility in New Orleans, but I guess I'm here until further notice."

"Father Wronka arrived just in time to oversee the major renovation of the old church," Lottie said. "The last hurricane did tremendous damage. It's been a huge job with many hurdles, but the work on the church is nearly finished. The overdue renovation of the rectory will begin soon."

Wronka grinned. "Thank God I've had Lottie here to help and guide me. She's not only my administrative assistant, she's also been my business manager, bookkeeper, and right hand. I didn't know the filing system in the office, had no clue which construction companies had good reputations, or how building permits were obtained and filed." He took a second helping of jambalaya and passed the serving dish to me. "I'm good at helping patients regain their strength in physical therapy, but I'm a lousy bean counter with no training in finance or construction."

I saw an opportunity to open the door to my investigation. "I do the financials and oversee repairs at my parish, Edwin, and wouldn't mind pitching in. I'd be happy to help you 'count the beans,' if you'd like."

He hesitated for a second, then said, "That would be wonderful. I just finished the quarterly statements, and I'd welcome a second pair of eyes. I'm in over my head and have no idea if the figures are even in the ballpark. I'd hate to get chewed out by my bishop again."

"I'm not doing anything this afternoon, Edwin. We could go over them after lunch. It shouldn't take too long."

"No, that's asking too much. You just arrived, and I don't want to ruin your vacation."

"I have no major plans and wouldn't mind at all."

"Well, okay then. I'll be away this afternoon but the parish financials are in the top drawer of my desk in the rectory study. Be my guest. I'd appreciate your help. Let me know if you find any problems. Lottie usually double checks me, but she already has more than enough to do running this place."

"It's not a problem, Father," she replied. "I was a bookkeeper before I was hired here."

After lunch, I took a stroll around the church grounds, stopping in the shade of a canopy of live oaks near a statue of St. Francis of Assisi to listen to birdsong and the soft whisper of a stream flowing into the bayou. Spanish moss hung from cypress trees like the long gray locks of a sea nymph's hair. My presence, however, must have disturbed a nearby heron because it screeched as it rose up and flew deeper into the marshland. A gator's eyes peered at me from the silky blue-green water fifty yards away, tracking my every movement. An osprey landed momentarily on St. Francis's outstretched arm, then took flight. As the patron saint of the environment and animals, his statue was ideally situated in the midst of the bayou's savage beauty.

I returned to the rectory, sat at the desk in the study, and got down to the business of reviewing the quarterly statements. All the repairs and new construction at the church had cost considerably more than they would have at my small town parish in Ohio. I wondered if labor and materials were simply more expensive near a major metropolis and tourist destination like New Orleans. The financials showed a depleted building fund, a lot of red ink, and the recent application for a bank loan signed by Wronka. Thumbing through the receipts folder, I realized that the Master Construction Company had done most of the work. In addition to doing basic items such as drywall and painting, they had structurally reinforced bowing walls in the church, which accounted for the lion's share of the expenses.

Lottie Trumble appeared at the door. "Since you're hard at work on your first day of vacation, I thought you might enjoy some coffee." She smiled and handed me a cup and saucer. "How's it going?"

"Looking at these figures, I'm wondering if it might have been cheaper to demolish the old church rather than spend so much on structural repairs."

"Father Wronka discussed that option with the bishop. The church is nearly one hundred and fifty years old. They decided it had important religious and historical significance and was worth preserving. The congregation agreed and gave generously to the building fund."

"What do you know about the Master Construction Company, Lottie?"

"It's been here for years, I think. I know that Father Wronka and the bishop looked at several other companies before selecting them. I've only been here two years but I've never heard a bad word about them. Why do you ask?"

"Just trying to justify some of their invoices. The previous quarterly statements would be helpful for comparison." I stood and tapped a finger on the file cabinet. "Are they in here?"

"I believe they're in the church office. I can get them for you, but would you mind if I did it tomorrow? I'm already late for an appointment."

I'd completely lost track of time. "That would be fine. I have one folder to finish and I've definitely had enough number crunching for one day. I'll see you in the morning."

It took forty minutes to finish reviewing the receipts. Father Wronka had mentioned a local restaurant at lunch that specialized in Cajun and Creole delicacies. I'd promised to pick up dinner for the two of us, so I called and placed our takeout order, then strolled outside as Wronka drove into the parking lot. He stepped from his car carrying his dry cleaning, said something to a worker who was loading paint cans and rollers into a pickup truck, and walked over to me.

I told him I'd be back soon with our meal, got into my rental, and was surprised to see Lottie Trumble slip out of the back door of the church, which was odd. She'd been anxious to leave the rectory, and yet she was still here nearly an hour later. She hopped into a beautiful, silver BMW and drove off—leaving a cloud of road dust in the air and my head filled with questions. It appeared that my first assignment as the investigator for the Camillian Order had me on edge, and maybe a touch paranoid.

CHAPTER EIGHTEEN

Thursday, May 1, 7:00 a.m.

I had called home on Wednesday night. As promised, Snapp had vacated the rectory and Colleen had moved in to stay with my nephew. Being the first time RJ and I had been separated since my sister's death, I'd worried about how he would react. At first he was brooding and sullen, but by the time I hung up he was back to his usual cheerful self. I, on the other hand, realized how much I missed the little rascal and was overwhelmed with guilt for leaving him. The sooner I completed this assignment the better. After we hung up, I'd been unable to fall asleep, so I'd read a Sterling Watson novel late into the evening before finally plunging into a fitful slumber.

I'd brought my Mass kit with me, so in the morning, I celebrated a private Mass alone in my room. When I had been in the Army as a young man and my comrades were dying around me, I had promised God that if He guided me through that valley of death, I would live my life as a tribute to Him. That solemn vow eventually lead me to the priesthood, so although the third commandment admonishes everyone to keep the Lord's Day holy, for me, having survived an overseas bloodbath, *every day* was the Lord's day, not just Sundays. One way I honored Him was to offer Mass whenever I could, even when I wasn't scheduled for a formal church service.

Afterward, I dressed in khakis and a t-shirt, made a pot of coffee in the rectory kitchen, and poured a steaming mug full. Father Wronka was not yet up and about, and Lottie hadn't arrived, so I walked over to the church.

Two workers were seated on a stack of roofing shingles chatting and smoking cigarettes. They spoke no English, so I explained in my broken Spanish that I was a priest and needed to enter the building. They nodded and one of them got up and unlocked a side door for me.

The interior of the church was attractive but not plush. I had absolutely no background in construction but wanted to get a sense of whether Master Construction's structural repairs of the bowing walls justified the high costs I'd seen in the financial statements. If anything seemed suspicious, my Superior General could hire a structural engineer for a thorough evaluation. Unfortunately, many of the interior walls were already covered with stucco or drywall, making evaluating the underlying structural repairs impossible. I was wondering what to do next when a tall, broad-shouldered man with a handlebar mustache ambled over.

"Can I help y'all, mister?" he said in a drawl as southern as pecan pie. "I'm the crew foreman."

"Father Austin," I replied, extending a hand. "Please guide me through the church and show me all of the work your company's done here." His brow furrowed and his gaze hardened, so I added, "My own parish church needs major repairs. Beside interior upgrades, our walls are beginning to bow, so I want to hire an experienced company."

He relaxed and pointed out where some corners had been tuck-pointed and relief joints had been added. "Them walls over there been steel-reinforced to fix the bowing. Cain't really see it now under that drywall. Stop on in at the office and the boss can show you the drawings and photos and tell ya how we do it."

"Can I see the structural repairs from the outside of the building?"

He scratched his chin and thought for a moment. "Ah, 'fraid not. We already stuccoed over that. Makes it look more finished and covers the repairs. Stucco's a masonry product, so it bonds real good to brick."

He told me what electrical work had been performed, showed me the few plumbing repairs that were visible, and I thanked him.

"Any time. Y'all have yourself a good day now, Father."

I circled the outside of the building slowly, looking for any continued bowing of the walls, but none was obvious. I had to admit that the stucco gave the reinforced areas an attractive rustic look in keeping with the rest of the church, but I would have much preferred to inspect the underlying repair.

Back in the rectory, I reloaded my coffee mug and was entering the study when Lottie came out.

"Morning, Father. I put the quarterly financials you requested on the desk—well, all but the two most recent ones." She ran her fingers through her hair. "Got no idea why they weren't in the church office with the others. Must have been misfiled. Sorry. I'll keep looking."

"Thanks, Lottie. There's fresh coffee in the kitchen."

I sat at the desk, opened the folder, and reviewed the statements. Prior to the church restoration, the quarterlies showed no red ink or discrepancies. I leaned back in my chair and considered that. If church funds really had been stolen, it probably occurred during the renovation, when financial shenanigans might easily have gone unnoticed amidst the chaos. I definitely needed the two missing quarterlies to complete my investigation.

"Hard at work already, Jake?" Father Wronka stood in the doorway wearing tan slacks and an emerald green golf shirt.

"Not too hard. Are you on your way to the links, Edwin?"

"No, running errands downtown."

I told him about the missing statements.

"That *is* odd. Ask Lottie. That woman is a magician. She's conjured up all kinds of mislaid things for me. It's like she has radar for lost items."

"I already asked. She doesn't know where they are and suspects they've been misfiled." I stood and pointed at the filing cabinet. "Do you mind if I look through here for them? Maybe I'll get lucky. The missing quarterlies would help me complete my review of the finances."

Wronka's eyes narrowed. "Worth a try, I guess."

He unlocked the cabinet and slid out the top drawer. "If Lottie can't find them in the church files, they may be in this drawer somewhere. Happy hunting. I'll be home in time to make us dinner." He started toward the door, then asked before leaving, "You ever had a crawfish boil?" I shook my head. "Then I'll cook up a steaming pot of 'mudbugs' for you tonight. It's messy and they're a lot of work to eat, but believe me, it's worth the effort."

I searched through the top drawer of the filing cabinet and removed a folder containing canceled church checks, which showed no discrepancies when compared to the bank records. The missing statements were not in the folder, so I worked my way through the lower two drawers. The bottom drawer contained a manila folder simply labeled "DC." Since it contained Wronka's personal Discover Card receipts, I put it back. When I failed to find the missing quarterly financials in the other files, however, I returned to Edwin's personal one. If significant funds were being siphoned from the church as my Superior General suspected, I needed to make sure Edwin wasn't living beyond his means at the expense of his parishioners—no better time to snoop than while he was away from the rectory and the filing cabinet was unlocked.

I found several receipts for recent repairs to Wronka's ancient Toyota Corolla. He had authorized automatic payments of his auto loan, and had a monthly Netflix subscription. He dined out only occasionally, always at moderately priced restaurants, and had spent almost nothing on his own clothing and personal items. Feeling guilty for snooping through his finances, I was about to close the folder when I came across a hand-written receipt from an independent bookstore for the purchase of two books, *The Secret Garden* and *Tales of a Fourth Grade Nothing*—both stories for children. I'd recently read the latter book to RJ. It was certainly possible that they were gifts for a niece or nephew, but then I found a receipt from the women's department at a Dillard's store for the purchase of two dresses.

Children's books and women's clothing? A Catholic priest? What the hell? I struggled to find a logical and innocent explanation but kept coming back to the possibility that Edwin had a secret family or a lover.

The head of my Camillian Order and my bishop had once interrogated me about my relationship with Emily, and I knew all too well how intrusive that had been and how violated I had felt. I was a member of the Catholic Church, not the Church of Perpetual Surveillance, and I didn't want to be their snitch.

On the other hand, Wronka's purchase of children's books was worrisome. The Vatican already had too many skeletons in its closet, and its willful disregard of the presence of pedophiles in its ranks had contributed mightily to our damaged reputation. It seemed logical to assume that if a priest who had taken a vow of poverty suddenly had new financial obligations, he might be tempted to dip into the church till. But before I invited the Vatican enforcers to stomp on Wronka's world, I needed to be certain his unusual purchases were related to the missing church funds and indicated that he had sullied his vows and was supporting a lover or secret family.

The Dillard's bill included a shipping charge, so I called the store's customer service number, posing as Edwin Wronka. I gave the clerk the information on the receipt and told her the package had never arrived. She said it had been reported as delivered ten days earlier. I suggested that it must have been shipped to the wrong location and asked where it had been delivered. She gave me an address on Severn Avenue in New Orleans. I told her I'd check with my neighbors to see if one of them had it, then thanked her and hung up.

I was pondering my next move when Lottie entered the study.

She looked around, then frowned. "Have you seen Father Wronka this morning?"

"He's running errands downtown and said he'd be home later this afternoon."

"Downtown? Again?" She pursed her lips, raised her eyes to the ceiling, and drew a deep breath before speaking. "Oh well, I guess church business gets shoved to the back burner once again." She began to walk away.

"Wait," I called out.

She stopped but remained mute.

"What is it, Lottie?"

She shook her head and turned away.

"What's going on? Tell me. I can help."

"Thanks for the offer, but Mr. Masterson at the construction company needs to speak with him. Something about unexpected expenses. I just wish Father Wronka spent less time downtown and more time at the parish!" She threw her hands in the air. "Sorry. I shouldn't have said that. Forgive me. Not for me to judge."

It was six o'clock before Wronka arrived at the rectory carrying two large shopping bags. As he began putting groceries away, he asked me to grab a large pot from an upper shelf that he couldn't reach. I handed it to him and he set about preparing a crawfish boil for our dinner. When he had finished, I started to set the dining table but Edwin told me to stop and led me into the kitchen. I knew I was in for a messy evening when he covered the kitchen table with three layers of newspaper, set a roll of paper towels nearby and a cardboard box next to my chair. He handed me a plastic bib and told me to watch and learn from a "mudbug virtuoso."

He plunked down two frosted mugs of beer, then set steaming bowls of spiced crawfish, potatoes, onions, and corn in front of us. We sat, rolled up our sleeves, and tied on our bibs. Edwin demonstrated how to twist and tug the tail free from the creature's head and then pinch the tail meat out of the shell. It was a lot of work and messy as heck, but the tiny morsels were delicious. When he showed me how to suck the juicy flavor from the crawfish heads, however, I briefly considered becoming a vegetarian.

Edwin was clearly in his element and in high spirits throughout this gastronomic debauchery. After the bowls were empty and the cardboard boxes full of shells and corn cobs, I cleared the table, loaded the dishwasher, and scrubbed the evidence of our barbaric meal off my hands.

When I'd finished, I joined him in the living room.

"That was quite an experience, Edwin. Thank you."

"My pleasure. You said you wanted to sample the local cuisine. Cooking is a passion of mine and a great joy. If I have time tomorrow, I'll prepare Coquille St. Jacques for a change of pace, so don't eat a big lunch."

He poured us each a snifter of brandy and we settled into armchairs near the window. The conversation was easy and amiable, and while he was relaxed and off-guard, I took the opportunity to ask about the peculiar Discover Card purchases I'd found in the filing cabinet.

"How was your trip to the Big Easy, Edwin?"

"Fine, though it's never *easy* this time of year with all the tourists in town."

"This is my first visit to Louisiana, so maybe you can help me. I want to buy a gift for my nephew. He's five and likes to read." I watched Wronka's expression for a reaction. "Is there a bookstore you'd recommend?"

"I have just the place, Jake. There's a wonderful Mom-and-Pop bookstore on Veterans Memorial Boulevard, off route 10, near Lake Pontchartrain. They have a large selection and it's easy to get to."

"I also need to pick up some new clothes. Any suggestions?"

"You're in luck. There's a Dillards in that same shopping mall."

Without hesitation, he'd given me the two stores where he'd purchased women's dresses and children's books. No tension was evident on his face, and he'd made no attempt at subterfuge. This was not the behavior of someone siphoning money from the collection basket to support an illicit relationship. I relaxed a bit, but decided to snoop around the next morning at the address on Severn Avenue where the women's clothing had been delivered.

I changed the subject. "By the way, Edwin, Lottie was looking for you. She seemed upset when she couldn't find you. Something about unexpected construction costs at the church."

"Boy, is *that* a common refrain. My bishop will not be happy. I'll call Master Construction in the morning."

When the conversation died, Wronka asked, "How about some mindless television? Anything you want to watch?"

"I don't look at much TV, but a friend recommended a movie on Netflix. I was hoping we could—"

"Let me stop you there, Jake. We only have basic cable. We don't get Netflix here."

His Discover Card, however, *was* paying for a subscription—interesting. Could it be he had Netflix at the address on Severn Avenue? Things were getting curiouser and curiouser.

CHAPTER NINETEEN

Friday, May 2, 7:00 a.m.

Bull gators bellowed most of the night in the bayou and woke me several times. I arose early, put on a clerical shirt and trousers, slid a Roman collar into my pocket, then read Lauds, the traditional morning prayer, from my Breviary. After I'd finished, I made a pot of coffee and strolled the grounds until Lottie arrived. She told me she hadn't yet located the missing quarterly financial statements, so I slipped into Sherlock Holmes mode and drove into New Orleans. If Wronka was stealing church funds to support a lover or secret family, I would need solid proof before I encouraged my Superior General to rain down hell on him.

I parked on the street across from the Severn Avenue address where Dillards had delivered the women's dresses to unit 105. The apartment complex had long since lost its luster. Three buildings flanked a small courtyard with several benches located around a central fountain in desperate need of repair. I walked toward it. Someone had painted blood-red tears on the concrete mermaid statue, which no longer streamed water. The fountain contained only green moss and the remnants of last week's rain. Behind it, two live oaks grew on either side of a magnolia tree, which had dropped most of its April crop of pink and white petals, leaving only their sweet perfume lingering in the morning air.

I had no real plan as I approached the main lobby. The entrance door was locked. As I began to leave, an elderly Asian woman came tottering up the sidewalk. I nodded to her and fumbled with my keys until she unlocked the door, then followed her in. I smiled at her but she cast a wary eye in my direction as she unlocked her mailbox, so I headed up the stairs to the top floor and waited for her to leave. When I heard her footsteps retreat and a door slam, I walked down to unit 105 on the ground floor. A straw sunhat rimmed in plastic flowers hung from a nail in the door. No name or identifying information was evident. I placed an ear to the door, heard no sound, and returned to the lobby. The mailboxes had no names listed, and the callbox outside of the entrance displayed names but no unit numbers.

Frustrated, I walked back to the courtyard, sat on a bench, and opened the novel I'd brought with me, pretending to read as I surveyed the deserted apartment complex. Each residence had a small patio or balcony facing the fountain. Most sported garage-sale tables and chairs. The lights were off in unit 105 and I saw no evidence of activity, but there was something next to the patio table. I closed my book, pulled my clerical collar from my pocket, and slipped it on. If caught snooping, I wanted to be able to play the "concerned clergy card."

I casually strolled toward the first floor patio. A pink bicycle, slightly larger than RJ's bike, was chained to a heavy wooden table—a child's bike with a personalized mini license plate affixed to the back fender that read JODI.

The window curtains were partially closed. I peeked into the apartment and saw a stuffed teddy bear on the couch.

"What the hell you doin', mister?"

I turned to face a muscular gentleman wearing shorts and an LSU t-shirt. Waving hedge clippers in my direction, he snarled, "Y'all best haul ass before I—" He stopped mid-sentence, lowered the clippers, and stared at my collar. "You a preacher?"

"I am. Sorry, I . . . ." Suddenly I wished I'd been a theater major in college rather than premed. I wiped a sweaty palm on my pants, swallowed hard, and hooked a thumb toward the window. "I'm, um, a family friend. Just got in from out of town and wanted to say hello." A venial lie in service of Mother Church. "Got a present for Jodi in the car. Doesn't look like they're home. Any idea where I might find them?"

"The girl goes to that special school down the street. I think it's called Cornerstone somethin' or other. She usually gets home in the early afternoon. Think that's why her mama moved in here, to be close to it." He frowned. "Ain't seen her mama for quite a spell. Think her uncle said she was in the hospital and he was looking after Jodi till she got home."

Time to play a hunch. "Would that be Uncle Edwin?"

"Don't rightly know his name."

"A short, stocky young man, about thirty with red hair?"

"Yeah, that's him. Looks like a roly-poly jockey to me, fingers fat as bratwursts. Seems to be a nice guy though. He comes a lot, brings food, looks in on that poor kid. She cain't really take care of herself too good."

"Jodi's father doesn't live here?"

"In all the years I've worked here, I ain't never seen Lucy, I mean Ms. Saroyan, with no man—other than the uncle." He eyed me with suspicion again. "None of my business though."

I had extracted as much information from the workman as I dared and was pressing my luck. I thanked him, said I'd stop back later, got in my car, and headed down the street. He stood there, watching me leave. As soon as I was out of his sight, I slowed and began looking for Jodi's school.

Cornerstone Preparatory Academy was located a few blocks away at the corner of High Street and Severn Avenue, easy walking distance from Jodi's apartment. I removed my clerical collar, strolled casually into the school, entered the office, and asked a young woman for information about the school.

She produced a saleswoman's grin and handed me a colorful brochure offering: *Individualized academic, clinical, and behavior-management solutions using a sensory-based curriculum.*

She asked me to register, and I wrote Jacob Smith, adding a fictitious address on Severn Avenue.

"Do you have a child whose needs are not being met in a traditional school environment?" she asked. "One who is navigating Autism, Asperger's Syndrome, Down's, or another learning challenge, perhaps?"

"I do," I answered, adding one more lie to my growing list, and another transgression for my next visit to the confessional. "Lucy Saroyan said her daughter is making progress here and recommended I stop by."

"Excellent. Does your child also suffer with Down's Syndrome?"

"Yes, he does. He's about the same age as Jodi."

"Well, Jodi's been a student here for several years now, but fourteen's not too late to enroll in our program. How about a tour of our facility … Mr.?"

"Smith." A few more lies and I'd qualify for a job as a used car salesman, a telemarketer, or a politician. "I'd love a tour."

She led me to a small kitchen where a teacher was showing several children how to safely use a microwave. "In addition to cognitive development, Mr. Smith, we emphasize activities of daily living to develop independence while fostering safe practices. We also offer speech and language therapy to enhance communication for those students who need it."

She then escorted me down the hallway to a classroom where a dozen children were working on basic addition and subtraction.

"We want our students to be comfortable handling money so they can perform essential skills such as grocery shopping and balancing a check book. Higher-functioning students are often able to find employment." She glanced around the room, then gestured to a teenaged girl in a pink dress with matching sneakers who was standing in front of a cash register. "We have high hopes for Jodi. She may well land a job as a cashier in a few years. Jodi's such a well-behaved young lady, always does what she's told. I wish all the children here were as well-mannered."

I wondered if *well-behaved* meant submissive, and if sedative medication was involved, but held my tongue and focused on Jodi. The bridge of her nose was flattened, and she had the slanted almond-shaped eyes and short, thick neck common in Down's Syndrome. Her figure indicated that she had already begun the transformation from a child into a young woman. Jodi's hair had a reddish tint and she was tiny for her age, about Father Wronka's height. I wondered how long he had known her mother and briefly considered the possibility that Jodi might be his daughter, but discarded the idea because short stature is common in people afflicted with Down's.

After touring occupational therapy, music therapy, and the rest of the facility, I left Cornerstone Preparatory Academy with a promise to return with my child—each little white lie becoming more dingy than the one before it.

On my drive back to Blessed Savior Church, I considered what I'd learned. Father Wronka was somehow involved with Jodi Saroyan, a teenaged girl with Down's Syndrome. The workman at her apartment complex had confirmed that Wronka stopped by frequently and had indicated that Jodi was his niece—certainly a legitimate reason for him to visit, especially if his sister or sister-in-law was in the hospital. The two children's books he had purchased might have been appropriate for Jodi's reading level given her genetic disorder, and the dresses he'd had delivered to her apartment may well have been for her.

Taken at face value, it appeared more likely that Wronka was simply a caring uncle helping his family through a crisis rather than a predator taking advantage of strangers. The trip downtown had definitely been worth my time. My fear that he had a lover or secret family in New Orleans now seemed unfounded, and I relaxed a little. Here I was investigating this poor man when I *should have been* supporting him in his time of need. Mea culpa.

CHAPTER TWENTY

Friday, May 2, 4:00 p.m.

Upon returning to the rectory, I asked Lottie, "Any luck finding the missing quarterly financial statements?"

"Sorry, no. But I'll keep looking."

"Thanks. But don't worry if you can't find them. I'll contact the bishop. I'm sure he keeps copies from all of the parishes."

She stiffened, then nodded.

"Not to worry, Lottie. Things get misfiled. No problem. We'll get this job done one way or another."

I heard noise in the kitchen and entered. The air was filled with an olfactory delight, and my stomach rumbled its approval.

Father Wronka smiled. "How'd your shopping trip go, Jake? Did you find what you wanted downtown?"

"I got everything I needed, thanks. What're you up to?"

"Preparing the Coquille St. Jacques I promised you for dinner. Hope you're hungry. It should be ready in about an hour."

"Perfect. I'll get cleaned up and join you then."

After my shower, I dressed and made my nightly telephone call home.

"How are things going, Colleen?"

"Splendid. RJ had a fine day at school and is watching the telly. Father Snapp continues to leave us in peace, so all is well. I've no idea where the man is, and no interest in finding out. *Gone* is where I'd prefer he'd stay."

RJ apparently overheard our conversation and commandeered the phone. He was weepy at first about my absence, but soon rallied. He told me all about the antics of someone in his class named Brandon, then went on in great detail to describe his latest TV cartoon discovery, something about a sponge who lived in the ocean—my viewing options ever expanding.

When Colleen called RJ to supper, I promised that I'd come home soon and hung up, feeling a touch guilty. There was still time before dinner and I hadn't spoken with Emily in four days, so I called her. Her voice told me that something was wrong.

"Are you okay, Em? You sound a bit … off. Not another paranormal incident in the snack shop I hope?"

"No, nothing like that. I just caught a cold from riding our usual topsy-turvy weather roller coaster. Remember how cool it was here before you left? Well, it got downright hot again, and then the darn air conditioning in the snack shop went on the fritz. Dad and I both have the crud. No big deal. How are things down south?"

I couldn't tell her about my investigation, so I gave her a sanitized version of my visit. When Wronka knocked on my door and announced that dinner was ready, I said, "I hope you feel better soon. I'll call you in a day or so. Say hello to your dad, and give RJ a hug for me when you see him. Bye."

Speaking with RJ and Emily reminded me of how much I hated being away from them, and reenergized me to finish my investigation and return home.

I joined Wronka in the dining room. My-oh-my, the man could cook! He was small in stature, but a giant in the kitchen. The Coquille St. Jacques was incredible. The sea scallops, bathed in Gruyere cheese and a heavy cream sauce laced with sherry, shallots, and mushrooms, literally melted in my mouth.

Wronka poured us each a glass of Vouvray and said, "Hope you enjoy this. It's made from Chenin Blanc grapes from the Loire region of France. I used a splash in the coquille. Been saving it for a special occasion." He chuckled, then added, "But I guess *you'll* have to do, Jake.

Drifting in gastronomic nirvana, we enjoyed a pleasant conversation. In light of what I'd learned earlier in the day, I wanted to offer Edwin any help I could with his family predicament. The problem was how to approach the subject without revealing that I had meddled in his personal affairs.

Wronka poured us each another glass of wine. "So, how's your visit to the Pelican State been so far?"

"The food's fantastic here, thanks to you, but I want to explore Bourbon Street and do the touristy things." I decided to make my move. "Truth be told, though, I miss my boy." He did a double take and his mouth dropped open. "Oh, I guess I never told you, Edwin. I became the legal guardian for my nephew after my sister died. Took some doing, but my bishop finally approved the arrangement. RJ is five now, and the center of my universe."

Wronka went speechless for a moment, then said, "That must be wonderful. The priesthood can be lonely at times, as I'm sure you know. Wish I had that option."

"No nieces or nephews to visit and indulge?"

"Sadly no, Jake. No siblings."

My muscles tensed. *Uncle Edwin*, huh? Why was he buying books and clothes for a fourteen-year-old teen, and who was Lucy Saroyan to him? If their relationship was innocent, why hadn't he shared it? Was it possible he had a lover with a child? Or was I sitting across the table from a predator priest who was preying on a vulnerable teenaged girl while her mother was hospitalized? Maybe Edwin was not only a master chef, but was masterfully cooking the books at the church to finance his extracurricular activities. Suddenly, my meal wasn't sitting well with me.

I tried to maintain my composure as I mulled over the possibilities. I certainly didn't want to accuse Wronka of anything until I had proof, but more bad press was the last thing the Church needed. It didn't seem to matter to the news media that approximately two percent of men in the general population were pedophiles, which meant statistically there were far more male teachers who were pedophiles than there were priests. If even one bad priest was discovered, it was splashed across the headlines. *All* professions dealing with children needed to be vigilant. The unforgiveable sin was the Church's cover-up, which should never have happened and could not continue—and that was exactly why I needed to further investigate Wronka's relationship with Jodi and her mother.

Wronka and I finished our supper, and I helped him with the dishes, then claimed fatigue and went to my room. I stared out of the guest room window as the sun bounced its last rays off of the bayou and an eerie dusk descended like a black shroud. Near the St. Francis statue, a flock of white ibises searched for insects and grubs in the grass with their long curved, red-orange bills. I was in a trance and lost in thought when my cellphone chimed: area code 414, Milwaukee—my Superior General's office number.

"Evening, Jacob," Demarco said. "How's your investigation going?"

Which investigation? Missing funds or aberrant behavior? How much should I reveal?

"Well, the renovation of the church has emptied the building fund, and the parish is deeply in the red. The cost here for labor and materials is considerably higher than at my church in Ohio. That may be due in part to structural repairs that had to be completed first, but I won't know more until we locate two missing financial statements."

I paused, trying to decide whether to bring up Father Wronka's involvement with Lucy Saroyan and Jodi. Demarco noticed my hesitation. He was a bright man and didn't miss much.

"What is it, my son? Don't hold out on me. Tell me what's going on."

Busted. It was vocational suicide to lie to this man. I heaved a sigh and told my boss what I'd uncovered concerning Wronka's connection to the Saroyan family.

"What are we talking about here, Jacob? An illicit relationship? A child molester?"

"That's the problem. I'm not sure, and I don't know what to do next."

"Well I do." He released a derisive snort. "Shove the missing money onto the back burner, and turn up the heat on Wronka! I've vowed to root out pedophiles from our order. You are my right hand, Jacob, so make a fist and bring it down hard on this man if he's abusing a child and soiling our faith. If he is, I want him gone—not only from the priesthood but from civil society, locked behind bars *forever and ever, amen.*"

I had been hoping that my first assignment as Demarco's investigator would be something less daunting than confronting a sexual predator. But my Superior General and I were on the same page when it came to pedophiles. As the son of a cruel alcoholic father, and now as the surrogate parent of a young boy, I was more than willing to take down anyone who mistreated children in any way.

"Hold the line for one second, Jacob." I heard computer keys clacking, then Demarco returned. "I pulled Father Wronka's file. I don't see anything improper or worrisome here, and there have been no formal complaints against him. It could be he's innocent … or maybe he's good at covering his tracks, or his bishop has turned a blind eye to him. Well, if he's guilty, I won't look the other way. I need an answer. The ball's in your court."

"You can count on me. I'll sort it out."

"Good. Call me when you know more."

I hung up and pondered my next move. Asking worshippers vague questions about Wronka's behavior would only inflame him and incite a firestorm among his parishioners, so I phoned local hospitals, asking what room Lucy Saroyan was in. After hearing a dozen receptionists say, "We have no one here by that name," I located her at the University Medical Center. I was uncertain how to approach her, but needed to ascertain her relationship to Wronka. Unfortunately, by the time I tracked her down, visiting hours were over for the evening.

I also wanted to find out whether there were any complaints about him that hadn't reached my Superior General. I knew if I asked the local bishop or Bishop Lucci in Ohio for help, the official inquiry would stir up a hornet's nest that could potentially bite an innocent man on the butt. Instead, I called a trusted friend who could check on Wronka's background without setting off the ecclesiastical radar—the sheriff.

When Tree Macon answered his cellphone, I explained the situation and asked him to run Edwin Wronka through the system. He and Sonya had raised three daughters, so he didn't even hesitate.

"I'll find out if he's a known sexual predator or on any watch lists, and also touch base with local cop-shops in Louisiana to see if anyone there is eyeballing him."

"Thanks, Tree."

"Call you tomorrow, buddy."

Out of ideas, options, and energy, I recited Vespers from my Breviary, got ready for bed, prayed Compline, and let exhaustion wrap its weighty arms around me.

CHAPTER TWENTY ONE

Saturday, May 3, 9:30 a.m.

I was sipping coffee at the kitchen table and reading an article in The Times-Picayune about hurricane preparedness when Father Wronka walked in, a wide grin on his lips.

"You look happy, Edwin."

"I am. There was a large turnout at morning Mass, and I mesmerized them." He laughed. "My sermon was perfection, like the ideal ladies dress—short enough to arouse interest but long enough to cover the essentials."

I chuckled along with him, then told Edwin I intended to contact his bishop to obtain copies of the missing quarterly statements.

He pursed his lips and cleared his throat. "You won't find him in his office over the weekend, though I may be able to track him down." He sat across from me and added cream to his coffee. "Be better if I approached him, Jake. I'm already in his doghouse over spiraling construction costs. Having an outsider inquire into this financial fiasco could send me from the doghouse to the guillotine. Okay if I contact him?"

"Sure, but the sooner, the better. I want to finish the financial review I promised you and slip into tourist mode. I'm looking forward to exploring the French Quarter and Jackson Square."

"Of course. Soon as I finish my coffee, I'll track him down. I'm grateful for your help. As I said, I'm completely out of my comfort zone with money matters."

I opened the sports section and handed him the rest of the newspaper.

Lottie Trumble appeared in the doorway. She smiled and waved a manila folder. "Morning, Fathers. Look what I found. The missing quarterly statements. Voilà! Misfiled, as I'd suspected." She set the quarterlies on the kitchen table between Wronka and me. "I'll be in the church office if you need me."

"Thanks, Lottie," I said as she walked away. I picked up the folder before Wronka could. "After I review these statements, Edwin, I'll leave them on your desk and we can discuss them this evening. I'll be gone most of the day. Would you like me to pick up dinner?"

"Don't bother. I'll rustle something up. I owe you for helping with the church finances. See you tonight."

In the study, I opened the folder, perused the missing statements, and found more of the same: high labor and material costs. The structural repairs to the church walls, which were performed over a two week period, accounted for most of the expense. I made copies of all recent financial statements in case my Superior General wanted to examine them, then phoned Master Construction and asked for an appointment with the owner to discuss the renovation and the repair of bowing walls in my building.

A perky voice said, "You're in luck. Mr. Masterson's last meeting of the day just canceled. Could you be here this afternoon by four?"

"Perfect. Thanks, I'll be there."

After crunching all the numbers, I had found no hint of theft, no secret slush fund, no sleight of hand. And yet, what should have been a routine building renovation had devastated the church finances. Was Master Construction taking advantage of Wronka, a bumbling fiscal rookie, or was Wronka in fact an expert financial manipulator? Maybe he was cooking up more than fine cuisine. Time to size up Mr. Masterson.

Having hit a dead end with the paperwork, I decided to look further into Wronka's relationship with Lucy and Jodi Saroyan.

I had no police badge to open doors for me, so I dressed for the part of a concerned clergyman in a clerical shirt and Roman collar. Who would suspect a priest of anything other than good intentions?

Looking in the mirror, I chuckled at the metamorphosis I'd undergone and the irony of it. Since returning to my hometown, I'd helped Sheriff Macon with several cases. Although I hated the violence, much to my surprise, I'd found I loved solving mysteries, reveled in the hunt and following the scent, and relished the challenge of assembling the clues like a jigsaw puzzle. It both excited and satisfied me in the same way that making the diagnosis in a gravely ill patient did. I could only wonder if being an investigator for the Church was my true mission in life, the reason I had been called to the priesthood. And I wondered what the heck the Almighty had been thinking when He assembled the bizarre collection of parts that made me tick—Soldier, Doctor, Priest, Spy. My life's journey read like the title of a dime novel.

I arrived at University Medical Center as visiting hours began, obtained Lucy Saroyan's room number and a visitor's pass, exited the elevator on the third floor, and thought, *Now what, genius?*

How could I determine if she and Wronka were lovers, just friends, or if he was taking advantage of her disabled teenaged daughter while she was hospitalized? According to Lottie, Wronka drove downtown frequently, so he might stop in regularly at the hospital to see Lucy, or they might be in contact by telephone. If he found out I'd spoken with her, it would unmask my role as Demarco's troubleshooter and make my investigation more difficult. He would also realize I'd invaded his privacy and undoubtedly be furious. On the other hand, if he was molesting Jodi or living a lie as a priest, stopping him was far more important than exposing financial fraud. And, if my cover was blown, my Superior General could always send in a horde of accountants to sort out the missing funds at the church.

I stopped at the nursing station, adjusted my Roman collar, and asked a white-haired woman, "How's Ms. Saroyan doing today?"

"Better, I think, Father. She just got back from physical therapy. They said she's gaining strength in her left leg." She shook her head. "Honestly though, I don't get it. The poor woman had nearly recovered from the first stroke when this one knocked her back down—and she's *still* dying for a cigarette!"

Having once smoked, I knew how strong the addiction was.

"I was asked to stop by and see her," I said. "Is Ms. Saroyan scheduled for anything else in the next hour?"

The nurse checked her computer. "Nothing until occupational therapy this afternoon."

I asked for a blank sheet of paper, scribbled Saroyan's name at the top and added a few fictitious names below it, walked to room 331, and peeked in. Lucy Saroyan was lying in bed, struggling to squeeze a rubber ball with her left hand. The ball slipped from her grip and rolled onto the floor. She moaned and ran her right hand through short salt-and-pepper hair.

I stepped into the room. "Let me get that for you." I picked up the ball and handed it to her. "I'm Father Smith, a chaplain here. Is there anything I can do for you," I pulled the sheet of paper from my pocket and glanced at it, "ah, Ms. Saroyan? We could pray together or chat for a while if you wish."

"No thanks, Father. I'm okay."

"Can I contact any family or friends for you?"

"Don't have any family except my daughter, and my friends know I'm here." She resumed squeezing the rubber ball.

"Is there anything I can do for your daughter?"

"Not necessary." She refocused on me, suspicion in her eyes. "An acquaintance of mine is looking after her till I get home."

An *acquaintance*. That didn't clarify anything, and I was getting nowhere fast. Time to change tactics.

"Saroyan? That name seems so familiar. Armenian, right?" She nodded. I stared at the ceiling, massaged my chin, and continued playing the bumbling fool. "Saroyan. How do I know that name? Oh, that's right. Someone I was in seminary with has a good friend named Saroyan. Do you happen to know Father Wronka?"

Her mouth dropped open and she appeared to relax. "I do! Father Edwin's such a nice man and a fine physical therapist. He helped me through rehab after my first stroke. Wish he worked here, but he's been reassigned. He's also been kind enough to look in on my daughter while I'm in the hospital. Brings groceries and cooks for her whenever he can. We got no one else to help us. Don't know what we'd do without him."

She had made no attempt to conceal their relationship, making an illicit affair unlikely. If Wronka was a threat to her daughter, however, she probably had no idea. I needed to speak with Jodi.

"I'm glad you have his support." I checked the sheet of paper in my hand. "Well, Ms. Saroyan, if there's nothing else, I'll stop in on the next person on my list. Hope you get well soon. Keep working on regaining your strength. You'll be in my prayers."

I stopped at Landry's Seafood House in the French Quarter and devoured a delicious Oyster Po'boy with remoulade sauce and a side of NOLA-style red beans and rice for lunch as the muddy waters of the Mississippi lumbered by, then parked my car down the street from Cornerstone Preparatory Academy. When classes were dismissed and Jodi began walking home, I stepped from the car and approached her.

"Hi, Jodi. I'm Father Smith."

She glanced at me. "Don't know you."

"I'm a friend of Father Wronka's."

Jodi continued toward her apartment, eyes straight ahead.

"He couldn't come today and asked me to stop by. Do you need anything? Groceries?"

She paused, then, "Um, I need Cheerios and milk … and pads."

"Pads?"

Jodi looked down. "You know … it's my time." She started walking again.

"Of course. No Problem." Talk about out of my comfort zone. At least it meant that if Wronka *was* molesting the poor girl, she wasn't pregnant. "I'll pick them up at the store and stop by your apartment when I'm done."

I drove to a nearby Piggly Wiggly supermarket. A priest buying any feminine hygiene products could only attract unwanted attention, so I removed my Roman collar, rolled up my sleeves, and entered the store. I placed a half gallon of milk and a box of Cheerios in my shopping cart, then went to the pharmacy department and gazed at the large selection of sanitary napkins. With no idea what I was doing, I chose a brand I'd seen advertised in a regular size, added a loaf of bread and a package of thin-sliced turkey, and went through checkout as nonchalantly as possible.

When I knocked on Jodi's door, she peeked in the grocery bag and scowled.

"Father Edwin always gets *Honey Nut* Cheerios. They're better."

"Sorry, I didn't know. Father Edwin's a real smart guy." I was wandering in the wilderness. "So, you like him? He's your friend?"

She wrinkled her brow and stared at me as if that was the dumbest question she'd ever heard. "Duh. 'Course. He's my main helper."

I wanted to keep her talking and inspect her apartment to see if it was clean and orderly, and to make sure Wronka wasn't leaving his personal items in the bedroom or bathroom.

I smiled and hoisted the bag. "Can I put the groceries away for you?"

"Nah." Jodi took it from me. "I'm supposed to do things myself."

"Want me to cook something for you?"

"No. I'm okay." She began to close the door, then added, "Thank you, Father."

Back in my car, I peered through the windshield at a hazy sky and thought about what I'd learned. Lucy Saroyan was unconcerned about Wronka's relationship with her daughter and was grateful for his help. When I'd asked Jodi if he was a friend, she responded with *Duh! Of course.* She was high functioning and capable for a teenager with Down's Syndrome, and the suspicious way she had reacted to me initially showed an appropriate wariness of strangers. I couldn't completely eliminate Wronka as a predator, but my fears had lessened. I was wondering how much further to push my investigation when I noticed the time. If I hurried, I could still make my four o'clock appointment with the owner of Master Construction.

CHAPTER TWENTY TWO

Saturday, May 3, 4:00 p.m.

Chance Masterson's waiting room was a study in opulence. The furniture was luxurious, the oil paintings belonged in an art museum, and the carpet was so thick it was like walking on marshmallows. By the time the secretary ushered me into his office, it was clear that his business was thriving.

As I approached, Masterson hung up the telephone and gestured toward an armchair. His face was tanned and seamed, framed by a nimbus of curly silver hair. He stood and shook my hand with a firm grip. Although within spitting distance of sixty, he was imposing, tall and muscular with a strong jawline.

I sat and surveyed the room. One wall was covered with before and after photographs of buildings. The transformations were impressive. Another was plastered with photos of Masterson smiling with various athletes and glad-handers whom I assumed were politicians. Framed building certificates and construction awards covered the third.

Taking a pen from the pocket of his dark-blue denim shirt, he sat at his desk, scribbled something on a legal pad, and offered a toothy grin. "What can I do for you Father Smith?"

"I've been admiring your restoration of Blessed Savior Church. The walls of my church are also beginning to bow and Father Wronka spoke highly of your company, so I decided to take advantage of your expertise. Our parish building fund is in its infancy. We're not ready to hire structural engineers and start the renovation, but I want to be prepared when the time comes. I was hoping you'd be kind enough to explain the process and options to me."

A smile spread slowly across his lips, "How versed are you in the repair of bowing walls and structural damage?"

"Not at all, I'm afraid. Please keep the explanation basic."

"Certainly. Did you bring any photographs, Father?" I shook my head and he sighed. "How old is the building and are the affected walls concrete, stone, or brick?"

"Our church is over a hundred years old and made of brick," I replied, heaping one more lie onto my growing rubbish pile of deceit, each one slipping from my tongue more easily than the last. Deception came with the job of investigator, but I doubted that I would ever get comfortable with it.

"Then the repair will likely be similar to what we did at Blessed Savior Church." He scribbled something and said, "Tuck-pointing and adding relief joints are only part of the process. I should warn you, though, that in areas without basements these projects can be tricky and expensive. Bowing is caused by moisture inside the brick expanding and contracting as the temperature changes. It's often necessary to drill channels through the walls to attach large steel plates and brackets, which are then anchored to the foundation."

He showed me pictures of several walls in various stages of repair to illustrate the process.

"Steel plates and brackets? That's pretty unsightly. Doesn't that destroy the beauty and elegance of the building?"

"That's why we cover the modified areas with stucco or drywall."

Although I am fairly fluent in Latin and medical jargon, I don't speak a word of engineering mumbo-jumbo. Within minutes, he'd led me deep into the weeds with technical terms, options, and costs until I was completely lost. I wondered if he had done the same thing to Father Wronka.

"Honestly, Mr. Masterson, wouldn't it be simpler and cheaper to demolish the structure and build a new church."

He frowned. "Let's not jump to conclusions. You have to consider the historical and religious significance of the building, and how important that is to the community and the parish. I always prefer renovation to demolition whenever possible, as do most of my clients." He handed me his card and a stack of brochures praising historical preservation. They contained photographs of prior projects and testimonials from satisfied customers. "How about I drive over and evaluate the situation at your church, and then we can talk specifics."

"Oh, I'm sorry if I gave you the wrong impression, Mr. Masterson. It's way too early for that. Our building fund is no were near ready to begin the work. I'm just gathering facts and researching the process." The smile fell away from his face. I stood. "It appears I've already taken too much of your time. Thank you for the information. You've been very helpful. I'll be in touch when the time is right."

I made my exit and drove away more confused than when I'd arrived.

CHAPTER TWENTY THREE

Saturday, May 3, 5:00 p.m.

When I pulled into the church parking lot, Lottie Trumble was kicking the front tire of her sleek, silver BMW. She scowled and slumped against the fender. I parked by the rectory and walked over.

"Problems?"

She looked up with surprise. "Oh Father, I didn't see you there. Sorry. I'm just frustrated." She tapped the hood of her car with an index finger. "This piece of garbage is only a year old, and this is the second time it's died on me."

I had to stifle a laugh. Lottie might be the best administrative assistant in the world, but she was a terrible judge of trash. For many years, I'd actually driven a second-hand, umpteen-year-old "piece of garbage." Her car was not just any BMW, it was a high-performance Z8 roadster convertible worth well over one hundred thousand dollars. With the top down, it was the kind of machine that demanded that the driver wear a long flowing scarf while on the way to the yacht club or an orchestra concert. In this vehicle, speed limits were optional and gas mileage irrelevant. When you'd taken a vow of poverty as I had, and filling your fuel tank was very much an issue, you tried not to notice such things—but at times, extravagant self-indulgence simply leapt out at you.

"Have you called for a tow truck?"

"That's the problem, Father. There's a twenty-car pileup east of here, and the highway patrol has commandeered them all. It'll be over an hour before one can get here and my dealership will be closed by then. I have a busy schedule tomorrow, so I guess I'll have to rent a car for a few days."

"Make the call, Lottie, and I'll drive you to pick up your rental. No problem. Dinner won't be ready for an hour."

On the way to the rental car company, I wondered how Lottie could afford such an expensive automobile on her salary. Family money or an excellent divorce lawyer seemed the most likely possibilities. Well, good for her! Vows of poverty are overrated. For all I knew, she might be so moneyed that she was *volunteering* her time at the church.

We arrived at the Avis rental agency and Lottie went inside. I waited to make sure there were no snafus and they could provide a car for her. After a few minutes, she came out, waved a thank you to me, and to my surprise, drove away in a Jaguar. Not a Ford or a Chevy… a Jag.

Paranoia raised its cynical head again, and the grin slipped from my lips. Wronka's relationship with Jodi was not entirely clear, but I'd found no indication that he was living beyond his means. It was possible he was a financial savant and had thousands of church dollars stashed overseas in a Swiss bank account—or *maybe* I was eyeballing the wrong person. Time to take a closer look at Lottie.

I gunned my engine and took off after her. A few minutes later, I hit the interstate and caught sight of Lottie's rental. A flashy emerald green Jaguar was hard to overlook. I followed five cars behind her, but when she took an exit into the rural Louisiana backcountry, tailing her became more difficult. If she spotted me, there was no logical explanation for my presence in this remote area.

Twenty minutes later, she made a hard right into a driveway. As I approached, the entrance gate closed. A security fence extended from each side of the gate. It was ten feet high with nasty-looking stainless steel spikes projecting from the top. All I could see from the road were her taillights disappearing down a long, curvy, tree-lined asphalt drive. I eased a hundred yards farther down the road and pulled off onto the berm where the fence made a right-angle turn into the undergrowth.

I called Father Wronka, told him I would be late for dinner, removed my Roman collar, and trudged through waist-high weeds toward a thickly wooded area. The ground was wet and soft, and my shoes and pant legs were soon covered with mud. Brambles scratched my face and hands, and tore a hole in my shirt. I passed through a stand of pine trees to where several weeping willows hung over the security fence. Through its steel bars I could see the side and much of the front of Lottie's house.

The two-story, stone-façade house, mansion really, was massive, at least ten thousand square feet. The number of chimneys indicated that there were four or five fireplaces. Several stained-glass windows upstairs glistened in the sunlight. Two stone lions guarded marble front steps leading to a magnificent stained-glass front door. Four round pillars completed the grand entranceway into the great house. If these columns were carved from marble, as they appeared to be, they had cost a fortune. Through a nearby first floor window, I was able to see massive bookshelves, an enormous television, and then an automatic door slid open and Lottie stepped into the room from an elevator.

The landscaping was meticulous. The green Jaguar rental was parked in the open door of a three-car garage on the far side of the house. I pushed farther into the marshland until I was stopped by a stream. An Olympic sized swimming pool and cabana nestled the back of the mansion, and in the distance two horses grazed in a paddock next to a large barn. I wanted to walk farther into the undergrowth, but the area was swarming with insects and I was already covered in mosquito bites. When something slithered through the brush to my left, and two workmen came around the corner of the house and began trimming the hedges, I crept to my car and drove to the rectory, my head filled with more questions than answers.

CHAPTER TWENTY FOUR

Saturday, May 3, 6:30 p.m.

It was 6:30 by the time I parked my car and entered the rectory. I changed out of my damp clothes and muddy shoes, then apologized to Father Wronka for being late. He ladled steaming beef stew into two bowls, and we sat down to dinner. He told me that Masterson had called from the construction company to say that some of the roof joists in the church needed reinforcing before the shingling could be completed, which would further escalate the renovation cost. When Edwin broke the bad news to the local bishop, His Excellency had rained down fire and brimstone on him and reported his financial "ineptness" to our Superior General.

Wronka stared down at his hands and said in a monotone, "Never saw that coming, Jake. I'm so out of my league with all this, I'm not even in the same area code." He leaned back in his chair, then looked up at me, hope in his eyes. "Did the last two quarterly statements from Lottie help explain the cause of this fiscal nightmare?"

"No, sorry. Nothing jumped out at me. As far as I can tell, your accounting is correct. The spiraling construction costs are the culprit and they're out of your control."

I finished the last of my stew, slipped into detective mode, and as casually as I could, I told him about Lottie's car trouble, watching his reaction.

"Her BMW's quite impressive." I took a sip of sweet tea. "It's brand new, Edwin, and even leasing it would be prohibitively expensive on an administrative assistant's salary. I assume Lottie comes from a wealthy family. Is she volunteering her time at the church?"

His expression remained placid. "No, as a parish employee, she's paid by the diocese." He thought for a second, then raised his eyebrows. "Actually, Lottie told me she was raised in an orphanage, so family money is unlikely."

I finished my tea. "Could be she received a healthy divorce settlement and is financially independent."

"Don't think so. She referred to herself as an 'old spinster' once when we were joking around."

A church drowning in red ink, a priest closely linked to a woman and her disabled daughter, and the church's administrative assistant living in a mansion? What the heck was going on here? I'd been thinking of the problems as separate, but maybe they were linked. Could Lottie and Edwin be working together?

I sighed. In addition to frustration with this case, I realized that my snooping was clouding my spiritual focus. I had vowed to love the Lord above all things, so I asked Edwin if I could celebrate Mass with him in the morning. He agreed. We cleared the dining table, retired to the living room, and he offered me a glass of brandy.

"I'd love one." I glanced at the time. "Give me a few minutes."

I entered my room and called home. To my surprise, Emily answered and told me she had relieved Colleen for the evening.

"How are things with RJ?"

"Okay, except he misses you something fierce. I'm doing what I can to take his mind off of it. Things are not so good with Dad and me, however."

"Is the snack shop air conditioner still broken?"

"Yes, for the gazillionth time, and it's hotter than Hades again, but that's not what I meant. Dad and I had another one of those episodes of dizziness, nausea, and anxiety. Dad nearly passed out and he's convinced the shop is haunted. We're fed up."

"I'm so sorry, Em. Wish I knew how to help."

"Me too. By the way, when I came over to the rectory today I ran into Father Snapp. Did you know he and his pet bird were living in his van in the church parking lot?"

"Long story, Em. Don't ask."

"Anyway, he was moving the bird temporarily into the basement of the church because the van gets too hot in the daytime. I told him about our recent problems in the snack shop and he offered to come and say cleansing prayers—you know, the way folks sometimes get their homes blessed. He thinks it might help, and he also wants to investigate the second floor of the hospital where you saw the Night Nurse. Dad and I have nothing to lose, so I said okay."

I had banished Snapp from the rectory in my absence. Now he was meddling at the hospital. Was the man truly trying to help Emily, I wondered, or was he *taunting* me?

The problem was, I had no explanation for the snack shop's bizarre occurrences, nor for Dorothy Margaret Clay's ghostly hospital appearances, and I knew that complaining to Bishop Lucci about Snapp would be ineffective.

"Cleansing prayers? Really? That's grasping at straws if you ask me, Em, but I understand your frustration. Let me know how things go at the hospital. Is RJ awake? I'd love to chat with him."

My nephew filled me in on his latest exploits at recess. As he wound down his detailed account, he paused and asked, "Are you okay, Daddy. You sound sad."

Sad, frustrated, lonely, and in need of a five-year-old's hug.

"I guess I am, sport. I miss you."

"Miss you too." He hesitated for a moment. "Bet I can make you laugh. Wanna hear a joke?"

"Definitely. Let's hear it."

"Why do priests wear collars?"

Somedays I wondered the same thing. "I give up, RJ. Why do priests wear collars?"

"So they don't get fleas and ticks, silly!"

He chuckled and I joined in, and the dark clouds cleared from my world.

"Good one, RJ. I feel better already." I scratched a mosquito bite and wondered if wearing my collar into the undergrowth today would have prevented me from being eaten alive. "Now, listen to Emily, go to bed on time, and I'll call you tomorrow. Okay? Love you."

After I hung up, the unanswered questions about missing church funds and Wronka's relationship with Lucy and Jodi Saroyan quickly ushered the black clouds of doubt back into my thoughts, and I plunked down onto my bed. The gears in my head were spinning, but not quite meshing. I called Tree Macon and told him about Lottie's car, her mansion, and my suspicions.

"Not enough to call in local law enforcement yet, Jake, but it sounds as if you're on the scent. What can I do?"

"Could you run a background check on her for me?"

A long silence.

"I could, but I won't. I'm not your personal private investigator. I only looked into Father Wronka for you because a child was potentially at risk. He came up clean, by the way. No wants, warrants, or any indication that he's a sexual predator." Tree released a disparaging grunt. "You're not police, Jake, and this is not an official case. I can't violate people's civil rights every time you have a hunch."

Over the years we had always been there for each other. I'd recently helped him with a murder investigation and the abduction of a teenager. I hated to lean on our friendship—but I did anyway.

"Come on, Tree. You needed my help on your last case, and I need you to look into her now for me. There's a six-pack of Guinness in it for you."

He drew a deep breath before speaking. "Well, as a strong, dark man I do enjoy a strong, dark brew now and again. Fine. Off the books. I'll see what I can do, buddy."

I gave Lottie's home address to Tree and hung up. I needed some quiet time to think, but my phone and my Superior General didn't care.

"Good evening Jacob. Father Demarco here." He lowered his voice. "Is our Louisiana colleague … fit for the priesthood?"

"As far as the parish funds goes, I have another suspect. And although Wronka's relationship with the girl and her mother is unusual, I have no conclusive evidence of wrongdoing. He was Lucy Saroyan's physical therapist, and as far as I can tell, he's been helping her disabled daughter until Mrs. Saroyan can be discharged from the hospital. Unfortunately, I had to invade his privacy and theirs, and I've pushed my investigation as far as I can without setting off a firestorm."

"Forget about his privacy. If there's any chance the girl's at risk, I need *certainty*. Take off the kid gloves, Jacob, and confront him."

"He'll go ballistic, and this will blow my cover for the fraud investigation."

"I don't give a flying fig about his feelings, and I'll handle any blowback. A child's welfare trumps fraud or theft. Not even close. Do it, Jacob, tonight!"

What could I say? My Superior General had spoken … and as his foot soldier, I had my marching orders.

CHAPTER TWENTY FIVE

Saturday, May 3, 8:00 p.m.

When I returned to the living room, Father Wronka was leaning back on the couch. Lost in a Brahms symphony, his eyes were closed. I poured a large snifter of brandy, sat across from him, and cleared my throat. He opened his eyes, gazed at me, and smiled. I tried for a neutral expression, but my anxiety must have bled through.

"Problems at home, Jake?"

I had once been an angry young man, which had led to my stint in the army and an unhealthy relationship with booze and bar brawls. After I found God, I'd spent the next two decades taming my inner demons—but the thought of Jodi's disability and vulnerability, and the possibility that a priest might be taking advantage of her, unleashed the beast.

"No, Edwin, but I may have a problem with *you*. I'm an investigator for the Camillian Order. Our Superior General sent me here to look into the missing church funds, but then I stumbled upon your relationship with Lucy Saroyan and her daughter." His eyes grew large. I took a swallow of brandy and let the heat burn its way down to my gut. "Who exactly are they to you?"

His nostrils flared and his hands became fists. "What are you implying?"

"It's a simple question. What is your involvement with a young girl with Down's Syndrome? I know you visit Jodi at her home even though her mother is in the hospital. Who is she to you? Does the Church need to be concerned?"

"How *dare* you question our relationship, you son of a bitch!" He jumped to his feet and pointed to the door. "Get the hell out of—"

I held up my hand. "I have the power of Superior General Demarco behind me." I rose to my full height and looked down on him. "I'm not going anywhere until I understand your relationship with Ms. Saroyan, and I'm absolutely certain you're not taking advantage of a defenseless teenaged girl."

"This is what you do for the Camillians? Snoop into colleagues' personal lives?" Wronka wagged a finger in my face. "You think I'm a predator? You couldn't be more wrong! But you *are* right about one thing. You bet your ass I'm involved with Mrs. Saroyan! I have been since she had her first stroke. I was her physical therapist. Her husband deserted them both, leaving them with no family here and no support in the area. What I did, what I am guilty of, is *helping*, so Jodi wouldn't be placed in foster care and taken out of a special school where she's thriving."

He took a step toward me and scoffed. "You're a priest, Austin, so maybe you've heard this one before: *Do unto others* … etcetera. And that's exactly what I did. I treated the Saroyans the way I'd want my own family treated. When you and I joined the Camillian Order, we took a vow to minister to the sick and infirm, and that's what I've been doing. So, go ahead and interview them. Investigate all you want and bring me up on charges. I wouldn't change a thing, and I won't apologize for doing what needed to be done!"

He started toward the door, then stopped. "And I'll be saying Mass alone tomorrow. You're not welcome in my church."

He walked out into the night and slammed the door behind him. The only sound in the room was the whirling blades of the ceiling fan.

I recalled all of the kind things Lucy and Jodi had said about Wronka. They hadn't been covering for him; they'd meant every word. I had followed the clues like the rookie sleuth I was, and I'd come confidently to the wrong conclusion and cast suspicion on an innocent man. Having been on the wrong side of the Inquisition concerning my relationship with Emily, I understood Wronka's anger and knew exactly how he felt.

Even worse, I'd come after a man for possibly having a family because he loved and cared for a woman and her daughter, when in my heart I would have given anything to marry Emily and raise RJ with her. What a hypocrite I was!

I topped off the brandy glass he had left behind, picked up mine, and followed him into the darkness. Except for the hum of insects, the evening was quiet as a nun at prayer. The sky hung heavy with stars, as weighty as my regrets over misinterpreting Wronka's kindness and mishandling my confrontation with him.

He stood between the statue of St. Francis and a giant bald cypress, silently gazing across the bayou. The moist night air was warm, smelled strangely sweet, and felt as soft as silk on my skin. Hundreds of feral eyes watched us across the marsh from the depths of the shadows.

I stepped next to him and held out his brandy. "I'm truly sorry, Edwin. I was dead wrong. Peace offering?"

He grabbed the glass, turned away, and took a swallow. After a long silence he asked, "What about the money? Do you still suspect me of theft?"

I stepped into his line of sight. "No, I don't. There's someone else I suspect, but I need to do more work to prove it."

He looked up at me, then spit on the ground. "Yeah? Well work a lot harder this time, so you don't accuse another innocent person."

"I deserved that. When I sort this all out, Edwin, I'll smooth things over with your bishop and our Superior General. As far as I can tell, you've handled the finances properly. 'Inept' is the last thing you are. They both need to know that."

I stared up at the night sky, and the stars winked down at me like ancient eyes that had witnessed mankind's many follies for eons.

"And our Superior General also needs to know what a fine, caring member of the Camillian Order you are, Edwin. Your exceptional commitment and personal sacrifice on behalf of Ms. Saroyan and her daughter raise the bar to a height most of us will never reach."

I finished the last of my brandy. "I'll leave you to your thoughts. I hope you'll accept my deepest apologies," I added and walked into the rectory.

CHAPTER TWENTY SIX

Sunday, May 4, 9:00 a.m.

While Father Wronka celebrated morning Mass with his congregation, I offered a private Mass in the small rectory chapel to nourish my own spirit. I wanted to give him space in the hope that he would forgive my intrusion into his personal life and the false accusation that had resulted.

It was not simply the proper thing to do; it was also the means to several ends. My Superior General wanted me to uncover the source of missing funds at Wronka's parish. Wronka wanted to be absolved by the local bishop of suspicion that he was, at best, fiscally incompetent and at worst, a thief. I wanted to wrap up this investigation and return home to RJ and a more serene life—but I would need Wronka's assistance to accomplish all three objectives.

I brewed a fresh pot of coffee, then left the rectory and walked to the church. A white egret and I stood sentinel at the entrance in a gentle morning breeze scented with the fragrance of jasmine and magnolia. At the end of the Mass, the organist launched into the exit hymn, and I trotted back to the rectory and began making eggs and bacon for brunch.

I'm a lousy cook. Although my breakfasts are usually edible, scrambled eggs can be bland and boring. Fortunately, Wronka's kitchen contained a vast assortment of condiments and a selection of spices to rival the McCormick Company. I sautéed diced onions in butter, added eggs and scrambled them, and finished with dried thyme and a dollop of sour cream, then sprinkled the meal with shredded cheddar cheese and garnished it with parsley.

When Wronka walked into the kitchen, I ushered him to his chair, handed him a steaming cup of coffee, and set a heaping helping of "Eggs a la Austin" on the table in front of him.

"Peace offering, Edwin?"

His look of surprise was followed by the hint of a smile, which promptly vanished. He dug in without a word, refusing to look at me.

Halfway through the meal, I made an attempt at small talk. "Offering Mass while the church is under construction must be challenging."

He ignored me, so I stood and refilled his coffee cup.

Wronka looked up. "What you did to me was hurtful and cruel." He pointed at his plate. "And it ticks me off even more that you did all *this*." He patted his protruding abdomen and a crooked smile danced on his lips. "Cooking a hearty meal for me makes it much harder to completely despise you."

"Truce?"

He shrugged. "Yeah, I guess—if you promise to take me to Antoine's in the French Quarter for supper. It's the Grande Dame of Creole restaurants in NOLA. Been in business a hundred and sixty years." He chuckled. "And dinner there is gonna cost you a bundle."

"Deal. Antoine's it is. With my vow of poverty, I'll have to sneak it past the Camillian bean counters into my expense voucher, but I'll get it done somehow." With all that I'd learned from Lucy and Jodi Saroyan, I had decided it was time to roll the dice and put my trust in this man.

I told him about Lottie's mansion. "Look, Edwin, I need your help. If church funds are being siphoned off here, the paper trail must be buried somehow in the structural repair costs. That means Master Construction is involved."

Edwin's eyes narrowed and his mouth opened, but he said nothing.

"Tell me about the repair of the bowed church walls. How were they fixed?"

"The structural repairs actually happened the two weeks I was in Colorado with my family for my mother's birthday celebration. Hadn't seen her in over a year. By the time I returned, the work was completed. The repairs were covered with stucco or drywall, so I didn't actually see how the company did it."

"How badly were the walls bowed?"

"Honestly, I never noticed anything. The company foreman pointed it out."

"Did you get a second opinion from a structural engineer?"

"I did. Lottie recommended one. I *was* here when he arrived. He hung a plumb bob from the roof, and the weighted end fell about a foot away from the base of the wall, indicating that the wall was leaning outward. He called the church a leaning tower, like the one in Pisa. Said it was a house of cards, and it was only a matter of time before the entire building collapsed."

"Who was the engineer?"

"Ah, let me think. He had the same last name as the Saints' quarterback ... Brees, that's it! Harmon though, not Drew. His invoice is in the filing cabinet."

I had so many questions I wasn't sure what to ask next. I cleared the dishes and refilled our coffee cups.

"Why did you choose Master Construction for the church restoration, Edwin?"

"I researched local companies online, compiled a list of possibilities, spoke with parishioners about their experiences, and reviewed my options with the bishop. I think it was Lottie who suggested I check out Master Construction. Anyway, Master came in with the lowest bid, making the decision a no-brainer at the time. Of course, that was before all the cost overruns for roof damage and bowed walls."

My mind was reeling. It was worrisome that Wronka had not been present to witness the structural repair of the church, though the plumb line falling away from the building gave credence to the bowing of the walls. Also troubling was the fact that Lottie had recommended both Master Construction *and* the structural engineer. As the church's administrative assistant, she would have known when Wronka was scheduled to leave town and could have alerted Chase Masterson. She and Masterson were looking more and more like a tag team, but how to prove it?

"How well do you know Lottie, Edwin?"

"She was here before I came. When I visited my predecessor after his cancer surgery, he spoke highly of her. He told me that even though Lottie had only been here a short while, she'd become his right hand. Called her indispensable. When I arrived, I was completely overwhelmed by the task and needed all the help I could get. Lottie jumped right in, and I leaned heavily on her out of necessity."

I fell silent.

Wronka's head jerked back and his eyes opened wide. "What? You think Masterson and she …." I nodded. He tilted his head to the side and thought about it. "Well, I have to admit, it does look that way. Okay, what can I do?"

"Let me check out a couple more things. If the evidence continues to suggest that Lottie is in cahoots with Masterson, would you be willing to help me bring them down?"

"It appears they saw my inexperience and lack of expertise and played me like a violin. If you're right, they've made me look like an incompetent fool in front of my bishop and our Superior General. No way am I turning the other cheek. If I did, they'd probably slap that side too. Damn right I'll help. I'm in."

CHAPTER TWENTY SEVEN

Sunday, May 4, 12:15 p.m.

After our Sunday brunch, I cleared the table, loaded the dishwasher, phoned my Superior General, and left a voicemail indicating that I wanted to speak with him. I downloaded my emails, then took a stroll along the bayou, hoping the fresh air and solitude would provide some new ideas. I was on my way back to the rectory when Demarco called me.

"Did you confront Wronka about his relationship with the Saroyan family, Jacob?" His voice took on a razor-sharp edge. "Do we have a sexual predator in our midst? Is he a wolf in … Camillian clothing?"

"No. I'm convinced he is not. I believe he was merely helping out a family in crisis. And I am fairly certain he's not involved with the theft of funds from the church either. It's beginning to look as if his administrative assistant is somehow involved with the construction company doing the restoration."

I brought Demarco up to speed on Lottie's extravagant home and car, and my conversation with Wronka, including the way she had manipulated him into hiring both Master Construction and the structural engineer, and may have alerted the owner of the company as to when Wronka would be out of town visiting his family.

"Sounds suspicious, Jacob. Now what?"

A good question. "Now I keep digging."

And possibly team up with Wronka, I thought, for our own little sting operation. I'd watched Tree Macon run sting operations in the past, and they'd worked because scumbags usually let greed outweigh their caution and common sense.

Shortly after I'd hung up with Demarco, Keri Novak phoned me.

"It's great to hear your voice again, Agent. Has the Marshals Service moved my dad to a new location? How's he doing?"

"Not so good. That's why I called."

"What's going on?" My muscles tensed. "Is he okay?"

"Yeah, but before we got him relocated, a car bomb went off in front of his house. Fortunately, your father forgot something and was stepping inside when the blast occurred. He's pretty shaken but has only a few cuts and bruises. One of the U.S. Marshals guarding him was not as lucky. He's dead. There was a lot of damage to the front of the house, so the bomber may think your father died too. The Marshals are trying to keep it that way while they relocate him. They carried a body bag filled with pillows out of the front of the house into a hearse and snuck your dad out the back door under cover of darkness."

"Damn it, Keri, the Witness Security Program was supposed to *protect* him!" Fear, anger, and helplessness all swept over me at once. "A car bomb? Wasn't that Giordano's signature, the way he eliminated his rivals?"

"Yup, and that's why I volunteered to investigate the incident. Organized crime that crosses state lines gets a lot of FBI attention."

"Is Giordano out of prison?"

"Nope, and never will be. This has his fingerprints all over it though, so he must be communicating with someone from lockup. But don't worry, we'll get the bastards who did this and keep your father safe." I heard someone shout her name. "Listen, I gotta go. I'll keep you posted." Click, and the line went dead.

I entered my room, closed the door, and plopped down on the desk chair. Where my father was concerned I was completely powerless, so I decided to deal with matters within my control.

I opened my computer and performed a Google search on Harmon Brees. He did, in fact, have a civil engineering degree from a school I'd never heard of near Wellsboro, Pennsylvania, a quaint town where I'd gone river rafting down the "Grand Canyon of Pennsylvania" as a young man. He was in solo practice in a small Louisiana city over two hours away, but it appeared that he had no formal training in *structural* engineering. Nothing else stood out, and I wondered if Tree Macon would be willing to run a background check on him as another favor to me.

Knowing nothing about construction or engineering, I researched plumb lines and plummets, wondering if it was possible to fake the result that Wronka had observed. It was simply a metal weight on the end of a string that was used as a vertical reference line, a technique that had been employed for centuries. No magic there; gravity doesn't lie.

Frustrated, I leaned back in my chair and sighed, then picked up a paperclip that had fallen on the floor. As I returned it to the cup on the desk next to the stapler, inspiration struck. A *metal* plumb bob on the end of a long line. *Metal.* Maybe there *was a way* to cheat gravity. I was about to ask Wronka for details about what he'd seen when my cellphone played "I Shot the Sheriff," my ringtone for Tree Macon.

"I looked into that Charlotte Trumble lady for you, Jake."

"Thanks. I have a bad feeling about Lottie." I realized what day it was and chuckled. "Wait, now you're working on Sundays too? I'm in fear for your immortal soul. Do you ever go to church, you heathen?"

"Yeah, yeah. Real funny. And *you're welcome*, Jake. This wasn't easy. There's not a whole lot on her as an adult. A few parking tickets and one DUI years ago. But apparently Lottie Trumble was a hellion as a teenager. The police in her small rural town always kept one eye on her. They called her 'Lotta Trouble.' Her juvie file showed an escalating series of offenses, ending with a conviction for purse snatching. The old lady she robbed tried to stop her and ended up in the hospital."

"How'd you find that out? Aren't juvenile records usually sealed?"

"They are, but I *am* the Grand Poobah of Law Enforcement. I have my ways. Don't ask. If Lottie had hung around town, she might have gotten her record expunged, but she left the state after she finished her two years of probation. Appears her younger brother, Harmon, followed in her footsteps, but he was more *rascal* than criminal." A clicking of computer keys. "The most trouble Harmon got into was leading a cow up to the fourth floor of Wellsboro High School. Cows won't go *down* stairs, so they had to kill and butcher the poor beast to get it out of there."

Harmon. An uncommon first name. My Google search on Harmon Brees, the engineer Wronka had hired, indicated that he'd gotten his degree near Wellsboro, Pennsylvania.

"Wait, Tree. Lottie and her brother grew up in Wellsboro? Is Harmon's last name Trumble?"

More clacking of keys. "No, it's Brees. He's Lottie's *half*-brother. Why?"

Jackpot! Lottie had recommended hiring Brees as the structural engineer to confirm that the church walls were indeed bowing as Master Construction had reported. When Wronka went away to visit his family, the walls were supposedly repaired during his absence and covered with stucco and drywall.

The puzzle pieces were beginning to fit together. Circumstantial evidence, but evidence nonetheless. I thanked Tree for his help, and began formulating a game plan.

CHAPTER TWENTY EIGHT

Monday, May 5, 11:00 a.m.

The next day, Father Wronka invited me to join him in celebrating morning Mass. It felt wonderful to share Communion and the Lord's many blessings with a congregation again. After the service, out of gratitude for my humble efforts in the kitchen the day before, Wronka prepared an Eggs Benedict brunch in a Hollandaise sauce worthy of Le Cordon Bleu in Paris.

As I cleared the table, I said, "I haven't seen Lottie today."

"She asked for the morning off."

"Good. I've been thinking about her relationship with Master Construction and wanted to talk with you."

Wronka chuckled. "I've been doing more than thinking, Jake. I pulled Lottie's job application from our files. She was hired here because she had experience. The file includes a letter of reference from the pastor at Holy Trinity Church, where she'd been an administrative assistant for two years. Holy Trinity is on the other side of New Orleans, about an hour east." A Cheshire Cat grin lit his face. "I called the pastor there last night and guess what? They'd had bowing church walls too and—wait for it—Master Construction performed the repairs."

"Way to go, Edwin! Nice job. So Lottie and Chase Masterson are working together like Bonnie and Clyde, huh?"

"Looks that way. And I'm not the first unsuspecting fool they've duped. There were large cost overruns at that church too."

"And by the appearance of Lottie's house, I'll bet they've run their scam more than twice." I smiled. "I was busy last night too, Edwin. I found out that Harmon Brees is Lottie's half-brother."

"What? That devious shrew! She set me up." Then a smirk crept across his lips. "But that means we got 'em!"

"Easy, my friend. The evidence we have so far is all circumstantial. But we're close."

"Yeah, well I have a feeling if we remove the stucco and drywall from the church, Jake, we won't find *any* evidence of structural repairs. I suspect the church walls were never bowed and our coffers were emptied for work that was never performed."

"You're probably right, but we have no hard evidence unless we start tearing off the drywall and stucco. I'm not ready to take that risk. What if we're wrong? You think you look bad in the eyes of your bishop now? Think how awful we'll look if we demolish much of the restoration that's already been completed."

"So what then, Jake?"

"Tell me what you saw when Harmon Brees dropped a plumb line along the supposedly bowed walls."

"It fell about a foot away from the base of the building." Wronka slumped onto a kitchen chair. "You're right, that makes no sense."

"It might. What else was near the wall when Brees dropped the plumb bob?"

He wrinkled his brow, then stared off into the distance, lost in a memory. "Well, I remember he brought a bunch of other equipment with him, besides the ladder."

"Was it a metal ladder?"

"No, it was wooden. He did take a lot of pictures of the wall with a camera, and he used some sort of gizmo to measure angles."

"And when Brees lowered the line down, was the metal plumb bob near anything? Think, Edwin, this is important."

"Now that you mention it, before he climbed up the ladder onto the roof, Brees set two duffle bags of equipment on the ground near the spot where he dropped the plumb line."

Bingo! Time to set a Tree Macon-style sting operation into action.

"I'm confused, Jake. What are you thinking?"

"I'll bet Brees had powerful magnets in those two bags that attracted the metal bob on the line and drew it away from the wall."

"Making it *appear* that the wall bowed outward. Son of a … a witch! But how do we prove it?"

"Unfortunately, we can't now without tearing the stucco and drywall from the church. What we *can* do is prove that Lottie and Masterson are working together. We already know that Harmon Brees is Lottie's half-brother, and that Lottie and Masterson were involved with another church with bowed walls and cost overruns. There may be other victims. We need to prove that those two are conspiring."

"How do we do that? I'm sure they don't want to be seen together, Jake, so how do we flush them out?"

"We give Lottie some damning physical evidence that puts their operation in jeopardy, and hope she takes it directly to Masterson—and we catch them in the act. But I'll need your help to pull this off. If we're successful, we'll prove your competence to the bishop and remove you from his doghouse, as well as show our Superior General what an asset you are to the Camillian Order."

"Count me in, Jake."

I told Wronka my plan, and our sting operation began to take shape.

CHAPTER TWENTY NINE

Monday, May 5, 12:30 p.m.

"I love the idea of laying a trap for those two weasels," Wronka said, "but we don't have any physical evidence to scare Lottie into running to Chase Masterson."

"True. No real evidence, but all we need to do is make her *think* we do. How well do you know the pastor at Holy Trinity Church, the one who also hired Master Construction for structural repairs?"

"We've spoken on the phone a few times, and we met once at a diocesan conference."

"Do you think he might consider joining our merry little band of Robin-Hoodlums, and help us return money stolen by the robber barons to our parishioners?

Wronka chuckled. "I suspect he'll be happy to play Friar Tuck to your Robin Hood. He definitely has an edge. If he was tricked the way I was, he'll want a pound of their flesh, though he might not be willing to put his career at risk if our plan backfires."

"I can work with that, Edwin. While I manufacture some physical evidence, call him and explain our theory and our plan. He doesn't need to be involved in any way other than allowing us to use his name. Let him know that if this blows up, it will be clear that I forged our evidence, and any fallout will be on me, and me alone. And tell him to steer clear of Chase Masterson for a few days while we make our move."

While Wronka set about enlisting the pastor across town in

our plan, I searched the internet for a large, out-of-state structural engineering firm. I found one, and with a little effort and the proper font, I reproduced their letterhead as best I could and concocted a letter addressed to me.

When Wronka returned to the study, he told me he'd just seen Lottie pull her BMW roadster into the church parking lot.

"And the pastor across town?"

"He's onboard, Jake."

"Good." I handed him the letter.

Dear Father Austin,

In response to your query, we do in fact have associates in Louisiana who can meet with you to evaluate the structural repairs at Blessed Savior Church. If your suspicion is correct and a construction company has perpetrated a fraudulent repair, we will contact the pastor at Holy Trinity Church and offer to evaluate Master Construction's repair of his church as well.

We have indeed worked with law enforcement in the past and served as expert witnesses in court. One of our Louisiana associates will be in contact with you soon. Thank you for your business and your confidence in our company.

A. Jones

Managing Director

Wronka looked up after he'd finished reading. "Heck yeah! That should light a fire under those two creeps."

I sealed the letter in a stamped envelope addressed to me care of Blessed Savior Church.

"It's best you not be in here, Edwin, when I drop the bombshell. Tell Lottie I'm in the study."

A few minutes later, Lottie entered the room.

"Good afternoon, Father. Sorry I was late today."

I ignored her, frowned, and sliced the envelope open with a letter opener, then pretended to read the note, mumbling "fraud" and "expert witnesses" as I paced back and forth across the study.

"Something wrong, Father?"

I stopped mid-stride and stared at her as if I'd been completely unaware of her presence.

"*Wrong* doesn't even begin to describe the situation, Lottie. I've uncovered a fraud perpetrated against this church so vile that I won't be satisfied until Chase Masterson is behind bars."

Lottie's mouth opened and she gasped. "Anything I can do to help?"

"There is, thanks." I handed her the letter. "The printer in the study isn't working and I need three copies of this, so I can send them to the bishop and possibly to the authorities. Please copy this letter in the church office for me immediately." I paused. "And Lottie, this is between you and me. I need you to keep this in the strictest confidence. Please don't mention the letter to Father Wronka until I'm certain he's not involved."

She nodded and glanced at the contents of the letter. Her eyes grew wide and she hurried off.

Wronka peeked in the door. "What now, Jake?"

"Now, you keep an eye on the parking lot. If Lottie gets into her car, follow her at a distance and call me. She thinks this investigation is all my doing. I told her I thought you might be involved with Masterson, so she won't suspect you if you get spotted—but don't get spotted."

As soon as Wronka walked out of the door, I called Tree Macon, explained the situation, and asked for his advice.

He chuckled. "Funny, you always get upset when I run a sting operation, but it's okay if *you* do it?"

"What can I say? I'm a walking contradiction."

"You're not wrong about that."

"I'm just following in the Lord's footsteps, Tree. Jesus was a fisher of men, so I've set the bait and cast the net. So, Grand Poobah of Justice, what do I need to do now to snare the fish?"

"Well, you already have everything you need to prosecute Chase Masterson. You got the paid invoices and if there are no structural repairs under the stucco and drywall, he's dead in the water. Especially if he's run this scam at other churches. My guess is he's also bribed building inspectors who might testify against him. His only option is to clean out his bank account and disappear."

"But all I have is circumstantial evidence against Lottie. She's living in a mansion off the backs of our parishioners, and I have nothing solid against her. This scam would have never worked without her involvement. I want to take her down too."

"True, Masterson needed someone inside the church to pull this off. So this is how I would play it." He then talked me through his version of *Sting Operations for Dummies*.

"One last question, Tree. If this plan works, *then* what do I do? The Vatican never issued me handcuffs, and His Holiness frowns on priests packing heat. If I work through Mother Church's usual maze of red tape, the two of them will be basking on a private Caribbean island before the authorities are even contacted. And the Louisiana police are not exactly going to jump to attention and call out the SWAT team when an out-of-state, Yankee priest walks in complaining of church fraud."

"Lucky for you, as a Majordomo in the Justice System, I have connections in Louisiana. One phone call from me will crank up the heat, and the local cops will cook up a mess of my favorite dish—southern fried perps. Call me when you have something concrete."

"Thanks, buddy. I owe you one."

I hung up the phone as Lottie entered the study.

"Here are the copies you asked for." She set them on the desk and coughed. "Sorry, Father, but I really don't feel well. I'd like to go home and rest, if you don't need anything else."

"No problem, Lottie. Take as long as you need."

After I heard the front door of the rectory slam, I headed to my room and called Wronka. "She's on the move, Edwin. Stay close but out of sight. Keep me posted on her whereabouts. I'll be right behind you." I grabbed my camera and car keys. "I'd love to record Lottie's conversation with Masterson as evidence, but my cellphone doesn't have a voice recording app. Does yours?"

"No, Jake, and I wouldn't know how to work it if I had one. Sorry. But I do have an old handheld Dictaphone recorder in the top drawer of my desk."

"That might work. Stay with Lottie. I'm on my way. I'll catch up with you as soon as I can."

And just like that, the game was afoot.

CHAPTER THIRTY

Monday, May 5, 1:45 p.m.

I slipped on a sport coat over my dress shirt and located Father Wronka's old hand-held Dictaphone in his desk. It recorded well, but it was big and bulky, and the mechanism was too noisy for my purpose. I took it anyway, and a few minutes later I was breaking speed limits, trying to catch up with Wronka's car.

I suspected that Lottie had made her own copy of my bogus letter, and I was hoping she would head directly to Chase Masterson. I wanted to take photos of the two of them meeting to demonstrate that they were working together.

Father Wronka phoned me to say that Lottie had pulled into the parking lot of the Grinning Gator Restaurant, twenty minutes north of Master Construction's headquarters. I told him to keep her in sight and gunned my engine.

When I arrived at the Grinning Gator, I spotted Wronka's car at the far side of the lot. I drove up next to him, got into his car, and handed him the Dictaphone. He pointed at Lottie, who was drinking coffee alone at an outdoor table. The lunch crowd was dwindling, and no one else was seated on the veranda. This scenario was better than I had hoped. It would be easy enough to get photographs of the two of them together when Masterson arrived, but I wanted more. I sat back and took a moment to fine-tune my plan.

"Now what, Jake?"

"Now we get creative. As soon as Masterson arrives, get some pictures of them with your phone. Use that live oak to shield yourself from sight. Then hop into your car and when I call you, put your cellphone on speaker and use the recorder to document everything you hear them say over the phone. I'll need a minute to get things set up."

I circled back to the Grinning Gator, bought a copy of the Times-Picayune from a newspaper vending machine, and was about to enter the restaurant when I realized that the hostess was seating Chase Masterson at Lottie's table.

I peeked around the corner of the building, snapped a couple of photos of them, then called Wronka and told him to turn on the recorder and remain on the line. I added that he should signal me if he was able to hear Lottie and Masterson talking. I left my cellphone on but shut off the ringer, rolled it in the newspaper, and walked into the restaurant.

When the hostess came to me, I lit up a cheery smile, took out my wallet, and said, "I need your assistance. I'm meeting an important client, a Mr. Chen from Taiwan, and wish to treat him to some southern hospitality at lunch." I pulled a twenty dollar bill from my wallet, handed it to her, and pointed to the table nearest to Lottie and Chase Masterson. "I'd like to be seated at that table under the Magnolia tree."

She took the money and beamed. "Certainly, sir. Please follow me."

"Actually, I need to retrieve something from my car first." I handed her the newspaper concealing my cellphone. "Please set this on our table. I'll be back soon." She reached out and I added, "Be very careful with this. I have a surprise gift for Mr. Chen hidden in the paper, and I wouldn't want it to slip out."

She nodded, and I watched her gently place my things on the outdoor table closest to Lottie and Masterson. I stepped outside and waved to Wronka. He gave me a thumbs up, and I walked to his car and got in.

I held a finger up to my lips. "Have they said anything yet, Edwin?" I whispered.

"They'd just begun talking when the waiter came to take Masterson's order and they stopped. Lottie did look nervous when the hostess put something on the adjacent table, but she relaxed when no one sat down," he replied softly.

We listened to silence until the waiter returned to their table. "Here's your martini, sir. I'll give you some time to look over the menu." His voice was faint but clear.

Masterson waited for the server to leave, then asked, "What the hell is going on, Lottie? What's so damned important that we had to meet in person? Someone could see us together."

"That new fucking priest, Father Austin, is on to us. He suspects something about the structural repairs." We watched Lottie hand him a sheet of paper. "Read it! He's thinking about hiring an engineering company for a second opinion."

"God damn it! This screws up everything." Masterson took a long drink of his martini and sighed. "Well, we always knew this could happen. We've had a good run, but I'm cashing in my chips. I'll be on a plane to Morocco in a day or two. I can live like a king there, and they don't allow extradition to the U.S."

"Don't you have to sell your house and office first?"

"All rented. Even the furniture is leased."

"What about me, Chase? I'll have to sell my home, my cars!"

"Not my problem."

"I need time! The housing market's in the toilet and I have a huge mortgage. I'll be lucky to break even. I can't just—"

Masterson held up a hand to stop her. "When we teamed up, I *told* you not to build that monstrosity 'cause we needed to stay nimble in case we had to disappear. You should have listened." He swirled his martini and took another swallow. "Look, it may take several weeks for the engineers to arrive and check our repairs. Take whatever you can get for the damn house and get the hell out of Dodge. A million bucks isn't worth shit if you're in prison." He laughed. "Been a fun ride, Lottie girl. If you're ever in Morocco, look me up."

Masterson downed the last of his drink, stood, threw cash on the table, then walked away. As he left, we could faintly hear Lottie sobbing. Finally, she stood, wiped her tears on a napkin, and left.

Wronka smiled. "Kinda fun watching the rats abandon the sinking ship."

I walked back to the restaurant, apologized to the hostess, and reclaimed my things from the table. When I returned to Wronka's car, I phoned Tree Macon and played the tape for him.

"Nicely done, Jake. A sting operation well stung." He chuckled. "But … what about that commandment, 'Thou shall not lie,' Father?"

"It's 'Thou shalt not bear false witness against thy neighbor,' you heathen, and everything I've said about the two of them is true. Their whole house-of-cards scam was built on falsehoods." I paused. "Okay, Tree, I maneuvered the fish into the net. Please have the good guys haul them in."

"I'm on it, buddy. Someone from New Orleans P.D. will stop by the rectory to take your statement and the evidence. Consider those two bottom feeders deep fried."

CHAPTER THIRTY ONE

Monday, May 5, 3:30 p.m.

When we arrived at the rectory, Father Wronka popped the cork on a bottle of champagne. We settled into armchairs in the living room and took a moment to celebrate our success.

We clinked glasses and he said, "Well, that's over. Thank the good Lord it went well."

"My job's not quite finished. Those two scumbags made you look incompetent with your bishop, and I inadvertently smeared your good name with our Superior General." He began to respond but I raised a hand to silence him. "Let me fix this, Edwin. I owe you. You'll be a rock star when I'm done."

I called the Camillian Order's headquarters and put my cellphone on speaker so Edwin could listen. I filled in Father Demarco on the success of our sting operation, suggested he send a forensic accountant to New Orleans to trace the embezzled church funds, and emphasized Wronka's critical role in our plan. Demarco was pleased.

"It appears I hired the right man as my troubleshooter, Jacob. Good job. I like the way your devious mind works. Very creative. You and Father Wronka *both* went above and beyond."

"Please contact his bishop in New Orleans and stress Father Wronka's critical role in ending the theft of church funds here." Edwin gave me a thumbs up. I cleared my throat. "And let me underscore that I was completely wrong about his involvement with the Saroyan family. That was an act of mercy on his part and nothing more. Father Wronka is a credit to our Order."

"Duly noted. His assistance in this matter will not go unrewarded. I'm adding a pair of 'atta-boys' to his record on my computer as we speak. Now if you'll excuse me, Jacob, I have a meeting to attend."

When I said goodbye, Wronka raised his glass. "Thank you, my friend. It's good to be out of the doghouse." He downed the last of his champagne. "Want another glass?"

"No thanks, I have some calls to make." On an empty stomach, the bubbly had already left me with a pleasant buzz, and I was feeling quite content with what we'd accomplished. Getting home to RJ, however, was now my priority. "My nephew should be home from school. I want to catch up on the latest playground gossip and arrange my flight home."

"Fine. That'll give me time to cook a thank-you dinner you won't soon forget," he said and entered the kitchen.

Just then my phone chimed. It was Emily. I grinned like a teenaged boy on his first date. Even the sound of her voice lifted my spirits. If I was honest with myself, I missed her as much as I missed RJ. I couldn't wait to get home to the two of them.

"Glad you called, Em. I was about to—"

"Jake, thank God I reached you!" She sobbed. "Father Snapp's been hurt! He was in the church parking lot, leaving for the hospital when his …. Oh my god, I don't even know how to say this! It makes no sense. His van just … blew up!"

"What? How'd this happen?" I jumped to my feet and began pacing. "Are RJ and Colleen okay?"

"The blast shattered a couple of windows in the rectory and they're both scared to death, Jake, but not injured. The police are there now taking their statements."

"How bad is Father Snapp? Is he conscious?"

"I don't know. He's in surgery." A soft whimper. "Oh Jake, this is all my fault! I asked him to come to the hospital to evaluate for paranormal activity in the snack shop. This would never have happened if I'd left things alone. I feel terrible!"

What I felt was *terror*. I remembered the phone call from Agent Novak about the car bombing at my father's house that killed a U.S. Marshal and forced my dad to be relocated. An icy chill slid down my spine; two explosions in less than a week involving people I knew? Coincidence? Not a chance!

Listening to Emily sob and blame herself, however, was breaking my heart.

"It's definitely not your fault, Em. Really. It was probably a freak accident. Maybe his van had a leaky fuel line and a spark set off the blast. I'll be home soon and we'll figure this out." Frustrated, I ran my finger through my hair. "Thanks for letting me know. I'd better call RJ now."

But first, I wanted to speak with Tree Macon. I made the call.

"Of course I heard about Snapp, Jake. Hell, the blast rattled the station house. The town's never had a major explosion, and everyone is on pins and needles. I'm on my way there now with our investigators. There are dozens of possible causes. The charging cycle of a car battery can cause highly flammable hydrogen to build up around the engine. If the electrical wiring is frayed or loose, a spark can ignite it." He paused. "Rotted fuel lines are the most common cause of vehicle fires. Could be Snapp's van had a gasoline leak and he tossed a cigarette out of the window?"

"His van didn't look old enough to have rotted fuel lines, and Snapp's not a smoker. I doubt this was an accident."

"Yeah, me too," Tree admitted. "Cars that catch fire don't usually explode immediately, and the blast was more intense than you'd expect. Have to say, Jake, I've been wondering if Snapp made an enemy doing exorcisms or some other hocus-pocus. He's a real strange dude. Think one of his exorcisms could have gone terribly wrong and a pissed-off family member decided to blow him into the afterlife?"

"It's possible, I suppose. Who knows with Snapp, but there's another possibility." I drew a deep breath, knowing I was right but hoping I was wrong. "I recently spoke with Agent Novak. A car bomb went off outside my dad's house. He's okay, but … this can't be a coincidence."

Tree went silent as he considered this.

"Wait a minute, Jake. You thinking Angelo Giordano's gang is retaliating for putting him in prison and shutting down their drug operation? Maybe, but I don't see the connection to Snapp. Makes sense the mob might go after your dad, but Snapp had nothing to do with that."

"True, but if Snapp was wearing a black cassock like I often do, it's possible they bombed the wrong priest. I received a death threat right after Giordano's trial. That's why I had a security alarm installed at the rectory. I'd nearly forgotten about it because that was months ago."

"Yeah, I got a threat too, Jake. But I doubt there's much left of Giordano's gang anymore. After Big Angie was locked up, the drug unit in Louisiana told me the Russian mob took his turf and killed or recruited most of his troops. But I guess it would only take one or two foot soldiers to go on a vendetta. Lemme see what I can find out. Talk with you soon. Take care, buddy, and watch your back."

I was more concerned about taking care of the two people at the rectory. I called RJ and told him I would be home soon. He was understandably shaken. I tried to calm him down, but he needed hugs much more than reassurance. When my boy finally passed the phone to Colleen, I asked her to take him to her apartment as a precaution until I returned. Next, I tried to book a flight home, but none were available for the next day. I phoned Demarco's secretary and told him I had a family crisis and needed to get home. I asked him to arrange for any fight that got me back as soon as possible.

After I hung up, I poured two fingers of scotch, plopped onto a chair, and took swallow. This was not the time for a champagne celebration.

CHAPTER THIRTY TWO

Monday, May 5, 6:00 p.m.

A car bombing had taken place at my father's house, and there'd been an explosion at the rectory—and with me, hundreds of miles from RJ, I was completely helpless! Good Lord have mercy!

With Father Snapp in the hospital, I phoned Bishop Lucci in Cleveland and arranged for coverage at Sacred Heart Church until I returned. Father Wronka was still preparing our meal, so I entered my room, knelt, and recited prayers of intercession for the recovery of Father Snapp, as well as for the protection of RJ, Colleen, and my dad.

Time slipped away until Wronka knocked on my door and announced that supper was ready. He had set the dining table with fine china and crystal, and had prepared Louisiana Shrimp Etouffee for our meal. The dining room looked and smelled like heaven. He ladled a medley of tender Gulf shrimp nestled in onions, peppers, and a blonde Creole roux over the white rice on my plate, and my taste buds went on a fanciful journey.

His mood over ensnaring Lottie and Chase Masterson in our sting operation was as high as mine was low. He tried for light conversation, but when I explained about the two car bombings, the celebratory tone of our meal cratered and we finished in silence.

Tree Macon's phone call to the New Orleans police department lit a fire under the investigation. A policewoman arrived after supper and took our statements, as well as the photos of Lottie and Masterson we had taken and the voice recording of their incriminating conversation. She told us that Masterson's passport had already been placed on a watch list and neither of them would be allowed to leave the country. After listening to the recording, she added that she suspected their arrest was imminent. The ball was now out of our hands and in the N.O.P.D.'s court.

After the officer left, I sat on a bench outside of the rectory watching the full moon carve a hole through the darkness, and listening to the bayou's mysterious evening serenade. I was lost in my thoughts when, from the corner of my eye, I glimpsed a dark specter rise up from the earth and ascend into the night. My heart began to pound. It looked like … a ghost. *What the heck?*

I leapt up and dashed to where I'd seen the apparition. It wasn't until the great blue heron shrieked mid-flight that I understood what had happened. The news of the car bombings had severely frayed my nerves, and I'd spooked myself.

But the incident reminded me of the Night Nurse, and the fact that I needed to call the nun in Tennessee who had introduced Dorothy Margaret Clay to her mysterious boyfriend shortly before her car's fiery plunge from the cliff. The question of why Dorothy's ghost continued to haunt the hospital after nearly four decades, and the reason she had chosen to reveal herself to me had been nibbling at the corners of my mind since I'd arrived in Louisiana. It was too late in the evening to contact her, but since I was stuck here with nothing to do until I could fly home, I decided to phone her in the morning.

My cellphone rang, dragging me back to reality: Tree Macon.

"Jake, we were both right. Snapp has been threatened in the past because of his exorcisms. His van was special-ordered and bulletproof. Not as fully armored as the 'Pope-mobile,' but it's the only reason he's alive. And as you suggested, he was indeed wearing black robes similar to your cassock when he was attacked. Given the bombing at your father's place, you're the most likely intended target for your part in sending Big Angie to prison."

"Good Lord, RJ could have been with me when the damn thing exploded!"

"I'm worried about him too. When Big Angie was king of the streets, he had no qualms about blowing up a rival mobster's car with the guy's kids in the back seat. It was Giordano's preferred method of retaliation. Overkill was Angie's way of emphasizing that he was really pissed off."

"I've already asked Colleen to take RJ to her apartment for safekeeping. Do he and I need to go into witness protection along with my father to keep him safe?"

"Hope not, Jake. I'd prefer to take whoever's behind this vendetta off the board and put them in jail … or in the ground. I told Agent Novak what happened, and she's requested an FBI team to investigate the rectory bombing. Gang activity across state lines tends to draw a crowd—which is fine by me. I'm happy to share my turf on this case. She also confirmed that the Russian mob dismantled Giordano's operation after Big Angie was locked in the slammer."

"Then who do you think planted the bomb?"

"Novak and I think Big Angie's son, Vinny. He's the only one who would be motivated to settle the score. He might have one or two hangers-on working for him, but there's no real gang left. Maybe it's a matter of family honor, and he's retaliating against everyone involved in putting his old man away and shutting down the flow of his drug money. Car bombings scream *personal* to me, not business. He wants us to know this is payback."

"Can't the police question him, place him under surveillance, or search his house? Something? Anything? This is life or death, Tree—for RJ, my father, and me."

"Problem is, Jake, this is all conjecture. We got no proof and need some hard evidence before we can shut him down. I contacted the Baton Rouge police chief and he tried for a warrant to search Vinny's home, but the judge refused. The local P.D. believes he's out of town, but even if Vinny's still around, they don't have the manpower to follow him 24/7 on a hunch."

"Whoa, hold on! Baton Rouge? That's where he lives? Heck, Tree, I'm staying at a church less than an hour from there on Interstate 10. What's Vinny's address?"

"No, Jake. *Hell* no! Don't go anywhere near that bastard. It's too damn dangerous. The guy's a drug dealer and a killer. Don't even think about it."

"If Vinny is behind all of this, you're right about one thing—this *is* personal. He tried to kill my dad and could have killed RJ! I'm here, one hour from his home, and I'm not walking away."

"Come on, damn it. Be reasonable. I know you've had military training, but you don't know a darn thing about explosives. Vinny does. He was an Army combat engineer and spent two tours as a demolitions specialist overseas before he became a lieutenant in Big Angie's gang. For Christ's sake, Jake, his house could be booby-trapped."

"Thank heavens I'm good with God."

"Don't be a smartass. It's too risky."

"I'm not going to wait for Vinny to realize he attacked the wrong priest and decide to blow up the rectory or the church. The police need to play by the rules and stay within the law, but when it comes to RJ, I've got no damn rulebook. I'm going. What's his address?"

Tree refused and I cajoled.

He resisted. "Think about it, Jake. You can't do this! What would happen to RJ if he lost you?"

That stopped me. Tree was right. I didn't want RJ placed in foster care if I died. I needed someone to be his guardian in case of an emergency. Colleen was nearing retirement age, which left only one logical choice—Emily. He was the child she'd never had. Emily loved him dearly and she already was a surrogate mother to my nephew. I had asked her in March if she would be willing to assume RJ's care if something were to happen to me, and she had agreed. Then all hell had broken lose with the human trafficking case, and my good intensions had slipped through the cracks.

But that didn't change the situation. A mad bomber was running around trying to kill me and those I loved, and I was already in Louisiana with an opportunity to help the police put him in prison.

"I can do this, Tree … and I *will*. Give me Vinny's address. I'll just have to make sure I don't get killed."

"There you go again being a smartass. Forget it, Jake. I'm serious."

"So am I, Tree."

Finally he relented and gave me an address on the west side of Baton Rouge near the Mississippi River.

Wondering what I might encounter, I added, "One more thing, Tree. Does Vinny have a wife or kids or live-in girlfriend?"

I heard pages rustling and computer keys clacking. "None listed. Far as we can tell, he lives alone." A pause. "Listen, Jake, if you wait to make your move, I could fly down and help you this weekend. A little backup might keep you out of the slammer—or the morgue."

"Thanks for the offer, buddy, but I need to get home to RJ as soon as I can. I'm stuck in Louisiana for only a day or two, so this happens tomorrow while I have the chance."

Years earlier, I had been to war, and I wouldn't hesitate to go to war again in order to protect my boy.

CHAPTER THIRTY THREE

Tuesday, May 6, 9:30 a.m.

I stared into my coffee, wondering how to gain entrance into Vinny Giordano's home in order to search for evidence of his involvement in the car bombings of Father Snapp and my father. If I wore my Roman collar and clerical shirt, I could play the priest card and claim I was performing a welfare check. The problem was, I had no parishioners of my own in Louisiana, and the media would have a field day if a priest was arrested, resulting in enormous blowback for me and the Church. If I was dressed in my civvies, however, it would be harder to gain entrance into his home, and I'd have no legitimate excuse for being there. Unfortunately, it was impossible to be two people at once. Or was it?

As Father Wronka entered the kitchen after morning Mass, I made a decision.

"What'd you have scheduled for today, Edwin?"

"A ten o'clock phone conference with the bishop about the stolen funds and how we can finance the remainder of the church renovations. After that, I'm meeting one of my parishioners for a pastoral counseling session about her philandering husband. Then I'd planned to get bids from several construction companies to complete the work on the church. Why?"

I smiled. "Now that your reputation has been restored, how would you like to put it at risk again?"

He gazed at me, confusion on his face. I handed him a steaming cup of coffee.

"The man suspected in the two bombings I told you about, Edwin, lives in Baton Rouge. He's a drug dealer, the son of the gang's kingpin, and dangerous as hell, but the police don't have enough evidence to arrest him or even get a search warrant for his home, so—would you be willing to help me put him behind bars?"

An impish grin slowly formed on his lips. "You're a curious fellow, Jake. It must be strange living inside your mind." He tilted his head to one side. "Well, your last cockamamie scheme turned out to be surprisingly effective … so, what'd you have in mind?"

I told him what I was planning. "It would be a lot easier with your help, Edwin."

He patted his belly. "You understand that I'm a short, fat man and won't be much help in a brawl, right?" He cleared his throat. "I have a question. Am I likely to be shot, blown up, or sent to jail?"

"No, your job will be mainly surveillance and snooping, but you may have to bend the truth a bit."

"My seminary never had a class on *spying and lying*, Jake, but I'll do my best. Before I was assigned here, I saw substance abuse every day at the hospital and sometimes in my parish. If we can put a drug dealer in prison, count me in." He thought about it. "Construction company bids for the church can wait a day longer. I should be free around eleven-thirty," he added and headed for the study.

With over an hour before we left for Baton Rouge, I threw a few items into my backpack I thought might be useful if a break-in at Giordano's house was necessary, then tossed the backpack into the trunk of my car and shifted my focus from killers to ghosts. I removed the note from my wallet that I'd written before leaving home. It contained the name and telephone number of the nun who had introduced Dorothy Margaret Clay to her mysterious boyfriend shortly before Dorothy's untimely demise.

Sister Maria Celeste had graduated with Dorothy in 1965 from the nursing program at St. Joseph's Hospital. A computer search revealed that she was working at a Catholic nursing home in Nashville, Tennessee. As she was probably in her sixties, I hoped she hadn't yet retired. I made the phone call and got lucky.

"This is Maria Celeste."

I introduced myself and explained that I was a priest looking into Dorothy's death.

"That was a long time ago, Father." I could hear the hesitancy in her voice. "Why now?"

I certainly didn't want to tell her about Dorothy's ghost roaming the hospital halls.

"I'm consulting with the Sheriff on the investigation, and unfortunately I'm not at liberty to say more at this time. He did share her police file with me, so I'm familiar with the details of the case." How to gain her confidence? "I've already spoken with Dorothy's sister, Sybil. They were quite close, as you might remember. She described Dorothy as joyful and caring."

"That she was, Father. As stressful as the training program was and as difficult as some patients can be, I never heard a harsh word from her lips."

"You two were good friends, then?"

"Oh yes, we were very close ... until she started dating that man. Nicholas Pappas was the hospital administrator and a big deal at St. Joe's, but truth be told, he was *not* a nice man. I never liked the guy and didn't trust his intentions." She released a bitter laugh. "To be fair, it's impossible to double date with a nun as your best friend. I was the unwanted third wheel in their relationship. Nick made it clear he didn't want me hanging around ... cramping his style."

She drew a slow breath. "As I think back, there were all kinds of rumors floating around in the women's dorm about his roaming hands. He never bothered me because I usually wore my habit, but his secretary told me he was *grabby* and wouldn't take 'no' for an answer. I heard similar stories from others. I have no doubt he was a womanizer, but in those days there was no such thing as a sexual harassment suit against your boss. Complaints just got swept under the rug. Honestly Father, I've always regretted introducing Dorothy to that man."

Bingo. Nicholas Pappas—the mystery man unmasked—but where to take the conversation?

"Dorothy's death was so sudden, so tragic. Any idea, Sister, why she would have been driving along the cliff road?"

"By Lovers Lane? Not exactly my area of expertise, Father, but knowing Pappas, I can guess. The only time I've ever been anywhere near there was when Nick took Dorothy and me to the country club, trying to impress us with his money and clout."

Sybil had mentioned that Dorothy's boyfriend had been teaching her to play golf. Now I had something to work with. But a woman in love plunging to her death from Lovers' Lane raised *several* possibilities. I had to explore all of them. There was nothing in the case report about her mental health, and the coroner had been unable to test her blood alcohol content due to the intensity of the fire.

"I hate to ask this, Sister, but could Dorothy have been drunk and accidentally driven off the cliff or … could she have committed suicide?"

"*No way* Dorothy would have taken her own life! She was a staunch Catholic, and I'd never even seen her depressed. Like her sister said, she was a joyful young woman, in love with life. Suicide? No, Father, I don't buy it. And the most I'd ever seen her drink was one glass of wine."

I'd taken the interview as far as I could, but at least I now had the name of Dorothy's boyfriend at the hospital.

I thanked Sister Maria Celeste and set about my last task of the morning. Months earlier, when I'd asked Emily if she would be willing to also become RJ's guardian, she had agreed, but I had never followed through with the paperwork. It's easy to procrastinate when tomorrow seems like a given. In light of the two recent car bombings, I could procrastinate no longer.

One of my parishioners was a lawyer who occasionally donated her services to the church. She had also helped me obtain legal guardianship of my nephew. I dialed her office number and asked to speak with her.

"Good morning, Father. How may I be of assistance?"

I explained the situation to her.

"So you want to add Emily Beale as a guardian for your nephew in case something were to happen to you? No problem. Easy-peasy. I can have the paperwork delivered to the rectory in a day or two. All you'll have to do is get her signature and I'll file the forms."

"Thank you, counselor. I'm afraid this is where I plead vow of poverty again."

"I do believe you're becoming a *pro* at pro bono, Father. Fine, just make sure that when my time comes, I bypass purgatory and go straight into heaven."

We said our goodbyes and I shifted mental gears, refocusing on Vinny Giordano. As I mulled over the problem of gaining entrance into his home, Father Wronka entered the room.

"I've wrapped up my morning, Jake." He chuckled. "Never imagined I'd ever say this, but … let's go put a drug dealer in jail."

CHAPTER THIRTY FOUR

Tuesday, May 6, 1:00 p.m.

Father Wronka and I were lost in our own thoughts with little to say on the drive to Baton Rouge. While I was contemplating my first move, he was probably reconsidering his decision to meddle in the life of a known drug dealer and suspected murderer.

"Let me reiterate, Jake, so I'm clear. I'd prefer not to be killed or arrested today. Got it?"

"Got it."

I parked a block away from the address Tree Macon had given me. I was surprised at the neighborhood. I'd expected a drug dealer to either live in a seedy apartment in a rundown part of town, or in a secluded house on the outskirts … wrong. Vinny Giordano lived in a middle-class townhouse on a quiet street not far from the Mississippi River. He appeared to be a chameleon criminal, blending in with his environment and hiding in plain sight. How many times on television had I seen the neighbors of a murderer describe the killer to a reporter as a quiet fellow they didn't know well, but who always seemed pleasant?

I told Wronka to stay in the car, watch Giordano's home, and phone me if he saw any activity. Setting my cell to vibrate, I got out, grabbed my backpack from the trunk, and sauntered past the front of the house as casually as I could.

The drapes on the first floor windows of Giordano's townhouse were drawn. Those on the second and third floor windows were open, but the rooms were dark.

I kept walking, and when I reached the end of the block, I rounded the corner and entered the alley behind his house. I didn't encounter anyone as I strolled down the alleyway, so I turned around at the far end and walked back to Vinny's home. Peeking through the back windows revealed an unoccupied kitchen on one side of the door, a darkened dining room on the other, and a third smaller window with frosted glass, presumably the downstairs bathroom.

I glanced again down the alley, saw no one, and slipped on latex gloves. Hoping that Vinny was out of town as the local police had told Tree, I tried the knob on the back door—locked. I attempted to force open the three sash windows from the outside, but they were also locked.

I had a putty knife and a hacksaw blade in my backpack to help open a window from the outside, as well as a crowbar to force entry if all else failed. But I wasn't anxious to add a breaking and entering charge to my resume, so I returned to the car.

Wronka asked, "Any luck?"

"No, but fear not, I brought my secret weapon."

"What's that?"

I chuckled. "*You*. Before I try to break into Giordano's home, it's time for some reconnaissance. Ring his doorbell and if anyone answers, pretend to be soliciting donations for Catholic Charities. If no one responds, see what you can find out about him and his whereabouts from his neighbors. Tell them you were supposed to meet him here and he's not answering the door or his phone, and you're concerned about his welfare. A concerned priest shouldn't cause any suspicion. I'll keep an eye out and call you if I see him coming."

Wronka nodded. It was not a particularly hot day, but sweat glistened on his forehead and upper lip. I hoped he wouldn't unravel if confronted with an unforeseen obstacle, or if Giordano was home. He put on his Roman collar, forced an unconvincing smile, and trudged to the front door of the townhouse like a death-row prisoner on his way to the electric chair. He knocked, then rang the bell. After a minute, he gave me a thumbs down, and began knocking on the neighboring doors.

As he did, I opened my backpack and removed the mugshot of Vinny that Tree had emailed to me. Although it had been taken several years earlier, I knew I'd have no trouble recognizing him. His head was clean-shaven and at some point in his life, he must have really pissed someone off. They had carved his face like a pumpkin. An angry red crescent-shaped scar ran from his pasty-white forehead past his left eye down to his chin. Most startling, however, were his cold, cruel pale-gray eyes.

I scanned the quiet side street in both directions looking for that ruined face, but saw only a young woman walking her toy poodle and an octogenarian reading the newspaper on his front step.

No one answered Wronka's knock at the first two doors he tried. An elderly man appeared at the third, listened patiently, then pointed down the block and closed the door.

Wronka gave me a thumbs up and walked to a door to the left of Giordano's house. An elderly woman answered. As they spoke, her congenial expression morphed into concern and she made the sign of the cross. She entered her home, reappeared with a ring of keys, unlocked Giordano's door, and led Wronka inside.

No security alarm rang out, so either he had none or the woman knew the alarm code. I relaxed a little until Tree Macon's remark about Vinny's military demolition training came back to me. I gasped. It was too late to warn Edwin. Father Snapp was already in the hospital because of me, and all I could do was pray that Giordano's house wasn't booby-trapped.

I held my breath and waited anxiously for what seemed like hours. Wronka and the woman finally reappeared on the front steps, and she relocked the door behind them. He shook her hand before walking slowly toward the car.

When he got in I asked, "How'd you get into the house?"

"One of the neighbors told me the old woman next to Giordano owns the whole block and rents out the townhouses. She has keys to all the units. When she answered the door wearing a crucifix around her neck, I knew we were in luck. A priest on a welfare check is a role I've played far too many times in the past … though I must say, my performance was award-winning. Anyway, she bought it completely and walked me through his place."

"Is there a security system inside?"

"Yup, but she had the code and disarmed it in a second."

"Damn, that puts an end to searching Vinny's place today. I could possibly manage a break-in, but there's no way I could shut down a security alarm. I'll have to come up with another plan."

Wronka shook his head. "Not necessarily, Jake. I think *1, 2, 7, 4* might be your lucky number today." He flashed a mischievous grin. "I watched her disarm the system."

I gave him a high five. "Way to go, Edwin." I grabbed my backpack. "Keep an eye out for Giordano. He won't be hard to recognize." I showed him the mugshot of Vinny's shaved head and scarred face. "Call me if you see him or the police. I'll sneak down the alley and try to break into his house."

"That won't be necessary. While on my welfare check, I had a sudden gastrointestinal emergency and needed to use the downstairs restroom." His grin returned. "The bathroom window is unlocked."

I burst out laughing. "Forget the priesthood, Edwin. You should have been a con artist." Clearly, I'd underestimated my partner in crime.

I stepped from the car, slipped on my backpack, pulled up my hoody to partially conceal my appearance, then reentered the alley behind his home. Within minutes, I'd pulled on latex gloves, opened the bathroom window, and entered the lion's den.

CHAPTER THIRTY FIVE

Tuesday, May 6, 2:00 p.m.

The security alarm beeped the second I entered Giordano's home through the bathroom window. Scampering to the front hall, I disarmed it with the code that Wronka had seen the landlady use. I relaxed a bit when I saw a pile of unopened letters on the floor below the mail slot. Vinny was out of town.

I saw no security cameras, but that didn't mean there were none, or that the alarm code turned them off. Time was of the essence. I glanced around the downstairs and saw an answering machine connected to a landline. A red light blinked the number "2," so I pushed the play button with a gloved hand. The voice of an elderly woman filled the living room.

"Mr. Giordano, your rent is late—yet again. We've been over this before, too many times. I don't want to evict you, but … if I don't receive your check by June 1st, I'll be forced to pursue legal action."

The next voice was male, low and gruff with a smoker's rasp. "Listen, man. I got no product for you to sell. With your old man in lockup and the Russians ruling the streets, you're radioactive. Get it? Supplying you is a one-way ticket to the morgue for me. Stop calling! You're on your own. You and me, we're done." Click.

The local police were right. With his father in jail, Giordano's drug operation had dried up, and so had Vinny's income and lifestyle.

I climbed the stairs and entered the study on the second floor. A stack of bills was piled on the desktop. Invoices from the electric, cable, and telephone companies peeked through clear plastic windows on the top of the pile. I thumbed through the rest of the envelopes, stopping when I came across a return address from Avon, Ohio, located approximately thirty minutes from my church in Oberlin. I opened it and found a bill for nine hundred dollars from Relentless Private Investigations for "target location, photography, and background." No names or further explanations were included, although I suspected I knew who the *target* was.

There was a computer next to the bills. When I turned it on, a rectangular box appeared requesting a password. I tried Giordano's name, then his address, and got nowhere. I didn't want to stay in Vinny's house any longer than I had to, so I gave up and closed the laptop.

The only other rooms on the second floor were a bathroom and an undisturbed guest room. I walked up to the third floor and entered the master bedroom, which looked like a combination of a man cave and a whorehouse after a busy night. There were mirrors on the ceiling and two walls, a stack of porn movies next to a large screen TV, and what had to be a sex swing hung from the ceiling over the king-sized bed. The swing was probably also good for flexibility, yoga, and core strength, but I doubted that was its primary function.

In contrast to the other rooms in the townhouse, this one was in complete disarray. Clothes were strewn everywhere and an open suitcase lay empty on the unmade bed. A locked gun safe the size of a car stood in the corner. I stopped dead in my tracks when I saw a dartboard hanging on the wall next to it with a photo of my father as the target, two darts stuck in his eyes. Undoubtedly, Vinny hated my dad for testifying against his father, but that wasn't evidence of a crime. I continued wandering through the chaos and clutter looking for something, *anything* the police could use.

Then the doorbell rang.

I hurried downstairs and headed for the unlocked bathroom window. Through the partially closed drapes in the living room, I glimpsed a man in brown overalls walking down the front steps toward a UPS truck, and my heart rate slowed.

I wasn't built for this kind of stress and desperately wanted to get the heck out of Giordano's house. But what had I found? A pile of unopened mail indicating that Vinny had left town, a suggestion that his source of drugs had dried up along with his income, a bill from a private investigator in Ohio, a dartboard with my father's photo as the target, and sexual-aids in his bedroom that made my skin crawl—but nothing to justify a search warrant, let alone get him arrested. I needed more.

Returning to the third floor, I reentered the master bedroom and rifled through his dresser drawers but came up empty. Many of the hangers in his closet were bare. He had been a man in a hurry. Had he left for good? Taking the flashlight from my backpack, I searched under the bed but discovered only a family of dust bunnies.

Frustrated, I opened the drawers in the nightstand. Beneath a stack of Hustler Magazines and a box of condoms I found a manila folder. Inside were photographs of my father with a U.S. Marshal taken through a telephoto zoom lens, pictures of Tree Macon and Special Agent Keri Novak, and several of me at the hospital, the church, and the rectory. In addition, three different private investigators had sent Giordano letters documenting all of our home and work addresses, as well as summaries of our daily activities. But what grabbed me by the throat were photographs of RJ at school during recess, and one of Colleen pushing him on a swing at the playground.

Unfortunately, everything made perfect sense, and the conclusion scared the hell out of me. First Vinny had car-bombed my dad, and thinking he had been successful, he intended to come after me and the others who had put his father in prison. There could be no doubt. Vinny Giordano was on a vendetta to eliminate all of us—and RJ, Colleen, and everyone around me were at risk.

My reconnaissance had confirmed my greatest fears, but nothing I'd found was valid in a court of law or could be used legally to obtain a warrant.

Not knowing what else to do, I snapped pictures of everything in the manila folder with my cellphone, took the folder down to the printer in the study, and made high resolution copies. Then I returned the originals to the nightstand before I climbed out of the downstairs bathroom window and got the hell away from the lunatic's lair.

CHAPTER THIRTY SIX

Tuesday, May 6, 3:30 p.m.

On the drive back to New Orleans, I described for Father Wronka what I had discovered on my search of the townhouse, then explained my part in putting Giordano's father in prison. Wronka stiffened and his mouth opened, but he remained silent as he took it all in.

Near the rectory, his stomach rumbled like an 8.0 Richter scale earthquake. He smiled and finally spoke. "Sorry. Guess my tummy isn't happy about missing lunch. How about I prepare an early dinner for us."

With everyone I cared about potentially in danger, I had no appetite, but I said, "Good idea, Edwin. I have a couple of calls to make, then I'll join you."

I phoned Tree Macon and filled him in on my search of Giordano's home.

"Sounds like Vinny is crazier than his old man. But with his military experience and explosives training, he's also more dangerous. And when I say crazy, Jake, I ain't kidding. He was discharged as 'mentally unfit for service.' Unfortunately, no judge is going to grant a search warrant based on your unlawfully obtained information." He thought for a moment. "What I *can* do is pay a visit to Relentless Private Investigations, lean on the PI, and threaten his Class A investigator's license or his statewide firearms permit. At the very least, I can make his life hell. If I rattle the cat's cage hard enough and long enough, maybe he'll cough up a hairball and some dirt on Giordano that we can use to get a search warrant for his home."

"I won't even ask if that's lawful."

"Don't. A punk-ass thug coming after me is one thing, Jake, but a *bomber* not only threatens me but also my wife and family, as well as innocent bystanders. I won't hesitate to color outside of the legal lines if it protects your family and mine, as well as the folks in town."

"One problem, Tree. Lawyers are willing to go to jail to safeguard their attorney-client privilege, and there's no way I'd break the seal of the confessional. Aren't private investigators required to protect their clients as well?"

"That's less clear. Depends whether the investigator is hired by a lawyer or by the client. Any information passed directly from the investigator to a client is not privileged. Have no fear, buddy. I can be very persuasive. Meanwhile, I'll find out if Vinny's still in Ohio. What I need from you are copies of everything you found in Giordano's house."

"I'm on it. Consider it done."

"Thanks. I'll have a patrol car regularly swing past Colleen's apartment and Sacred Heart Church, but I don't have the manpower to station deputies there for protection, so get your butt home soon."

"I'll be on the first available flight. Keep me posted, Tree. And, thanks."

The instant I was off the phone, I called Demarco's secretary and asked, "Any luck getting me a flight home? I'm desperate."

"I booked you on Delta for tomorrow night."

"That's the first available flight? Heck, I'd get home sooner if I drove."

"Well, Father … exactly how desperate are you?"

"Extremely."

"I've been looking at your file. You were military, right?"

"Yes, Army."

"Then I have both good and bad news. The good news is that there's a flight from Barksdale Air Force Base in Shreveport to Wright-Patterson in Dayton at nine tonight. With your military background and my boss's clout, I can get you on it."

"If I leave now and drive like a lunatic, I can make it. What's the bad news?"

"It's a transport plane and you'll probably have to sit on a jump seat in the back with the cargo."

"I'll take it."

"Leave your rental car at the base, Father Austin, and I'll have someone pick it up. There'll be another rental waiting for you in Dayton. Good luck and God speed."

I threw all my things into my suitcase and stopped in the kitchen on the way to my car.

"I'm sorry to leave like this, Edwin, and sorry I won't be able to stay for dinner tonight or take you to Antoine's for the supper I promised."

He patted his protruding belly. "A mad bomber is about the *only* excuse I'd accept for missing a four course meal at Antoine's. Maybe next time you're in New Orleans, okay? Now, go protect your nephew, Jake. And be safe."

CHAPTER THIRTY SEVEN

Tuesday, May 6, 4:15 p.m.

I hopped into my car and made the five hour drive to Barksdale Air Force Base in Shreveport in four and a half hours, then rattled my way through rough air all the way to Dayton, Ohio in the bowels of an ancient, twin-prop cargo plane. It was definitely a "red-eye flight" because it was nearly impossible to doze off while strapped to a transport jump seat amid crates of pharmaceuticals, airplane parts, and military jeeps as gusting winds shook us like maracas.

When we touched down before sunrise on Wednesday morning, I picked up my rental car and sped north on the interstate, arriving at Colleen's apartment in time to wake RJ for school and get him dressed while Colleen made breakfast. My assignment in New Orleans had been the first time my nephew and I had been apart since my sister passed away, and the separation had been hard on both of us. Our reunion was tear-filled and joyful.

As we finished eating, RJ looked up at me. "Daddy, can we go home now? I miss my room and my toys."

Colleen took a sip of tea. "Yes, Father, may we … and more importantly, *should* we?" She glanced at my boy, choosing her words carefully so as not to frighten him. "Would that be prudent? Are things finally back to … normal?"

Normal? What was that? I'd completely lost touch with any semblance of normality when a bomber had blown up Father Snapp's van near the rectory thinking he was killing me.

As for *prudent*? A great question. I had no clue. Was it safer to leave RJ with Colleen and hope Vinny Giordano wouldn't decide to target them, and possibly level an apartment building full of innocent people in the process? Or should I take my nephew on an unplanned vacation somewhere far away for a few weeks, and let the church and the hospital fend for themselves while I was gone? Or was it better to return to the rectory with him, hope Giordano believed he'd killed me and left town, and become hyper-vigilant in case I was wrong. I was a man of peace, but not where RJ's safety was concerned.

I gazed into the living room, where a blanket and pillow lay on the couch. Colleen had given her bed to RJ and had been sleeping on the couch since the bombing. I considered proposing that she sleep with him in her bed while I slept in the living room, but dismissed the idea. Within days, rumors about a priest shacked-up with his housekeeper would be circulating through town. Worse, RJ was a restless sleeper and sharing a bed with him would be like sleeping inside a washing machine. The poor woman would be black-and-blue after one night.

I made my decision. "Okay, RJ, we'll move back home this afternoon." Although I would be completely lost without her, I said to Colleen, "I would understand if you resigned or took a leave of absence until things are resolved."

She flushed and her voice hardened. "Honestly Father, have you not met me? I don't quit on the people I care about! You and RJ are my family. I'll not be forsaking either of you, so let me hear no more of *that* nonsense."

She stood, walked over to me, and much to my surprise, did something she had never done before. Colleen gave me a hug.

Then just as suddenly, she frowned and wagged a finger in my face. "But let me be clear. I'll not be taking care of that infernal bird one day longer! No feeding or cage cleaning. That creature is *your* problem until Father Snapp is out of the hospital."

"What are you talking about? Moarte? I assumed it died in the explosion. How in the world ...?"

"Father Snapp couldn't leave it in his van during the heat wave, so he'd been keeping it in the church basement during the daytime. Sister Catherine complained, so I moved its cage into the rectory living room, but I'll have nothing more to do with that revolting beast!"

Just what I needed. The care and feeding of Snapp's vile pet.

I thanked Colleen for all of her help, dropped RJ off at school, exchanged the rental car for my own, and drove to the hospital.

Father Snapp had been moved from ICU to the second floor. I knocked softly on his door and entered. Lacerations on his forehead and cheek had been sutured, and a nasty-looking plumb-colored bruise painted the left side of his neck. An IV dripped silently on the far side of the bed. Wrapped in bandages and miles of gauze, he had the appearance of an Egyptian mummy.

Snapp looked up and frowned. "Ah, the prodigal son has returned." His voice was raspy and raw, suggesting he'd been on a ventilator in the ICU.

"I came as soon as I could, Phineas. Is there anything I can do for you?"

He scoffed. "Think you've done quite enough. The cops tell me the bomb was intended for you." As I searched for something to say, he added, "I will, however, need a place to stay when I get out of here, since my van is in a scrapyard and I've been *banished* from the rectory."

"I'm so sorry, Phineas. You're more than welcome to move back in with us."

"Yeah, well I'm not interested. Wish I'd never been assigned there."

He scowled and pointed to the door.

"You have every right to be angry, Phineas, but I am *truly* sorry … about everything. Just so you know, Moarte is at the rectory with me, and I'll take good care of him until you're released from the hospital."

His expression softened. When I turned to leave, he heaved a deep sigh and said, "Wait. I should tell you what I found at the hospital before my … accident. My investigation revealed absolutely no evidence of paranormal activity in the snack shop. Zero. But room 232 on the second floor is teeming with the aftermath of pain and violence. The atmosphere there is so thick with evil it's like walking through lava. And you should also know," Snapp closed his eyes, then continued, "I met the Night Nurse."

I was speechless and could only stare.

"I was awakened last evening from a deep sleep by the sound of a crying baby, screaming really, and the smell of smoke. The Night Nurse was standing at the foot of my bed. When she opened her mouth, the crying stopped and she spoke one word, clear as day. 'Club.' Then she was gone."

His voice was raw and fading. "But I can tell you one thing for certain, Jake. She's angry, very angry. Maybe she wants us to be the instrument of her revenge, or at least deliver justice for her. I'm not sure, but she did *not* look merciful or forgiving."

Snapp opened his eyes. "Strange, huh? Of all the people who work here, she's sought out two priests. Wish I knew what that meant. But that's *your* problem now. I'm done with this fiasco." He rolled away from me onto his side.

Club—so that was the word Dixie Carter's voice recorder had picked up on the second floor amid the static and background noise, the word that had been repeated over and over again; not "glub" as she had believed, but *club*.

I left Snapp's room and rode the elevator down to the ground floor trying to make sense of what he'd told me, but my thoughts kept drifting to the threat that Giordano posed. I searched every face I passed in the halls for an angry red scar. The idea of an impromptu vacation with RJ in Canada was sounding better and better.

Lost in my thoughts, I found myself approaching the snack shop. Although I'd only been out of town a week, I had to admit I'd missed Emily almost as much as my boy. Fine example of a priest I was. Perhaps I ought to hear my own confession while looking in the mirror.

To avoid temptation, I should have walked away—and yet, my hand was reaching for the snack shop door as my phone rang and Tree's name appeared on the screen.

"I come bearing gifts, Jake. Got me a big old bucket of good news for a change."

"That's exactly what I need. Pour it all over me. Baptize me in positivity and renew my sagging spirit."

"Well first off, Lottie Trumble was arrested at an open house at her mansion in front of dozens of people. One of them snapped a lovely picture of the police slapping steel bracelets on her wrists, which ended up on the front page of the Times-Picayune."

"I'm feeling better already, Tree."

"Then you'll love this. New Orleans P.D. dragged Chase Masterson out of his first-class seat on an overseas flight before takeoff and escorted him to their one star iron-barred accommodations downtown. We were able to freeze one of his bank accounts, and secret compartments in his luggage contained a bunch of diamonds and thousands in cash. Any money stashed overseas will be harder to recover, but at least Masterson will be too old to enjoy it by the time he gets out of lockup. He and Lottie are done."

"You made my day, buddy."

"As they say on late-night TV ads: *But wait, there's more!* I put tracers on Giordano's credit cards and cellphone. As of yesterday, he hadn't used his credit cards, but his phone's GPS shows him in Illinois heading west. He's no longer in Ohio, Jake, so maybe he thinks you're dead. I have an all-points bulletin out on him. Hopefully, he'll continue to be stupid or arrogant enough to keep using his phone and plastic money, so we can track his ass down and put him away."

I relaxed—but only a little. I wanted that lunatic off the streets permanently. "Any luck getting a search warrant for his townhouse? I sent you everything I found there."

"I tried. The judge wasn't buying my 'anonymous tip' story but if we locate the bastard, I'll think of some reason to arrest him. I can be very creative. I've also been leaning hard on the private investigator Giordano hired in Ohio, but so far he's claiming *client confidentiality* and hasn't budged. I may have to get nasty with him. Listen, buddy, gotta run. I'll keep you posted."

Inside the snack shop, I sat at a table with Emily and her father and told them what Snapp had said.

Emily shook her head. "No evidence of paranormal activity here? I don't buy it. What about our bouts of dizziness, nausea, and dread? It's not only affected Dad and me, but some of our customers too. How do you explain that, Jake?"

"I can't." The room was uncomfortably warm and I wiped sweat from my brow. "The air conditioning's not working again?"

"This is an old part of the building, and the AC is ancient. The hospital fixed it twice for us, and each time it died again in a few days. They finally ordered a new one and are installing it today."

"About time, too," her father added. "Been terrible for business *and* for our health." He stood and redirected the oscillating fan in our direction. "Good thing we still had this old relic. It's not AC, but it's better than nothing."

We said our goodbyes and I left to visit several hospitalized parishioners, then grabbed lunch in the cafeteria. Before heading home for the day, I stopped in Administration to speak with Harvey Winer.

Although he was nearing retirement and worked long hours, Winer always wore a tailored suit, silk tie, and a yarmulke that partially covered his bald spot. When I entered his office, he was staring at his computer screen.

"Got a minute, Harvey?"

He looked up and waved me in. "Yup, but not much more."

I told him what Snapp had said about room 232.

He tilted his head to one side. "Ghosts, Jake? You surprise me. Not really your style." He tugged gently on an earlobe that drooped like melted candle wax. "Yeah, I've heard complaints about that room for years from nurses and patients. But honestly, it's complete nonsense. When I first started work here as an assistant to the CEO, that part of the building used to be the administration wing. Room 232 was my boss's office. My tiny cubbyhole of a workroom was next door, and I was in and out of 232 every day. Believe me, the only *dread* I ever felt in that room was when Nick Pappas gave me my performance review. Although, I definitely got *spooked* the few times he unleashed his legendary temper. The man had a short fuse and could go off like a roman candle."

Nicholas Pappas. Dorothy Margaret Clay's boyfriend. The fellow that Sister Maria Celeste regretted introducing her to because, as she'd said, "he wasn't a nice man." Interesting.

Winer continued. "I have to say, Pappas was a hard worker. With no wife or kids, he was married to his job. Definitely a workaholic."

I pointed at the stack of papers in Winer's inbox and laughed. "Looks to me as if you're the pot calling the kettle black."

"At least I don't sleep here. Pappas had a couch in his office with a fold-out bed, fridge, and minibar." He glanced at his watch and stood. "Sorry, Jake, I have a meeting with a major hospital donor at the country club. Wish my MBA program had had a class in putting. I will greet him warmly and let him beat me on the links again. Losing to duffers annoys the heck out of me, but it's part of the job."

Country Club, huh? Pappas probably also did business on the links. He'd been teaching Dorothy how to play golf, and the Oak Ridge club wasn't far from Lover's Lane, where she had plunged to her death.

"No problem, Harvey. Just wanted to let you know I'd returned to town. You can schedule me in Urgent Care starting on Friday."

He patted me on the back and went off to schmooze a hospital donor on the golf course, and I left to do my homework on Nicholas Pappas.

CHAPTER THIRTY EIGHT

Wednesday, May 7, 3:00 p.m.

After I left the hospital, I picked RJ up from school and moved his things into the rectory. I'd barely slept on the flight back from New Orleans, so I took my miniature tornado in tennis shoes to the park, hoping the playground equipment would take him from a category five twister to category one. My plan backfired, and I was the one who was completely exhausted by the time we got home. I grilled hotdogs for dinner, and finally cajoled him into the bathtub before his bedtime.

After he fell asleep, I brewed a pot of strong coffee, booted up my computer, and googled the name 'Nicholas Pappas.' There was a lot of information about his rise to CEO at St. Joseph's Hospital and his successful thirty-year career there, but little about the man. He retired twenty years after Dorothy's untimely death in 1965, which would make him around eighty years old.

Three online photographs showed a middle-aged man with ebony hair, dark sleepy eyes, and a winning smile who looked a lot like George Clooney, the movie actor. In one picture he was wearing a suit and tie and hoisting a champagne glass in a toast. Another showed him standing on a putting green, leaning jauntily on a golf club. In the third, he was dressed in too-tight black bellbottom trousers, platform shoes, and a neon-purple silk shirt unbuttoned to his navel, with several gold chains dangling from his neck—quite the dashing man-about-town back in the disco era, but nothing useful in linking him to Dorothy Margaret Clay's death.

Frustrated, I logged out, slipped into my recliner in the living room, and surfed through the TV channels. What caught my eye were the words POLTERGEIST OR POPPYCOCK? above a cartoon image of a white ghoul inside a red circle with a crimson slash across its body, similar to the logo for the movie Ghostbusters.

A young man wearing a tweed sport coat, bright orange bowtie, and wire-rimmed spectacles stepped from behind a curtain and was greeted with a riotous ovation. When the applause died down, he grinned at the camera and began his introduction.

"The world is full of ridiculous theories about occurrences we don't understand. Things that go bump in the night morph into spooky ghost stories around campfires. Unexplained lights become UFOs. Weird events that seem impossible to explain send our imaginations into overdrive. Apparitions, poltergeists, phantoms, and evil spirits raise the hairs on our arms and send shivers down our spines. But even the creepiest incident can be debunked with logic and science by asking the right questions and employing careful observation." He let a moment pass. "Scared of spirits? Paralyzed by poltergeists? That's why I'm here. Tonight on Science Rocks, I will make a ghost vanish before your very eyes—right after a word from our sponsor."

It was unlikely that this guy could explain why a nurse killed in the 1960s was haunting the hospital nearly forty years later. Then again, I had no rational explanations either, so I walked into the kitchen, poured a bottle of Michelob into a frosted mug, and returned as the host resumed his spiel.

"Let's look closer at two unexplained occurrences. In the first, rumors of a haunting surfaced at a laboratory in Great Britain during the late 1990s. Workers there were often overcome by unexplained waves of fear, anxiety, and shivers, and one scientist reported seeing a terrifying dark apparition from the corner of his eye. Spooky?" He laughed. "I think not."

"In the second incident, much of the audience at a recent concert described the onset of sadness, dizziness, and overwhelming fear. Was it simply that the songs were dreadful? Had Beethoven clawed his way back from the grave to express his disdain for the music? No, what it was ... was an experiment."

He walked over to two tables and stood between them. One had a glass of water and a fan on it. The other held a fencing foil with the handle grip of the foil secured in a clamp.

"Haunted laboratories and concert halls? No. The explanation, ladies and gentlemen, is the same in both cases."

The words RESONANT FREQUENCY appeared behind him.

"Let's repeat the experiment that the scientist in England performed to explain these events." He raised a finger to his lips. "I'll need complete silence from the studio audience."

He turned on the fan and the camera focused on the tip of the fencing foil. As he moved the fan closer, the tip of the foil began to vibrate.

"A skeptic might think that the breeze from the fan is shaking the foil." He rotated the fan away but the foil continued to vibrate. "No, it's *not* due to the wind."

He chuckled. "It's almost as if a ghost is shaking it—except …." He turned the fan off and the foil stopped vibrating. "The *fan* is the culprit. This one emits low-frequency sound waves below the range of human hearing, so we hear nothing at all."

He ran a finger around the edge of a water-filled crystal goblet and a clear ringing sound filled the room.

"All objects have what's called a *resonant frequency*, which makes them vibrate. The frequency of this fencing foil happens to be nineteen hertz, that is, nineteen vibrations per second—the same frequency that the fan is emitting. Which also happens to be the frequency that vibrates the human eye—hence the apparition that the scientist in Great Britain saw from the edge of his vision."

Interesting, I thought, but that *doesn't* explain the Night Nurse. I was looking directly at her, not from the corner of my eye. And I could smell her cigarette smoke. That encounter had nothing to do with frequencies or vibrations.

He smirked. "Not convinced? What about the anxiety, sadness, and fear the people experienced both in the concert and in the lab, you might ask?"

A photograph of a concert hall came into view on the screen behind him under the words FEAR FREQUENCY.

"What the heck is the so-called Fear Frequency? That's what the concert was designed to explain. The music that they played contained frequencies of 17 to 19 hertz, just below the range of human hearing, called *infrasound*. Even without the music, the fear, sadness, and anxiety that the audience experienced can be reproduced whenever these frequencies are introduced into a room. Not only does infrasound vibrate the human eye, it affects the entire body. Experiments have convincingly shown that strong infrasound frequencies can repeatedly produce these symptoms, as well as nervousness, nausea, dizziness, panic attacks, and loss of balance—all of which can make people feel like they are in the grip of something unnatural, as if they're being *haunted*. Hence the term, Fear Frequency."

I had once read something similar in a scientific journal, which at the time seemed irrelevant to my medical practice, so I'd skipped on to the next article. The TV host's conclusions, however, was logical, plausible, and suddenly felt extremely relevant.

The camera zoomed in on the host. "And that, ladies and gentlemen, debunks the existence of ghosts—well, at least in *these* two instances." A video of bright, flashing lights on the horizon appeared and he add, "Tune in next week when we demystify the existence of UFOs."

I leaned back in my recliner, drained the last of my beer, and focused on recent events at the hospital. A smile creased my lips.

CHAPTER THIRTY NINE

Thursday, May 8, 6:00 a.m.

That night I dreamt of Emily. She was running toward me through a field of wildflowers. She wore only a sheer negligee, which was backlit by the setting sun, highlighting her long legs and lovely figure, leaving little to the imagination. When she reached out and embraced me, I awoke drenched in a cold sweat.

I had been having sexually-charged dreams about her more frequently since I moved back to town, and they unsettled me every time—not the way I wanted to start my day. I hopped out of bed, showered, dressed in a clerical shirt and trousers, and recited my Morning Prayers.

After getting RJ off to school, I tried to set aside the lingering threat from Giordano and focus on morning Mass, but I kept scanning the crowd, looking for a man with a scared face and a shaved head. Even in his absence, he was upending my world.

After the service, I placed Holy Oil, the ritual book, my stole, and my gold-plated pyx containing the Blessed Eucharist into my traveling burse. With one more day off before returning to work in Urgent Care on Friday, I drove to St. Joe's to minister to my hospitalized parishioners. Walking from room to room, I heard confessions, offered Communion, and asked patients if they wanted to receive the Anointing of the Sick, providing what comfort I could. Then I stopped in at the snack shop.

"Morning, Em."

Emily lit up the smile that had melted my heart since grade school. "Morning, handsome."

"That would sound more sincere if you weren't visually impaired."

She laughed, then filled a large cup with coffee and handed it to me. It's good to have once dated the store manager.

We chatted briefly at the counter about various hospital events, but when she leaned in to tell me about an upcoming fundraiser, the scent of her perfume ignited a host of memories from our high school romance and touched off a painfully desperate longing. I took a step backward, gathered my emotions, then said, "I see the fan is off. Does that mean the new air conditioner's been installed?"

"Went live this morning. Which means our weather will probably go from sweltering today to snow tomorrow. You know how unpredictable Mother Nature can be around here."

"That I do. I have a question, Em. Have those intermittent bouts of anxiety, dizziness, and dread you and your father have been experiencing ever occurred in winter?"

She considered that for a moment. "Come to think of it, no. They happened mostly in the summer. Why?"

"I have some good news." I told her about the television show I'd watched the night before, and explained the Fear Frequency. "My guess is that old fan is emitting infrasound that no one can hear, and *it's* the source of your problems."

"You mean the fan caused the symptoms Dad and I had?"

"I think so. Remember, Em, Dixie Curry and Father Snapp both found paranormal activity on the second floor, but *none* in the snack shop."

"Vibrations? Fear Frequency? Are you positive?"

"Pretty sure. It's logical. I can't be positive without running experiments on it, but with the new AC system, I doubt you'll have any more trouble. If you ever need a fan in here, buy a new one and throw that antique out—or at least, don't give it to anyone you like." I took a sip of coffee. "I'm glad you and your dad didn't quit your jobs over these frightening incidents. Where else would I get free coffee?"

She chuckled, and with no other customers in the snack shop, we commandeered a corner table. I filled her in on RJ's latest antics. But with Giordano on the loose, it was time to get down to business. Who knew where he was or what he intended to do next? I had many responsibilities at the church and the hospital, but RJ was my most important one.

"Remember when we talked about you becoming RJ's guardian a couple months ago, Em?" I slid the legal documents my parishioner had drawn up across the table. "Well, I brought the paperwork. I was hoping you're still willing to be his guardian."

The urgency I felt must have been evident.

"Are you okay, Jake? Has something happened?" She leaned forward. "Are you ill?"

Tree had last reported that Giordano had left Ohio and was headed west, so I didn't want to frighten her unnecessarily. "No, I feel fine."

"Thank God! You scared me."

"I just want a backup plan. RJ's already gone through so much with the loss of his mother. And it's clear that he loves you, and you love him. There's no one I'd trust more with his welfare. So, will you … sign the papers?"

"Of course, Jake." She reached across the table and her hand found mine. "I'd be honored."

I handed her a pen and the legal documents and offered to read them to her, but Emily declined and signed them with a flourish.

And with that, my burdens became a bit lighter. We turned to more carefree topics, and when we ran out of small talk, I drove to the rectory, traded my clerical attire for a polo shirt and matching slacks, and headed to Oak Ridge Country Club.

CHAPTER FORTY

Thursday, May 8, 2:00 p.m.

Except for a few areas, Ohio is as flat as a billiard table. The Oak Ridge Country Club, however, was nestled on a rise above the Vermillion River. A meandering, tree-lined driveway led to the venerable clubhouse with its stately pillars, giving it the feel of a southern plantation manor house. The building was constructed of sandstone from local quarries and fronted by a yawning porch furnished with rocking chairs overlooking the manicured front lawn.

Hoping no one would recognize me from the church or the hospital in the middle of the afternoon, I drew a deep breath and walked through the spectacular mahogany entranceway. The grand foyer's crystal chandelier and elegant furnishings conveyed a rich history of money, breeding, and power. Without a doubt, I had crossed the threshold into a world that was completely foreign to me.

A young, chestnut-haired woman wearing a tailored pantsuit strode up to me, her heels clicking across the polished white marble floor.

"How may I be of assistance, sir? My name is Moira. I'm the assistant manager at Oak Ridge."

"I'm moving to the area soon, and I'm looking for a club that might suit my needs. A cousin of mine was a member here in the 1960s and spoke highly of Oak Ridge. I'd love a tour to decide if the facility is a fit for me."

"We're always happy to add another legacy member. What was your cousin's name, sir?"

"Nicholas Pappas."

"Pappas? I'm afraid I'm new here and don't recognize the name." She cocked her head to one side. "I'd be happy to give you a tour, but I think you'd be better served if Mr. Howe did it. He's a senior member and may have known your cousin. I believe he's just finished lunch. Let me see if he's available. What may I say is your name?"

Glancing at the finery surrounding me, I was certain that none of the club members had taken a vow of poverty. The alias "John Smith" seemed too mundane, uninspired, and blue collar for these hallowed halls. I needed a name that spoke of yachts, private jets, and Rolex watches.

"Smyth. Alistair Smyth."

She nodded and marched into the dining room. I followed her to the door. The room offered a lovely view of the 18th green and the gently rolling countryside. Bright white table clothes, navy-blue linen napkins, soft music, and the lingering aroma of flame-grilled filet mignon mixed with the faint scent of cigar smoke.

Moira spoke briefly with an elderly gentleman at the bar who looked to be in his eighties. He glanced at me, drained the amber liquid from a tumbler, snuffed out his panetela, and tottered over, leaning heavily on a cane.

He extended a hand and a salesman's grin. "Vernon Howe. Moira asked me to show you around. It's a pleasure to meet one of Nicky's family. What a small world. The old boy was a close friend of mine."

A *close* friend. What luck! Maybe Howe could not only give me insight into Pappas, but also his relationship with Dorothy Margaret Clay.

We shook hands. His was cold, the bones as thin and frail as glass rods. "Alistair Smyth, of New York. Nice to meet you, Vernon."

He wrinkled his already deeply furrowed brow. "Nicky was proud of his Greek heritage and demanded that the bartender stock ouzo here at the club. Guess I expected you to have a Greek-sounding name. Can't say I recall him mentioning any New York Smyths."

"Nicholas was a distant cousin on my mother's side. We visited him when I was a lad. He was quite a lively chap, as I remember."

"Ah, that he was. The man was a real scamp. I miss Nicky. It's hard for me to get into any real mischief now without him." He lit up a roguish smile. "Back in the day, we were double trouble, you might say, both on and off the links … and with the ladies." His eyes twinkled at the thought.

He pointed to his cane. The head was a sterling silver lion. "Once upon a time, we were a pair of young pumas, always on the prowl."

"I'm not surprised. I've heard rumors of Cousin Nick's … shall we say, exploits." I produced a lusty leer of my own. "I'd like to think I have a few more decades of the hunt left in me."

I paused, hoping this aging alpha male would consider me a lion cub and fill the silence with tales of Pappas's escapades. He chuckled amicably, but didn't take the bait.

Time to shift gears. "Might I have a look around then, Vernon?"

He led me down the hall to the library. Ashtrays on the tables indicated that non-smoking social pressure had not yet scaled the walls of this private club. Towering bookshelves were filled to capacity with leather-bound volumes, although other than the Wall Street Journal and Kiplinger's Personal Finance, I doubted that any reading took place in the room. I asked if some of the club members were authors. He laughed so hard I was afraid he might cough up a lung, the implication being that most authors couldn't afford the price of dinner here, let alone the hefty initiation fee.

The billiard room continued the masculine theme. Oil paintings featured snarling hounds and red-coated fox hunters bounding across the wood-paneled walls. I wondered where female members, if there were any, might actually feel comfortable relaxing after eighteen holes on the links.

Howe led me across the hallway to the ballroom. The intricate herringbone pattern of the oak floors, its towering ceilings and chandeliers, and the Steinway grand piano spoke of magnificent galas and fundraisers.

"I imagine some spectacular parties have been held in here," I said, my voice echoing through the enormous hall. "Was Nicholas a good dancer?"

"Oh my yes. The gals stood in line for a spin or two. The old boy had a way with the ladies," he added, the impish twinkle returning to his eyes, "both on and off the dance floor, if you know what I mean."

"Did any particular lady ever catch his fancy?"

"My dear boy … they *all* did. No, Nicky was many things, but never monogamous … or monotonous. Never married, never had children—at least none that he knew about."

Strike one. I stepped back up to the plate. "I believe my father once mentioned a lady that Nick was particularly fond of. He was teaching her to play golf, as I remember. What was her name? Dorothy … that's it, Dorothy Clay. Did you know her?"

"Might have, once upon a time, but he gave *personal* lessons to so many gals in those days it's impossible to remember names. I don't think any of them held his attention for more than a few months."

Strike two. "You mentioned that Nick was a good golfer."

"That's an understatement!" He stopped walking and turned to me. "He was a *scratch* golfer, the best the Club ever had. Won most of the tournaments, even though he wouldn't give up his damn *hickories*."

"His what?"

"Hickories. You know, the old wooden-shaft clubs. He was a purist, nostalgic about the early days of the sport, when everyone used them. If he had purchased a new set with steel or graphite shafts, the man could have gone pro. But no, Nicky wouldn't hear of it. What a waste of talent." Howe shook his head. "Here, let me show you."

He led me into the Cup Room, which looked like a shrine to golf. Engraved plaques on the walls and glass cases filled with trophies dominated the room. The floor covering was a synthetic putting green with a cup sunk in the center of the room, complete with a red flagstick.

Howe pointed to a photograph. "That's Nicky after he won the club championship in 1966."

In the picture, Nicholas Pappas stood on the 18th green raising a large golden trophy above his head. He had the face of a young George Clooney and the body of a weightlifter. No wonder the man was a lady magnet. Rich, powerful, and movie star handsome—which made me suspect and detest him all the more.

"Those were the days," Howe added.

Yeah, carefree days not long after the tragic death of his girlfriend in a car crash less than a mile from the county club. Apparently, he had recovered nicely from his overwhelming grief.

Howe pointed to the far wall. "Those are Nicky's clubs. We retired them after he gave up the sport."

"Gave it up? Why?"

He shrugged, then tapped his cane on the floor. "Father Time gets us all eventually. Let me show you his hickories." We walked over to a set of vintage golf clubs encased in glass. "Relics from a bygone era. The old boy could hit 'em long and straight, even with those outdated sticks."

By the reverential silence that followed, it felt as if I was standing before the golf god's sacred altar.

"You're probably too young to realize what you're looking at. Those babies were handmade in the early 1920s with forged steel heads and hickory shafts, a few years before metal-shaft clubs became legal for tournaments. They were produced by the St. Andrews Golf Company of Scotland, the world's oldest club manufacturer. It's a shame the mashie is missing."

"Mashie?"

He laughed. "That's what we called a five iron back in the day." He pointed at the display case. "See, all the clubs are there, except the mashie."

Lights flashed and alarm bells clanged in my head. I remembered what Father Snapp had told me about his encounter with the Night Nurse, and the word she had uttered. *Club*. Had she been referring to this country club or that particular five iron—or both? Was she pointing her lifeless finger at Nicholas Pappas?

Old man Howe had delivered more than I could have hoped for. It felt as if Raguel, the archangel of justice and vengeance from the ancient Book of Enoch, had landed on my shoulder. I knew what I needed to do.

I glanced at my watch. "Sorry, but I really must be going, Vernon. Thanks for the tour. I'm quite impressed."

We shook hands and I walked to my car. The moment I left the county club grounds, I telephoned Tree Macon.

CHAPTER FORTY ONE

Thursday, May 8, 3:30 p.m.

Tree Macon answered on the second ring.

"Perfect timing, Jake. I was about to call you with some good news. We tracked Vinny Giordano's cellphone to a motel in Ames, Iowa. I contacted the local cop shop and they're on the way to take him into custody. Fingers crossed. If we put the bastard away, life goes back to normal and we can all relax again."

"Let me know the minute you nab him. I've been on edge since Father Snapp's van was bombed. Every time the rectory creaks or groans at night, I jump out of bed, grab my Louisville slugger, and sprint to RJ's room to make sure he's okay. I'm getting cranky from lack of sleep."

"Will do, buddy."

"Listen, Tree, I need your help with something." I told him about Pappas's missing five iron. "He was giving Dorothy Margaret Clay golf lessons. According to the police file you loaned me, some sort of metal wedge was found in the trunk of her car after it plunged from the cliff near Oak Ridge Country Club. I think he could have killed her with that club, then disposed of her body and the murder weapon in the fiery crash. How long do the police store evidence?"

"Anywhere from a year until the end of time. There are no real state guidelines. Depends on the prosecutor, the investigating officer, and the crime. If they suspected it was a murder, the evidence box may still exist. If not, it's gone."

"Can you find out if the evidence from the investigation is in storage? If Pappas killed her with his five iron, the wooden shaft would have burned up, but the metal club head might have survived the fire."

"Come on, Jake, she died almost forty years ago. What's with you? This is the *coldest* cold case of all times, and I have a desk full of ongoing investigations. Why are you on this like a hound on a hambone? Is it that hospital ghost nonsense?"

"The Night Nurse isn't nonsense. I swear to God I *saw* her, and in this case seeing is truly believing. She also appeared to Snapp and spoke the word 'club.' It all fits."

"You're killing me, man. Eyewitness testimony from ghosts is not admissible in a goddamn court of law!" He grumbled something unintelligible. "Even if we prove Pappas killed her, he has to be a geezer by now, if he's not already dead. Why bother?"

"Oh, so it's okay to get away with murder if you're on Medicare?"

"All right, all right, you win. I'll see if her evidence box is around, but don't get your hopes up. If anything metal survived the fire, I'll have it examined."

"Thanks, buddy. I owe you."

"That you do," he replied and hung up.

I spent a quiet evening teaching my boy how to play checkers. He beat me every time, resorting to cheating repeatedly. We would definitely have to work on his devious nature but that night, I was too tired to care. Fortunately, as a priest, I could absolve my little double-dealing rascal.

I'd given RJ a bath and put him to bed when Tree phoned.

"Don't shoot the messenger, Jake, but the news isn't good. The Iowa police tracked Giordano's cellphone to a motel in Ames, but he wasn't there. A runaway teenager found it on a Greyhound bus. Vinny finally wised up. He must have figured out we were tracking him and played us. Which means he'll go deeper underground. He's probably using a burner phone now. Remember when I said we could all relax? Well, don't. Giordano's in the wind and could be anywhere."

Every muscle in my body tensed. "Crap. Now what?"

"Now we're back to square one. So far, the BOLO I put out on his SUV has come up empty. He may have had it repainted and is using stolen plates. But if he gets sloppy or uses a credit card, we'll pounce on him like a cat on a mouse. Otherwise, prepare for the worst and hope for the best."

Tree released a sigh befitting his size, then went silent.

"What? More bad news?"

"Afraid so. Dorothy Clay's evidence box is missing. The investigating officer signed it out seven years ago, just before he retired. He never brought it back. I left him a voicemail, but he hasn't returned my call. Not a good sign. I'll let you know if I get ahold of him."

CHAPTER FORTY TWO

Friday, May 9, 9:00 a.m.

The scheduling gods had smiled down on me and assigned Maya Ruiz to assist me in Urgent Care. Having a third-year super-resident at my side made my shift much more pleasant knowing I didn't have to continuously look over her shoulder. I was completing a patient chart at the nursing station when she approached, lips pursed, eyebrows knitted together.

"Please look at a patient for me, Dr. Austin. I think he has a bad case of the flu but … something feels off."

"And his bloodwork?"

"Pending. I'll go put a rush on it."

I had come to trust Maya's judgment and instincts, so I didn't hesitate. I entered room four and introduced myself to Mr. Singh, an elderly gentleman who spoke little English, and to his grandson. Mr. Singh was lying under several blankets but shivering violently. He had a high fever, his face was sweat-covered, and his eyes had a distant listless apathy, as if he was hanging on to life by a thread and no longer cared. That made me very nervous.

Severe cases of the flu in the aged can be lethal, and it was easy to understand why Maya was leaning toward that diagnosis. The problem was, flu season typically lasts from December through March. Cases did occur as late as May, but that was unusual.

I asked Mr. Singh if he'd had a flu shot this year. He merely shrugged, so I turned to his grandson.

"Yes he did, Doctor. I took him in late December, just before he left for his annual trip to India. He was complaining of headaches and muscle aches when he got home last month. I wanted to drive him to his physician, but my granddad can be stubborn." He hung his head. "He's taken a turn for the worse this last week. This is my fault. I should have forced him to come in sooner."

I performed a physical exam. Mr. Singh's respirations were rapid and his heart rate galloping. I reviewed Maya Ruiz's chart note and agreed with all of her findings, but there was one thing she hadn't noticed. Although he was dark-skinned, his nail beds were quite pale and his eyes had a yellowish tinge, suggesting a rapid destruction of red blood cells. Combined with his flu-like symptoms and his recent travel to Southeast Asia, I was reminded of a few patients I had treated years earlier while I'd been overseas as a medic in the Army.

Just then, Maya entered the room with Mr. Singh's lab work. I looked up and asked, "How bad is his anemia?"

Her jaw dropped open. "Severe, but how…?"

We excused ourselves, stepped out of the room, and I took her through my reasoning.

Her eyes grew wide. "Malaria? I've never seen a case before!"

"And in all probability, you won't see another in this country unless your patient has traveled to an endemic area. Untreated, however, it can lead to kidney failure, seizures, confusion, coma, and death."

We reentered the room and explained the situation to the patient and his grandson, then took a drop of Mr. Singh's blood from his finger, added Giemsa stain, and examined it under the microscope at the nursing station.

Maya stared at me. "My god, it's like the textbooks. Purple-stained parasites inside both his red and white blood cells." She cast her gaze down. "But … I would have missed the diagnosis and failed Mr. Singh."

"No, not true. Many doctors would have dismissed the case as a run-of-the-mill flu and hurried off to their next patient—and Mr. Singh could well have died. *You* were alert and thoughtful enough to consider other possibilities and ask for a second opinion. You didn't let the heavy workload or your own ego get in the way. That makes you the kind of physician I would love to work with when you've finished your training in two months."

"Thank you." She blushed. "That's kind of you, Dr. Austin. So, what's our next step?"

"Given his condition, start him on Chloroquine now, order a stat chest x-ray, admit him to the hospital, and call an infectious disease consult. We may need to add doxycycline to the treatment regimen if the strain is resistant. Hopefully, we can get his malaria under control."

She nodded.

"Then read up on everything you can find about malaria, Maya, so you can present the case at Grand Rounds. This is a tremendous teaching opportunity. All of the interns and residents here can learn a great deal about parasitic illnesses from your presentation." She lit up a huge smile. "And I'd be happy to help you write up the case, Maya, if you want to submit it for publication in The Journal of Infectious Diseases."

She was out of the door before I finished the sentence. I called Harvey Winer in administration, summarized my many positive experiences working with Dr. Ruiz, and strongly suggested that the hospital offer her a staff position in July.

Maya and I were cruising through the rest of day when Tree phoned me.

"Ready for some good news for a change, Jake?"

"More than ready. Fire away."

"I visited the home of the officer who'd investigated Dorothy Clay's death. He'd signed out her evidence box before he retired because he'd always suspected Nick Pappas was dirty and he couldn't quite let go of her case. Unfortunately, he had a stroke shortly after his retirement and lost the ability to speak and walk. His wife didn't even know the box was stored in their basement until we searched for it."

"And?"

"That strange metal object discovered in the trunk of her car after her accident was in the box. It was damaged in the fire, but my lab geeks were able to detect what looks like an engraving of a clay pipe that a leprechaun might smoke, and the words 'St. Andrews' and 'Mashie.' You were right, Jake. It's definitely the head of an old golf club, presumably a match for Pappas' missing five iron at the country club. So my guess is he used it to *mashie-in* Dorothy's skull. The fire, of course, destroyed the wooden club shaft and any blood or hair evidence that might have been on it."

"So we got him!"

"Not yet. We can place his missing club in her car, but we have no proof he killed her with it."

"The police report you showed me indicated that Dorothy had a depressed skull fracture, Tree. Maybe the coroner could match the club head to the shape of the depression in her skull."

"Whoa, Jake, put on the breaks for a minute. I want Pappas locked up too, but the coroner says that matching the skull fracture is a long shot. To do that, we'd have to exhume Dorothy's body, which would be traumatic as hell for her sister and family. And a defense lawyer could easily claim that the trauma of the car crash caused the fractures. I have a better idea. I found Pappas's address, so how about we go confront the bastard with the evidence, catch him off-guard, tell him the coroner believes his club is the murder weapon, and see if he panics. You in?"

"Darn right I am. My shift's over in twenty minutes. Pick me up at Urgent Care."

CHAPTER FORTY THREE

Friday, May 9, 5:00 p.m.

I phoned Colleen, told her I'd be home a little late, and asked her to stay with RJ until I got back. When my shift ended, I dropped off my white coat in the doctors' lounge and jumped into Tree Macon's cruiser. Twenty minutes later we arrived at 5560 Park Street.

We looked at each other for a moment, then Tree said, "Not exactly what I expected."

Royal Buckeye Retirement Community was a cluster of three-story, brick buildings located far out in the country. We entered the lobby. Tree showed his badge to the receptionist and said he needed to speak with Nicholas Pappas.

She mumbled, "Good luck with that," and handed us two visitors' passes. "Just follow the green arrows."

The arrows led us to the nursing wing where the residents were having dinner. Nicholas Pappas was seated in a wheelchair at a table with an elderly woman who was half-asleep. He was unshaven and bald as a full moon. A nurse was taking turns shoveling spoonfuls of pureed meat and vegetables into each of them. Pappas tried to speak with his mouth full, speckling his plastic bib with saliva and food particles.

We walked over. Tree flashed his badge and said, "Mr. Pappas, we need to talk."

Pappas slowly raised a vacant stare in our direction, then returned to his meal.

The nurse shook her head. "Sorry officer. Nicholas hasn't been able to communicate in over a year." She gently wiped drool from his chin. "It's so sad. We've tried everything we could to help him, but his Alzheimer's has been relentless."

It was Tree and I who became speechless.

We thanked her and stepped away. Tree whispered, "Well, we tried. No point in it now. This is worse for him than any prison sentence." He shrugged. "Time to go, buddy. We'll let God judge him."

I remembered the photograph of the strapping, young George Clooney look-alike raising the championship trophy above his head, then focused on the withered husk of a man before me.

"Maybe God already has, Tree."

I was certain Pappas was a womanizer and a murderer, and probably the kind of man who had abused his authority over his subordinates all his life. So many powerful people in this world, including priests, had exploited and sexually abused the vulnerable in their care and had gone unpunished. I thought about Dorothy Margaret Clay, a joyful, trusting young woman in the hands of this predator, and it turned my stomach. Yes, Pappas had been sentenced to solitary confinement inside his head and broken body for the rest of his miserable life, but just walking away seemed pathetically weak-willed and unjust.

I had spent a lot of time wondering why Pappas would take the risk of killing Dorothy rather than simply casting her aside for his next conquest. Clearly, she had been in possession of damaging information about him. But in those days, there was not much an apprentice nurse could have done to threaten a hospital CEO, let alone topple him. Yet she must have known something about him so potentially destructive that he'd been compelled to murder her.

Finally, all the jigsaw pieces had fallen into place. A fiery car crash; the smell of smoke in the elevator when I'd first met Dorothy; the crying baby that woke Father Snapp; and the infant's footprint in the steamed-up bathroom mirror that Dixie Carter had witnessed. It all made sense.

I believe in a merciful God, and I know I should try to walk in the Lord's footsteps. But knowing what I did about this vile creature, I didn't feel the least bit merciful. The only person who had the right to forgive him for what he had done was dead.

When Tree started to leave, I put up my hand and said, "Give me a second."

I returned to the table, smiled at the nurse, gently lifted Pappas's gaze up to mine, and said, "Dorothy Margaret Clay sends her regards, Nicky."

For an instant, I thought I saw something spark in his eyes, a brief neurologic flash of lightening. Was it pain? Fear? Anger? Regret? I didn't know and didn't care. While the nurse was feeding her other patient, I leaned over and whispered softly in his ear, "You got her pregnant, didn't you, you bastard? Then you burned them both alive until they were nothing but ashes. Well, Nicky boy, there's a blistering inferno in Hell waiting for *you!*"

The emotion in his eyes, whatever it was, sparked again. I should have felt guilty about my malicious attack on a helpless being, but instead I took pleasure in every syllable. It was the most *unchristian* thing I'd done since becoming a priest. I had my many recent lies in service to the Church to confess, and now this vicious, vindictive attack on a defenseless old man … but I felt no regret. I didn't know what Dorothy had intended or what she wanted of me, but I hoped that she approved of my action.

As the nurse turned back to Pappas with another spoonful of pureed beans, I thanked her for taking such wonderful care of our dear Nicky, then rejoined Tree. We drove to town without a word, surrounded by the silence of the dead.

CHAPTER FORTY FOUR

Saturday, May 10, 11:00 a.m.

Not scheduled to work at the hospital on Saturday, I wanted to leave behind the stress of church fraud and vengeful ghosts and spend time with RJ. After celebrating morning Mass, I drove him to an amusement park. I spent most of my cash on ride tickets, hot dogs, and cotton candy, and was rewarded with giggles, grins, and hugs—terrible parenting, but worth every penny.

I had hoped he would nap on the drive home to give me a break from the commotion of the park, but he was so revved up on sugar that he chattered endlessly about the miniature roller coaster, spinning teacups, and the carousel horses.

Halfway to the rectory, he became quiet.

"What's up, RJ. Are you okay?"

"My tummy hurts, Daddy."

I heard a gagging sound and glanced in the rearview mirror. His face was pale and he was covering his mouth with his hands. I had visions of cotton candy-covered hotdog chunks spewing all over the inside of the car, so I parked off of the road and we walked in the fresh air. When his nausea settled down, we continued the drive home with the windows down.

I was beginning to relax again when Tree phoned.

"Jake, where are you?"

"On Route 10, headed home. Why?"

"Is RJ with you?"

"Yes, he is. What's going on?"

"We got problems. I'll meet you at the rectory. See you there."

When we pulled up to the rectory just before dusk, a sheriff's cruiser was parked in the driveway. Tree was leaning against the fender. While I unlocked the rectory door and turned off the security alarm, RJ hurried over to Tree. My little guy greeted my favorite big guy with a high-five and asked if he could come in and play with us.

"Sorry, RJ, I can't today. Next time, okay?"

My nephew made a pouty face and raced inside. Tree stared off into the distance. His expression and mood said, *We need to talk.*

I withered inside. "What?"

Without a word, he opened the cruiser's door and removed a metal pole with a mirror attached to one end.

"What the heck is going on, Tree?"

"When the FBI examined Snapp's van after the explosion, they found evidence of a UVIED."

"A what?"

"An Under Vehicle Improvised Explosive Device. It had been attached to the bottom of the van with a magnet. It was a clever contraption with a mercury switch. When the van started to move, a bead of mercury slid into the two detonation wires, completed the electrical circuit, and set off the explosion."

"Dear Lord! What—"

Tree held up a hand to stop me. "There's more. Because of the death threats you and I received after Big Angie Giordano was sentenced to prison, I had camouflaged security cameras installed at the station house, my home, and at the rectory."

"Here? Where?"

"Damn right, *here*. Don't bother; you won't find them. That's the whole point of camouflage. But don't run around outside the rectory naked. I'm paid to protect and serve, and that includes safeguarding you and RJ. I have no intention of losing either one of you on my watch. I'm also paid to be paranoid, and my paranoia peaks when my own ass is on the line. Unfortunately for Snapp, the surveillance coverage didn't include the church parking lot where his van was parked."

The big man heaved a heavy sigh. "Anyway, Jake, I have a deputy check the footage from the motion-activated cameras systems every morning.

Today he burst into my office and played the video from last night. It showed Vinny Giordano attaching a bomb under *my* cruiser. Took the bomb squad hours to defuse the damn thing. It had the same mercury switch detonator as the bomb that took out Snapp's van." He shook his head. "Vinny's in town, Jake, and he's after us both. You and RJ need to get out of here till we catch the bastard."

I gazed at the fading blush of daylight and considered what that would mean. "I can't leave my duties at the hospital and church, any more than you can run and hide out at your brother's home in Florida. And I won't move RJ in with Colleen and put her and the whole apartment complex at risk."

Tree wagged a finger at me. "And he can't stay here and continue going to his school without putting all those kids in danger."

"All right, all right, Tree. I get it. I'll find somewhere safe for him until I can leave, then the two of us will disappear. But … what about Mass here tomorrow?"

"Fine. I can station a deputy here till the service is over, but after that, you're on your own, Jake." He glanced around, then reached under his jacket and pulled out a pistol. "Take it, Jake. It's a throw away, untraceable. Serial number's been filed off. Giordano's nuttier than squirrel shit. Who knows what he might do. You should have a piece."

God knows, I *wanted* to take it—but I couldn't.

"I told you Tree, I shot a man in the throat at close range during the war. A man who had a child waiting at home for him. Sometimes when my nightmares grab *me* by the throat, I can still see his face, hear that pitiful gurgling sound he made with his last few breaths. That day, I swore to God and myself I'd never again fire another weapon. Never." I pushed the gun away. "And I meant it."

He stared at me for a long time, then slid the handgun back under his jacket and handed me the mirror attached to the metal pole.

"If you're gonna be pigheaded and stay in town, Jake, then use this to look under your car every time you're going to drive it. Also, check the top and sides of all four tires. Now, let me give you a crash course on detecting vehicle IEDs."

He walked over to my car. "It's good that you have a tamper-proof gas cap that unlocks from the inside. But remember, Giordano was a demolitions expert in the Army. Not all devices are attached magnetically like the ones he used on Snapp's van and my cruiser. Before getting into the car, always look inside through the windows for anything that shouldn't be there. Park on soft ground in well-lit areas, and look for footprints or bits of tape, wire, or string in the area. If you see anything unusual or evidence of forced entry around the trunk or doors, get away and call me immediately."

He showed me how to check the engine compartment and the ignition wiring. When he'd finished, I asked, "What about Giordano?"

"Every cop in the state is looking for him and his SUV. We'll nab him—soon I hope. With the video of him planting a car bomb, getting a warrant for his home and financial records was easy. Baton Rouge police raided his place today. He had nothing of value and everything was rented. Vinny had less than a hundred bucks in the bank, so I doubt he's planning on returning to Louisiana. He probably has cash stashed somewhere safe, like in the Cayman Islands. He took off in a big hurry, so I suspect he had an easy-to-carry, grab-and-go bag ready, packed with money and essentials."

Tree placed a hand on my shoulder and looked me in the eye. "I know you, Jake. I know you're thinking you don't want to desert the church and hospital, and that you can tough this out because of your military training—but don't. You're out of your league with this guy, and I don't have the manpower to protect you. Please, buddy, get the hell out of Dodge till this is over."

I didn't want to scare RJ, so after Tree drove away, I slipped on a neutral expression and went inside. Moarte was hopping around inside his cage, making a racket. Hoping he'd go to sleep, I fed him a couple of grapes and threw a blanket over the cage, then RJ and I read a book until bedtime. Exhausted from a day of running from one amusement park ride to another, he crashed into a deep slumber. I, however, got very little sleep.

CHAPTER FORTY FIVE

Sunday, May 11, 5:00 a.m.

I spent most of the night sitting bolt upright in bed every time the house creaked, but at five in the morning I was awakened by what sounded like a gunshot or a car backfire. I jumped out of bed and grabbed the autographed Cleveland Indians baseball bat the previous pastor had given me as a gift, then rushed downstairs. I walked from window to window, Louisville slugger in hand, until daybreak, wishing I still had the sidearm from my Army days.

I felt relief when I saw a Sheriff's cruiser slowly circling our block, and even better when the bomb squad arrived early in the morning to sweep the church for explosives before Mass. Tree had come through for me. But law enforcement resources were limited and wouldn't be available forever—and there was no way I was willing to live in the shadow of a death threat indefinitely. The long night of tossing and turning had given me plenty of time to think, and I'd decided what I needed to do.

From the photographs I had discovered in Giordano's home, it was clear that Colleen was on his radar and needed to disappear.

Emily, on the other hand, hadn't been to the rectory in weeks and had not been photographed by the private investigator Giordano had hired. She was an early riser, so I phoned her at seven and told her what Tree had said.

"Oh my god, Jake! Car bombs? What're you going to do?"

"First, I need to get RJ out of danger. Because of my connection with St. Joe's, the police and FBI have added additional protection at the hospital.

You weren't involved in Angelo Giordano's trial, Em, and you're not on his son's radar. Can RJ stay with you for a few days? I don't want him here with me even one more night."

"Of course. There's always room for RJ. But … what about school?"

"I'll let his teacher know he'll be away for a while."

"All right. Bring his workbooks with him and I'll do what I can." A moment of silence. "But what about you?" A faint sob. "I almost lost you in the war, Jake, and I don't know what I'd do if …."

"I'll be okay, Em. Not to worry. As soon as I get coverage at the hospital and the church, I'll pick up RJ and we'll go on a little vacation somewhere far away until this is over."

We said our goodbyes, then I telephoned Colleen and brought her up to speed.

"Jesus, Mary, and Joseph! So the hounds are baying at our door, are they? What are we to do, Father?"

"*You* should drive to Toledo immediately and stay with you sister until the danger has passed."

"I can't just pop in on her unannounced, Father. What if she has plans? Perhaps I could go after the Legion of Mary meeting tomorrow night."

"No, Colleen. You're in danger. Leave *today*. Please!"

"But Father, I promised I'd bring a tuna casserole to the meeting. I'll not be breaking my word and shirking—"

"No 'buts.' I mean it, Colleen. This man is dangerous and he's seen you at the rectory. Please pack a suitcase and leave now. I'll call you when things are safe again."

"But what about yourself, Father?"

"RJ and I will be leaving town soon. Now go. Start packing."

"Okay, okay, Father. If you insist." She grumbled something unintelligible in Gaelic, then hung up.

My next call was to the hospital administrator. I was scheduled to be on-call overnight to guide the interns and residents through any difficult cases they might encounter. In light of the bombing of Snapp's van and the risk my presence posed to the hospital, Harvey Winer approved my impromptu leave of absence from Urgent Care, and agreed to ask another physician to cover my night call.

Bishop Lucci was less accommodating.

"If I wasn't short of priests, I'd have sent you back to the Camillian

Order a long time ago. This will only worsen my staffing shortage. Since the day you arrived in my diocese, Father Austin, you've been nothing but trouble. Your Superior General will hear about this."

I wasn't the least bit concerned about his threat because I was Demarco's right-hand man, and he outranked Lucci in the ecclesiastical pecking order. My concern was the safety of those around me.

"But your Excellency, I can't in good conscience put my parishioners at risk, to say nothing of the church itself."

He filled the ensuing silence with a disgusted snort. "Fine, fine. I'll have Father Vargas fill in at Sacred Heart. You're on sabbatical after Mass today, but the instant this criminal is apprehended, I want you back at the church, hard at work." He slammed the phone down with a loud thud and was gone.

It was the second Sunday in May. As I polished my Mother's Day homily, I thought about my *chosen* family and how my sister's death had changed all our lives. I'd become a stand-in father, Emily a surrogate mother, Colleen a grandmother to RJ, and Tree an uncle to my boy. It wasn't a classical nuclear family, but it was loving and stable, and RJ appeared to be thriving. I felt truly blessed—and I'd be damned if I'd let Giordano tear our world asunder.

I was pouring my second cup of coffee when I heard RJ stirring. I walked upstairs and entered his room. He'd already dressed in a Ninja Turtles t-shirt and jeans—not my choice of attire for Sunday Mass, but I let it slide.

As he brushed his flaming red hair, I said, "Emily's been feeling lonely, RJ. She wondered if you'd be willing to spend a few days at her apartment to cheer her up."

"Would I! You bet. She's fun." He began bouncing around the room like a human pogo stick. "Can I, Daddy? Pleeease! Can I?"

"Of course, sport. Maybe you can even miss a couple days of school. Help me pack your things."

When RJ and I arrived at the church, I saw Officer Kearney stationed at the entrance. He and I had met a few months earlier.

I sent my nephew inside and asked, "You know what's been going on, right?" He nodded. "I need a favor, officer. I don't want to put my nephew in the car with me for obvious reasons, so after Mass would you drive him to Emily Beale's place." I handed him the address and RJ's suitcase. "She's expecting him. Sheriff Macon will back me on this."

He hesitated for only a second. "Sure, Father. Happy to."

I dressed in my vestments and walked to the altar. As usual, RJ was seated in the soundproof Quiet Room in the rear of the church. To my surprise and frustration, Colleen was sitting next to him. The woman was nothing if not devoted. Her loyalty was only exceeded by her stubbornness. I had hoped she would be on the way to her sister's home by now, but I suspected she wouldn't leave until she had delivered her tuna casserole to the Legion of Mary meeting. Once she'd made up her mind, she was downright immovable.

I heard a commotion near the entrance. Fearing the worst, I stiffened, but it was only Mr. and Mrs. Becker squabbling. Despite the three counseling sessions I'd had with them, they'd made little progress in communicating. Colleen referred to them as the *Bickersons*.

Before beginning Mass, I scanned the nave looking for Giordano on the chance he might be reckless enough to ignore the police presence. I knew he might be in disguise, but it would be difficult for him to hide the angry red, crescent-shaped scar that marked his face. Attendance at church had been low since the bombing of Snapp's van in the parking lot, and I didn't see him in the gathering. Refusing to let fear spoil my precious time with the Lord, I placed my fate in the hands of Tree Macon, the bomb squad, and the Almighty, and began the service.

Deacon Lyons was assisting me, my altar girl was competent, and all went well. My Mother's Day sermon was uplifting and hit the mark, and to my relief, RJ nearly leapt into the police cruiser after Mass when Officer Kearney offered to let him run the siren on the way to Emily's apartment.

When they drove out of the church parking lot, I was awash in conflicted emotions—relieved that my nephew was safe, but anxious that I no longer had police protection. I returned to the rectory as satisfied with the situation as anyone being stalked by a killer could be.

I thought about loading the car with our things, picking up RJ, and leaving the state, but rejected the plan. Giordano had failed to kill me when he blew up Snapp's van, and he'd been foiled in his attempt to bomb Tree's cruiser. Undoubtedly, he was frustrated and knew we were on to him. He'd be desperate to complete his mission. As a matter of family honor, it was unlikely he would quit and walk away from his vendetta. But desperate people do desperate things, and I worried about what he might try next.

If I disappeared, Giordano might take out his frustration on the innocent people in my life. Emily and her dad were easy targets if he stumbled across my relationship to them, and Colleen couldn't hide out at her sister's home indefinitely. I had no doubt that if I vanished, Giordano would focus his vendetta on Tree and his family, and possibly the church.

No, better for me to remain a visible target and be on my guard. The rectory and I could be replaced, but not a school full of children, or a church filled with the faithful. The idea of a deadly confrontation with Giordano was a little easier to accept because I knew Emily, Colleen, and Tree would care for RJ if I was gone.

I began to prepare for the worst, and hope for the best. That evening, I locked the doors and windows in the rectory, darkened all the rooms except for my bedroom upstairs, brewed a pot of strong coffee, then wandered the first floor from window to window peering out, armed with my baseball bat, a butcher's knife always close at hand. By three a.m., the coffee's effect was waning and my eyelids were losing the battle with gravity when my phone rang.

CHAPTER FORTY SIX

Monday, May 12, 3:00 a.m.

Maya Ruiz said, "I'm sorry to disturb you in the middle of the night, Dr. Austin, but I have a patient at the hospital in cardiac distress. He was brought in due to fainting and lightheadedness, and I'm not sure what's going on. I know it's not your night on-call, but could you come in and give me your opinion?"

"Sorry, I can't. Who's the staff doctor on-call?"

"Dr. Ballestra."

"Okay, so call him, Maya. I know it's late, but it's his duty to come in."

"I did, but he had an attack of food poisoning tonight and he's sick as a dog. That's the problem. He's also the cardiologist on-call tonight."

"Nobody else is available?"

"Sorry, no. No one. I've tried everyone I can think of."

I didn't know what to say. Was she taking advantage of our friendship, knowing other physicians might be furious with her for dragging them into the hospital before sunrise? The silence lingered.

"Please, Dr. Austin, I really need your help. My patient's extremely short of breath on 100% oxygen, but so far his EKG and bloodwork show no evidence of acute MI."

"Chest pain?"

"Sharp as a knife he says, but more in his *back*. Worse with deep breaths and when he lies flat."

"Hypertension?"

"No, that's the thing. His blood pressure is *low*. I put him on meds to raise it and I'm pouring in IV fluids, but I'm not getting anywhere. The poor guy's only thirty years old. He doesn't have a history of cardiac problems but his heart is enlarged on x-ray. He's also having short, intermittent runs of ventricular tachycardia. I don't know what to do. Please, Dr. Austin, I'm afraid I'm going to lose him."

A young man who might be dead before morning, and a colleague in need of assistance. Maya was a bright, well-trained resident who rarely asked for help. I couldn't leave her in the lurch.

"All right. I'll be there as soon as I can. Get a stat CT scan of his chest to rule out a dissecting aortic aneurysm, Maya, and keep trying to contact a cardiologist. I'm on my way."

I checked my car carefully for signs of tampering, then ignored the speed limits and wheeled up to the hospital emergency room in record time. Maya introduced me to a muscular young man sitting bolt upright on a gurney. Although the oxygen valve was wide open, he was breathing at twice the normal rate, making it difficult for him to answer questions. His skin was parchment pale, his eyes wide with panic, and his face glistened with sweat. What caught my attention, however, were the markedly distended veins in his neck.

"We should have his chest CT scan results any minute, Dr. Austin," Maya said.

"How's his blood pressure?"

"Dropping."

The EKG showed a rapid heart rate but no definite evidence of a heart attack. After checking his bloodwork, I placed my stethoscope against his chest and listened. His heart sounds were extremely faint, partially obscured by an abnormal rubbing noise. *My* heart skipped a couple of beats. The young man was knocking on the Pearly Gates.

I sent the nurse for a pericardiocentesis tray, then said to Maya, "He has Beck's triad: low blood pressure, bulging neck veins, and faint heart sound muffled by a distinct rubbing sound. There's fluid in the pericardial sac around his heart, constricting it, preventing it from filling normally. There's nowhere for returning blood to go. That's why his neck veins are so distended."

She gasped. "Damn. So there's very little blood available to pump out to his body. *That's* why I couldn't get his blood pressure up and he's so pale!"

"Exactly." I listened to his lungs and heard crackling sounds on both sides. "The back-pressure on his lungs is filling them with fluid and he's going into congestive heart failure. There's no time left for cardiac consultants or more tests. We have to relieve the pressure around his heart by draining the fluid."

I told Maya to get gloved and gowned, and explained to the young man that he might feel a needle stick but that his breathing should soon get better. I eased him onto his back, then prepped and draped his chest and upper abdomen.

When the nurse returned with the pericardiocentesis tray, I said to Maya, "Find the notch between the bottom of his breastbone and his left rib cage and inject the area with local anesthetic. Good, now slip that thin catheter over the needle and slowly advance the two together at a forty-five degree angle through the skin toward his left shoulder."

Maya was usually cool under pressure, and she didn't disappoint. I kept one eye on the EKG monitor to make sure the needle tip didn't make contact with the man's heart.

"Excellent. Now apply gentle suction with the syringe as you advance the needle."

When she pulled back the plunger on the syringe, there was a flash of fluid. I said, "Perfect. Stop right there, hold the needle completely still with one hand, and with the other hand slide the thin plastic catheter off the needle into the pericardial sac. That's right, now remove the needle."

When she did, yellowish liquid poured out of the catheter. We affixed it to our patient's skin and attached a bag to collect the fluid. With the pressure around his heart relieved, it began pumping blood normally. His blood pressure normalized, his respirations grew less labored, and his EKG slowly returned to a normal rhythm.

I looked a Maya and smiled. "Well, that was more exciting than I would have liked. With the resistance to blood flow relieved, his congestive heart failure should clear rapidly. I suspect a viral infection caused the fluid around his heart, but let's send it to the lab for analysis to be certain." I told the young man that he would soon be fine, then said to Maya, "I have to leave now. Admit him to cardiology. If all goes well, we can remove the catheter and send him home in a day or two."

I was about to walk to my car when she said, "Oh, I nearly forgot, Dr. Austin. A man asked me this morning if you'd be working in Urgent Care tomorrow. Said he was a friend of yours. I told him your name had been crossed off the schedule for the entire week and that I didn't know when you'd return."

"What was his name?"

"Sorry, I don't remember. He was wearing scrubs, so I assume he works here. A big guy with a southern accent and a nasty scar on his left cheek. He said he'd give you a call."

All my muscles tensed, and my hands became cold and clammy. Giordano!

"Maya, that man's a dangerous felon."

Her eyes grew large. "Oh my god!"

"As soon as you get our patient admitted to the hospital, go to the security office and identify him on the surveillance footage. Tell the security officers to call Sheriff Tree Macon if they spot him in the hospital again, and to use my name so Macon will take their call. This man is armed and shouldn't be approached by anyone but the authorities. And Maya, call me if you see him again."

I said goodbye and headed for the garage. I was dizzy with fear and anger. This changed everything. If Giordano was freely wandering the hospital, my presence made me a walking time bomb and a danger to everyone around me, including Emily and RJ. I needed to disappear immediately. I hopped into my car and hurried toward home to pack my things. RJ and I would be gone by morning, somewhere far away.

Angry black clouds hung low in the sky, obliterating the moon and stars, mirroring my mood. I drove home through perpetual night, the darkness pouring down as thick as tar. Near the rectory, fat raindrops began to slap my windshield. When I stepped from the car, the storm howled an ominous tune and the sky opened up. I sprinted to the back door as rain fired down at me like bullets.

When I entered the kitchen, the security alarm beeped its cautionary warning. I punched in the code to disarm it, relocked the door, and threw off my wet coat as the downpour pounded on the roof. Moarte must have heard me come home and started shrieking, "Demon be gone!"

God, I hated that damn bird and couldn't wait to be rid of the vile creature.

I poured a cup of coffee to bolster myself for more sleepless hours, picked up my baseball bat, and entered the living room just as Moarte screamed, "Evil!"

I heard a familiar sound from my Army days, a metal *clack* as Giordano racked the slide on his weapon a second before I saw him sitting on the couch. A wicked grin full of malice slowly spread below his dark dancing eyes.

CHAPTER FORTY SEVEN

Monday, May 12, 4:30 a.m.

"Well, ain't this an unexpected surprise, Father," Vinny Giordano said in a southern drawl as thick as molasses on a frosty winter's morning. He spoke in a velvet-soft monotone and was dressed all in black. Lamplight glistened on his shaved head.

The television remote control rested on his lap. What the hell? Watching TV? That made no sense. He set it gingerly on the coffee table, then stood.

He was even taller and beefier than Tree Macon, about the size of a great white shark, with the same merciless, icy-cold eyes.

Giordano pointed his gun at me; it was like looking down the barrel of a cannon.

"I'd given up any hope of meetin' y'all face to face. Come on in and join me." He waved me farther into the room.

I did as directed. Moarte was in his cage to my right, squawking and leaping around wildly. I'd walked into a trap, and my baseball bat was worthless against a semi-automatic. I wished to God I'd taken the pistol Tree had offered.

Surveying the room for something I could use to my advantage, I noticed a roll of duct tape, pliers, and a spool of electrical wire lying next to the television set.

Giordano followed my gaze. "I was just about to leave, Father, but runnin' into ya like this makes me happier than a tick on a fat dog." He released a thin humorless laugh. "I'd planned on torturing you some before I killed you, but y'all weren't here when I arrived. So I decided on a more *explosive* ending for you and that fuckin' bird of yours." He gestured with his weapon at Moarte. "Damn thing's been screamin' its fool head off ever since I got here."

We locked eyes. Suddenly the paraphernalia around the television and the careful way he'd handled the remote control made perfect sense. He'd rigged the TV to detonate when I turned it on.

I felt blood rush to my cheeks, raw anger rising within me. What if RJ had decided to watch cartoons, or Colleen wanted to catch a soap opera? The bastard didn't give a tinker's damn who he killed. I gripped the bat tighter.

"Damn you! My boy could have—"

"I don't give a flyin' fuck about your kid. It's you and your old man I'm after—and that nigger Sheriff. Y'all put my pappy in prison, trashed our business, and ruined my life." He stepped toward me. "Now, if y'all wanna swing at me with that bat, go ahead. Take your best shot. My money's on my Glock. Otherwise, drop that useless piece of lumber and we'll have ourselves a conversation."

Moarte was clinging to the cage door shrieking, "Evil! Evil!" The damn bird was right about that. For an instant, I considered lunging for the remote and blowing us both up. Anything was better than letting a stone-cold killer walk out of here to murder Tree and his family, and maybe RJ or Emily. I tossed the bat onto my recliner, not too far out of reach, and moved back toward the bird cage.

"That's better." He inched cautiously toward me.

Up close, his pale gray eyes appeared cold and soulless, devoid of compassion. The crescent-shaped scar on his face looked much angrier than it had in his mug shot. Bright red, it wrapped around his left eye and extended down to his chin.

"This here might be a good time for y'all to start prayin', Father." He pursed his lips and tilted his head to the side. "I wanted to slice and dice your daddy with my Bowie knife, make him pay for being a snitch, but I couldn't get past them damn Marshals. But if you don't do exactly what I say … you can bet I'll use the blade on *you*."

He spit on the rug. "I hear your old man lived through the blast. That's too bad, but it makes no never-mind. He's gonna die along with the rest of y'all. It's just a matter of time."

He had me dead to rights. If I even thought about grabbing the bat or diving for the remote, I'd be dead before I finished the thought. I needed to find a distraction to buy some time.

"How the hell did you get in here? My security alarm—"

"Yeah, that was a lot harder than I figured."

Then I realized the alarm had been *armed* when I'd arrived from the hospital, so he hadn't disabled it. And yet, he was inside. He'd somehow turned it off and then back on. The breath froze in my lungs. Only five people knew my code. RJ, Colleen, Emily, Snapp, and Tree.

"That's top-of-the-line security ya got there, Father. But there's more'n one way to skin a cat—or a nasty old Irish whore." A smirk surfaced on his lips, then disappeared like a shark's fin.

"Irish whore? What are you talking about?" Then it hit me. "Colleen?"

"Damn right, *Colleen*. Spit at me, she did, and wouldn't say a word. But that just pissed me off." He snickered. "I tried to play nice but…."

He pushed up a shirt sleeve, revealing arms that must have spent hours at the gym. He pointed to teeth marks above his wrist.

"But when that she-devil bit me and called me a stinkin' grease-ball guinea, well what can I say? No more Mister Nice Guy." He patted the large knife in the leather sheath hung from his belt, then shook his head. "Gotta admit, she was one tough bitch. Didn't even flinch when I pulled out my blade … and even after I cut her, it took forever 'fore she gave up the house key and the alarm code."

I leapt toward my recliner and reached for the baseball bat. Giordano got there first and pistol-whipped me with the butt of his gun. I staggered backward, blood running down my forehead into my eye.

"Not so fast, tough guy." He tossed the bat on the floor by the couch. "We're not done here."

I retreated. "Is Colleen … all right?"

"Well, let's just say she's been better." He released a phlegmy laugh that would have curled Satan's toes. "Though, she didn't look so good when I left her."

Anger exploded inside me like a landmine. The fiery rage I'd once felt as a young man during the war burst into flame. No matter what happened here, this bastard couldn't be allowed to walk away.

I started in his direction, but he leveled his weapon at my chest. I stopped and eyed the TV remote again. If that was my only option, then … God forgive me, so be it.

"That's enough chit chat, Austin. Times a-wasting. Tick tock. Call your buddy the Sheriff, and have him get his black ass over here. Tell him to come alone or I'll kill your kid."

Dear Lord! Could he have been to Emily's place and taken RJ?

"RJ!" I yelled. Not a sound. "Bull! You don't *have* my boy."

"Makes no never-mind, 'cause if you don't do zxactly what I say, I'll find your kid and slice and dice him like the Irish bitch." He bared his razor-sharp, ocher-colored teeth. "Whatcha waiting on. Tick fuckin' tock! Make the call, and be convincin'. If the Sheriff brings the damn *po-lice* with him though, well … boom! There's only one safe way out of this here house, and I'm the only one knows it. The rest of y'all will be smoke and ash. So call him … now!"

Damn it! If I phoned Tree, I'd put him in danger. If I didn't, this lunatic wouldn't hesitate to kill RJ and Emily. It was a lose-lose situation. I took a step back and bumped into the bird cage. Moarte leapt around inside it, screeching, "Demon be gone!"

I speed-dialed Tree's cellphone, but with my other hand I reached behind me and unlocked the cage. When he answered, I shouted, "Giordano's here," and flipped the cage door open.

Moarte flew from the cage like a surface-to-air missile straight for Giordano's head, but Vinny sprang away just in time. When Moarte made another pass at him, I threw myself on the floor and grabbed the Louisville slugger. As Giordano fired wildly at the bird, I swung the bat and shattered his ankle.

He howled, collapsed to his knees, and fired at me. Lightning shot from my thigh down my leg, and blood poured onto the carpet.

He reached for the TV remote detonator. In my mind, I saw Colleen and what this monster had done to her. I raised up and gripped the bat with both hands. When he turned his head toward me, the scar on his face became the bright red seams of a baseball hurtling toward home plate—and I swung for the fence.

His blood was everywhere before his body hit the floor.

I crawled to my cellphone and dialed. "Tree, the rectory's booby-trapped! Use the kitchen door in the back."

The room began to spin faster. The phone slipped from my hands. I used my bloody fingers to scrawl Colleen's name on the beige couch, then collapsed onto the floor. Moarte swooped past me, landed on what was left of Giordano's face, and pecked at his eyes. The plaintive wail of sirens rose in the night, then faded as my world went dark.

CHAPTER FORTY EIGHT

Monday, May 12, 12:30 p.m.

I felt woozy, as if I'd had one too many drinks. Great swells of nausea rolled up toward my throat, then receded like ocean waves. I tried to move but couldn't. Something heavy seemed to be sitting on me. Every time I drifted off into merciful oblivion, a damn beeping noise woke me again. My eyelids felt glued together—but when I heard sobbing, I forced them to open.

At first, I thought I was in Rome, looking at Michelangelo's Pietà sculpture of Mary staring down at Jesus, her dead son nestled in her arms. As my vision and mind cleared, I realized Emily was sitting on a chair near me with RJ asleep in her lap. She wiped a tear away.

My leg throbbed, dragging me closer to consciousness. Looking around, I realized I was in a hospital bed, an IV dripping into my right hand. When I lifted the covers, I saw a surgical dressing on my left thigh.

I lowered the blanket and tried to recall what had happened. Images of the gaping maw of a gun inches from my face morphed into Giordano's malicious grin, then slowly gave way to the weight of the baseball bat in my hands and his head exploding like a crimson paintball.

Then I remembered Colleen. I gasped and sat bolt upright.

Emily heard me. "Jake?" she whispered.

"I'm here, Em."

"Oh, Jake, RJ and I were so afraid!" she said softly. "You'd lost a lot of blood. They took you straight to the operating room. We've been here all night."

I wanted to hug them and say something reassuring, but I couldn't contain the question any longer and it burst from my lips. "Colleen?"

Emily shook her head. "It's not good, Jake."

"She's alive?"

Tears began to flow again. Emily bowed her head. "She's out of surgery, but .... Dad's at her bedside. He doesn't want her to be alone in case she ...."

A weighty silence passed between us. I tried to imagine my life without Colleen.

Finally, I managed, "Does RJ know?"

Another head shake. "He was so scared, Jake, so afraid he'd lose you," she whispered. "We both were. You were in the O.R. a long time. They had to give you two units of blood, and the surgeon said if the bullet had been a few millimeters over, you'd ...." She cast her eyes down, then took a moment to gather herself. "It was too much. I couldn't bring myself to tell him about her."

Silence engulfed us again. I stared at the two people I loved more than life itself. But Colleen was the linchpin, the glue that held us all together. Without her ... what were we? How could we go on? RJ had already lost his mother. Now the grandmother figure in his life? How could I possibly tell him about Colleen?

When RJ's head lolled backward and Emily turned toward him, I again thought of Michelangelo's Pietà—and I realized how close I had come to losing them. If RJ had used the booby-trapped television, or if Giordano had stumbled across the two of them, they might both be dead.

Then a terrible thought took shape. If Giordano had actually had RJ in his clutches when I entered the rectory, would I have phoned Tree and knowingly led him into a trap trying to buy time to save my boy? Would I have traded my best friend's life for RJ's? The answer was too painful to even consider.

RJ stirred and brushed a mop of red hair away from his face, then his eyes popped open.

"Daddy!" He jumped from Emily's lap and climbed up into my bed, landing, of course, on my incision. The pain, however, was short-lived, and the hug he gave me was more healing than any drug they could have put in my IV.

He snuggled against me. "I was scared, Daddy!"

"I know, buddy. Me too. But I'm okay now. Everything's going to be fine." As the lie left my lips, I cringed. Things were far from fine, and I wasn't sure they would ever be anywhere close to it again. But somehow I had to make a terrible situation better for him.

Deacon Lyons knocked at my door and peeked in. He was Father Vargas's right hand man, besides assisting me occasionally when I needed help. "Bad time, Jake?"

"No." I waved him in.

After Lyons greeted Emily, he said, "Father Vargas and I heard what happened. He wanted to stop by, Jake, but was called to perform Last Rites, so he asked me to look in on you. How're you feeling?"

"I'll be fine in a week or two."

He walked over and extended a hand to my nephew. "And you must be RJ. I've heard good things about you, young man."

A grin flickered on RJ's lips and they shook.

Lyons turned to me. "Father Vargas thought you might like to receive Communion?"

I would have loved to, but self-defense or not, I'd tried to kill a man—and deacons cannot hear confessions.

"No thanks, Pat. But please ask Father Vargas to stop by when he's available."

"Will do. Well, I best be getting home. My daughters are probably running my wife ragged by now. I suspect my afternoon will be filled with tea parties and Barbie dolls. May the Lord offer you strength and a speedy recovery, Jake. You'll be in my prayers."

As he walked away to join his family, I gazed at RJ and Emily, and jealousy raised its envy-green head. In many ways, Lyons had everything I wanted—an active role in the church as an ordained clergyman in addition to a wife and children. The thought left me feeling as if my heart had been ripped out of my chest, leaving a gaping void at my core.

But I couldn't dwell on what wasn't, on the life I *might* have had. My thoughts shifted to Colleen … and how I had failed her. I should have recognized how much danger she was in and *forced* her to leave town immediately.

My regret must have bled through. RJ stared at me.

"Are you okay, Daddy? You look so sad."

Sad didn't come close to how I felt. Miserable, guilty, depressed and terrified were closer, but mostly I was despondent at the prospect of explaining to RJ that another person he loved might soon be dead. A warm tear ran down my cheek.

"Daddy?"

"I have some sad news, RJ."

The expression on his face broke my heart.

CHAPTER FORTY NINE

Monday, May 12, 1:00 p.m.

After my sister died and I took guardianship of my nephew, I'd read every book I could find on helping children cope with death. Kids process grief in bite-sized chunks over time, not all at once, and in different ways than adults. The many conversations I'd had with RJ were far more painful than any bullet wound. Given time and support from Colleen, Emily and Tree, however, we'd eventually rebuilt his world and mine.

Now Colleen? Here we were again, standing on the precipice, looking down into the abyss. Would it be better to tell my boy how grim things appeared, or should I dance around the situation, only to have to break the sad news to him later out of the blue?

I was never much for dancing, or dodging the truth.

"I have some sad news, RJ." He glanced at Emily, then peered up at me, his face a question. I swallowed hard. "Colleen's in the hospital. She's hurt bad."

I paused to give him a moment to digest my words. His eyes filled with tears, then the dam broke and they streamed down his cheeks. We hugged each other for a long time. Finally, he pulled away. His mouth opened and closed but he said nothing. What can any of us say when tragedy strikes?

"I know you're feeling sad and scared, RJ. I am too."

I didn't fight my tears because over time I had, in fact, come to love Colleen, and I wanted my boy to know that expressing grief was normal.

"Can I go see her, Daddy?"

"Not right now, buddy."

He stared at me, hope in his eyes. "She'll be okay, right?"

"I don't know, RJ. We're all praying for her and—"

"No, no, no!" He sat up, his eyes wide. "We prayed for Mommy and she *still* died!"

His little hands fisted. "Don't let her die, Daddy! Please!" He punched my pillow. "It's not fair!"

Not fair indeed—from the lips of children to the ears of God.

"But why, Daddy? Why?"

Why? How do you explain vengeance, greed, and violence to a five year old? And as to the question of why those we love are taken from us, is there even an answer that an adult can understand? In seminary, I was told that if we all lived forever, no one would appreciate God's incredible gift of life—but that didn't begin to address the *emotional* turmoil that loss triggers, and it was certainly not the kind of thing you say to a child.

RJ waited for me to respond. When I didn't, he gazed off into the distance and was quiet for a while, then finally asked, "If she dies, will she … go to heaven with Mommy?"

"Yes, RJ," I replied. "I'm sure of it. They'll be best friends because they both love us so much and we love them too." I pulled him closer. "And if that happens, our sadness will heal slowly over time, but we will never forget her. Healing doesn't mean forgetting the people you love. It means *remembering* all the good times with love."

He wiped away a tear. "Well, at least Mommy wouldn't be so lonely anymore."

Now who was comforting whom?

Then the light went out of his eyes again. "But who will drive me to school and take care of me?"

And there it was, our crisis summarized in one practical question. And as critical as the answer was, it caught me off guard coming from him.

"I, ah … *I* will, RJ, whenever I can. And I'm sure Uncle Tree and Sonya will help out, and …."

As I struggled to find a cogent response, Emily snapped her collapsible cane to full extension, tapped her way over to the bed, and said, "I could stay with you when your daddy's working. And maybe you and I could take a taxicab to school together once in a while. That might be fun, right?"

The village to the rescue … but without Colleen, I had my doubts it would be enough.

RJ nodded hesitantly, then looked directly at me. His eyes grew as large as quarters. "Don't die, Daddy! Promise me. Please!"

I forced the lump from my throat.

"Don't you worry about me, RJ." I conjured up an unconvincing smile. "I plan to be here until I'm very, very old, and you're all grown up. But … I'll need you to be my number one helper now. Can you do that for me?"

He nodded again, then went quiet. I waited, uncertain what he would ask next, but he remained mute.

Grateful that he'd run out of questions for the time being, I turned to Emily. "You two look exhausted. You both should take a nap and come back after dinner."

RJ stiffened and shook his head, red locks snaking from side to side. "No! I wanna stay with you, Daddy. I don't need a nap. I'm not sleepy."

Emily ran a finger around her braille watch. "Wish I could, but I have to help out in the snack shop for a while." She stood. "But your daddy's right, RJ. We both need some rest. How about this? When I'm finished working in an hour or so, I'll come back and then you and I can sleep until suppertime. Deal?"

He nodded. "Deal."

After Emily left, a far-off look drifted across RJ's face. I braced for another barrage of unanswerable questions.

He bit his lower lip for a moment, then asked, "Daddy, can we get a kitten?"

I almost laughed. Who can understand the workings of the five-year-old mind?

"Maybe, buddy. We'll see."

My boy grinned, then did what I least expected. He snuggled up close to me and fell sound asleep—leaving me to ponder how to mend his shattered world and mine.

CHAPTER FIFTY

Monday, May 12, 2:30 p.m.

Not long after Emily returned and took RJ to her place for a proper nap, the surgeon stopped in to check my wound and change the dressing, then she upgraded my liquid diet to some sort of nondescript purple gelatin with less taste than tap water. I had pushed it aside and was sipping a cup of coffee when Tree walked in.

He forced a smile. "Dumb question, but how're you feeling?"

"Like I was shot. But all things considered, it could've been a lot worse."

His smile disappeared. "I'm so sorry about Colleen. I just spoke with her doctors. All they'll say is that *if* she makes it, she'll have a long road to recovery. That bastard, Giordano, stabbed her and left her to die. But if you hadn't scrawled her name on the couch in blood to alert us, Jake, she wouldn't have had any chance at all."

Tree plopped down hard onto the chair by the bed. "Until you find someone to take her place, Sonya and I will do anything we can to help out with RJ." He looked down. "I know you don't want to hear this, buddy, but let me tell you what I think."

"It's not as if I've ever been able to stop you before, Tree."

"Colleen was a *gift*. Even if she lives, she's not coming back any time soon, if at all. It's gonna be damn near impossible to replace her, and without her there's no way the whirlwind of your current life can continue." The big guy hesitated before continuing. "I said it when you became RJ's guardian, and I'll say it again. Emily is your soulmate. Marry the girl, Jake, raise RJ, and focus on your medical practice. I know you love the priesthood, but you can't be everything to everybody. Give it up and move on. It's not that complicated."

"The hell it's not! Thanks for the wisdom, Socrates, but you don't know a damn thing! After God guided me safely through that valley of death during the war, I made a *commitment* to Him and to my Catholic faith." I felt blood rush to my cheeks and realized I was yelling. I lowered my voice. "Since then, I've invested as many years becoming a priest as I did becoming a doctor. The Church has come to be my home, my culture, my community. It's my identity now. This isn't a simple matter of quitting my current job. I'd be abandoning an essential part of *who I am* … but more importantly, I'd be breaking a solemn oath to God."

How to explain? "In a way, it's a little like a loving couple who have grown apart but still care about each other. If I decide to leave the priesthood, I need to believe it's for the best in God's eyes as well as mine. Please don't pretend that you have the vaguest idea of what this decision means to me."

"All I'm saying, Jake, is the Church has endured great hardships and challenges for over two thousand years and survived. They'll be fine if they lose you as a priest. But after his mother and now Colleen, *any* more loss for RJ could be devastating. He'll need you present in his life more than ever. It's simply cost vs. benefit. Your love of the priesthood in exchange for a child's well-being. You need to make the sacrifice for RJ's welfare." The big guy shook his head. "That's how I feel. Sorry if I'm out of line."

"Damn right you are! My life, my decision. End of discussion, Tree." I was seething because he had opened a door I was trying to keep closed. But he wasn't wrong. I drew a deep breath. "Any other life-changing wisdom you wish to impart?"

"No, but I do want to thank you for the warning. Your phone call saved my ass. My deputies and I would been blown to kingdom come if we'd come charging in the front door of the rectory last night, and half the neighborhood would be rubble. Giordano had rigged the place with enough explosives to level a small third-world country. Took the bomb squad all night to disarm it." He laughed. "They even had to call in a damn animal wrangler to cage Snapp's crazy-ass bird. The thing was dive-bombing everyone, and they were afraid it would accidentally blow the joint up."

"That crazy-ass bird saved my life." I paused. "And Giordano?"

"He made it to the hospital just in time … to be pronounced dead. I'm not gonna shed one damn tear for that piece of shit, Jake. What you did was clearly self-defense. There won't be any inquiry or charges, but …." He handed me the Cleveland Plain Dealer and the Lorain Journal. "Thought you should see these. The press is having a field day. Didn't want you to be blindsided."

My photograph was on the front page of both newspapers. The headline of one read PRIEST KILLS KILLER! The other, ONE SWING OF THE BAT. I read the first paragraph: "Father Jacob Austin played high school baseball in Oberlin where he developed his killer swing. Last night he knocked a murderer out of the park."

"Is this garbage on the television and radio too, Tree?"

"Yeah. The damn reporters are swarming all over town like locusts."

"Unbelievable." I tossed the newspapers on the bedside tray table.

Tree's cellphone chimed. He checked the screen, then silenced it. "I got a meeting with the City Manager in an hour, and a phone call with the Governor later this afternoon. Lunatic bombers running around with explosives make voters nervous and politicians worried about their reelections. They want to cover their own behinds, which means I'll be on the hot seat. You're not the only one in the spotlight." He stood. "Gotta run, buddy. Hang in there. I'll stop by later."

After dinner, Maya Ruiz peeked in and said, "I heard what happened, Dr. Austin. I'm so sorry. Is there anything I can do for you before I head home?"

"There is. Please check on Colleen Brady's condition. She's a close friend who had surgery earlier today."

"Will do."

After she left, I complained to the nurse about post-op pain in my thigh. She gave me a whopping dose of pain medication, and that was the last thing I remember until the sun came up the next morning.

CHAPTER FIFTY ONE

Tuesday, May 13, 8:00 a.m.

I had just finished breakfast when Maya Ruiz entered my room.

"I looked in on Colleen Brady as you asked, Dr. Austin. Her vital signs have stabilized, but she lost a lot of blood and was in the operating room a long time. The stab wound to her belly did serious damage." She shrugged her shoulders. "At her age, who know? The long term prognosis is decent, but her recovery will likely be rocky and protracted."

I knew from experience that recovery from that type of injury would be prolonged and difficult for a young person, let alone someone in her sixties. But Colleen was one of the toughest people I knew. My money was on her.

"Thanks for the update, Maya. I appreciate it."

"She asked about you. Said she wanted to talk with you when you're feeling up to it." Maya's beeper screeched and she checked the number. "Sorry, duty calls. Gotta go."

I'd finished praying for Colleen's recovery when RJ, Emily, and her father entered my room. Their visit lifted my sagging spirits. They made an early exit, however, when Bishop Lucci appeared at my door, a scowl on his face.

Wrapped in his enormous robes and the purple sash indicative of his rank, he waddled his great bulk over to my bed, the gemstone-encrusted cross hung from a gold chain around his neck swaying as he came. Although he had the appearance of a chubby cherub, I knew from experience that his starched piety was a disguise he wore to conceal the ruthless, domineering autocrat that he was. Any visit from His Excellency boded nothing good.

His voice was warm, his eyes ice cold. "I heard what happened, Father. I've been praying for you." He glanced at the newspapers. "Praying not only for your recovery, but also for the Lord to give you guidance and clarity."

He shook his head, his jowls wobbling side to side. "Jacob, Jacob. What am I to do with you?" He pointed at the headlines. "The Church has had enough bad press without *this*. From the day you arrived, you've brought nothing but chaos into my once tranquil diocese." He removed his tortoise-shell glasses and rubbed his eyes. "And then there's the matter of your … lady friend. Have you burned that bridge to your past yet?"

I must have hesitated too long.

"Come now, my son, we've discussed this. You must shed these feelings and commit one hundred percent to God."

Commanding me to stop caring for Emily was like ordering the sun not to shine or the wind not to blow. It was far too late to unlove her.

"We're not lovers, Your Excellency, if that's what you're implying. I haven't broken my vows. But … I *do* love her, and always have. I care deeply for her, and *that* will never change."

He returned his glasses to his nose, the thick lenses magnifying the dark bags under his eyes. "I'm sorry to hear that your … dilemma remains unsolved. And the boy? Why haven't you put him up for adoption to a good Catholic home? A loving *two parent* family would be best for the child."

The two parent family I envisioned would require the Vatican to grant me permission to marry Emily, and that was never going to happen. Was loving *both* her and the Lord being selfish?

"RJ *is* my family, Your Excellency. He's the only family I have left. I refuse to warehouse him in foster care, or entrust his care to strangers. I promised my sister on her deathbed that I'd look after him, and that's exactly what I intend to do."

He stepped closer, his dark eyes boring into me.

"Then we have a problem, Jacob. The woman, the boy, and the scandal you bring to my diocese … and now taking a man's life! It's more than I'm willing to tolerate. You've become a distraction and a hindrance, rather than an asset. You should submit your request for an indult of laicization from the priesthood, and petition the Vatican to release you from you vows."

Perhaps the bishop was right. Maybe I *should* resign from the priesthood. But I loved serving the Lord. How could I give that up? It was as much a part of me as an arm or a leg!

He *was* right about two things, though. First, Emily and I couldn't continue our bizarre hokey-pokey relationship—one foot in and one foot out. We loved each other, and living this way was Purgatory on earth. And second, RJ needed a stable home, and I couldn't provide that by myself. Colleen had been the only reason I'd been able to raise my nephew and still serve the Church, as well as my hospital patients.

Bishop Lucci walked to the window and looked out. When he turned toward me again, sunlight twinkled on his balding pate.

"As badly as I need priests in my diocese and the hospital needs doctors to treat the poor, Jacob, I believe you are no longer fit for the priesthood. I will be in contact with your Superior General to discuss your future. I'm certain my good friend, Stefano Demarco, will agree with me that your time in service to the Lord is over."

Lucci strode out of the door without looking back.

CHAPTER FIFTY TWO

Tuesday, May 13, 1:00 p.m.

Word of my injury was out, and afternoon visiting hours brought a parade of friends, parishioners, and colleagues. My room soon began to fill with flowers, cards, and wishes for a speedy recovery.

Although their love and support was appreciated, when visiting hours ended, the specter of Bishop Lucci's visit came roaring back to haunt me. He'd rattled me, not because he wanted me out of his diocese and the priesthood, but because everything he had said was true. Maybe I *wasn't* fit for the priesthood.

I'd joined a religious order to place my life in service to God. Yet my feelings for Emily would *always* be a potential impediment to my vows, and knowing that she felt the same way about me made living without her all the more painful.

Corinthians tells us love is patient, but that's not always true, at least not for me. Even after all these years, my desire for her was so fierce that at times it caused me to tremble. But that didn't mean I didn't love the Lord fully and completely, only that when it came to my passion for Emily, my head would always be at war with my heart.

I also took pleasure in supporting my parishioners, guiding them through good times and bad in the same way I enjoyed caring for patients at the hospital. Wasn't that an expression of love? How could I give that up? The heart's capacity for love is endless. One love does not preclude another—but in the eyes of the Church, it did.

And without a doubt, RJ was the greatest blessing I'd ever received. God had placed this precious child in my care for a *reason*. He definitely deserved a better childhood than I could provide alone. But even with help from what remained of my chosen family, caring for him without Colleen at my side would be nearly impossible. And if Bishop Lucci convinced my Superior General to reassign me elsewhere, what would I do? Emily couldn't leave her elderly father, and Tree had a family and career here in town. Moving with RJ would totally eliminate my boy's support system, and I would lose my two best friends.

I was ensnared in a damn Catch 22 of my own making. I'd made two conflicting sacred promises: one to my sister to care for her child, and one to God—and I couldn't bring myself to betray either one—yet the conflict was preventing me from committing fully to either.

I sat on the edge of the bed, my head in my hands, praying for a solution and brooding over my predicament. My cellphone's chime dragged me back to reality: Milwaukee area code. I suspected that Bishop Lucci had lit a fire under my Superior General, and Demarco had wasted no time calling me.

"I heard what happened to you, Jacob. You're in my prayers. I've placed you on a leave of absence until you're feeling better."

"Thank you."

He cleared his throat. "I just had an unpleasant conversation, however, with Bishop Lucci. He's convinced you're unable to perform your duties, that the Church is no longer your priority."

"That's not true! Celebrating the Sacraments, consecrating the bread and wine, holding the body and blood of Christ in my hands is the miracle and the joy that gets me out of bed every morning. When I entered the seminary, there was *zero* chance that I'd be responsible for raising a child—but then when my sister died, suddenly I was." I massaged the back of my neck. "I refuse to believe that Jesus would have wanted me to turn my back on my nephew, or on *any* child. The only reason I've been able to perform my duties at the church and the hospital, and still provide my nephew with a stable home life, was because his nanny, Colleen, loved him as much as I did. But she's been severely injured and may not survive. That changes everything."

"I know it's hard, Jacob, to live the solitary life of a priest with one foot in this world, and one in the next. Many priests struggle, but there's Grace in the struggle itself, and great blessings that come with serving the Lord." Demarco cleared his throat. "I understand *your* situation is unique and complex, but there are options. You could hire someone else to care for your nephew."

"Who? Some teenager who's more interested in the latest pop song or the color of her prom dress than in RJ's well-being? Or an elderly person who could die within a year, adding more upheaval to his young life? How many temporary babysitters would I have to audition before I was lucky enough to find someone who cared for him the way Colleen did. No, with all that's happened, I can't put RJ through that kind of turmoil." My voice had risen and I ratcheted it down a notch. "But if I focus on RJ's welfare and leave the Church, I'll be breaking my solemn vow to God, and failing to be the man I hoped to be. I'm being pulled in two different directions and don't know what to do."

"Don't lay that kind of burden on yourself. We all have struggles and failings. Yet God somehow manages to work through *imperfect* people in imperfect churches to bring Divine Grace to this imperfect world. As for your nephew, Jacob, I consider your commitment to him an act of Christian charity, and I fully support your effort. But with all you do at the hospital and the church, bringing up a child alone will be nearly impossible. Is there no one in your life now who can help raise him?"

"There is." I drew a long, slow breath. "My friend, Emily Beale. She loves RJ and has been a second mother to him since my sister died."

"Oh, I see." Demarco went silent, "You'll need someone every day and at all hours to care for your nephew. Knowing how you feel about her, I cannot sanction that. A woman, one you have strong feelings for, in the rectory? Impossible. For that, you'd have to leave the priesthood. I would hate to lose you as a priest and as my investigator, but I see no other way out of your predicament." He sighed. "The Almighty gave us this world, but it's our job to serve Him by making our small part of it as close to perfect as we can. Only you can decide *how* to do that."

Demarco paused. "Think long and hard about your needs, desires, and priorities, Jacob. There are many ways to embrace the sacred, many ways to serve the Lord. If you act with integrity and faithfulness, God will make use of your gifts. Pray hard on the matter. God will respond. Maybe not with the answer you'd hope for, but He will guide you. Whenever you are conflicted and discouraged, *that's* the time to listen deeply for His whisper."

CHAPTER FIFTY THREE

Tuesday, May 13, 4:30 p.m.

My head was spinning after my encounter with Bishop Lucci and the telephone call from my Superior General. My entire world seemed upside down, yet all I was doing was lying in bed feeling sorry for myself and worrying about the future.

I asked the nurse for a wheelchair, then rolled myself to Colleen's room and peeked in the door. She looked as if she'd aged two decades since I'd last seen her. Her white hair was in complete disarray, and there was a nasty bruise on her cheek. A thick post-operative dressing bulged the covers over her abdomen, and two IV lines hung next to her bed.

I fought back tears and knocked on the door frame, then wheeled up next to her bed. "Colleen, I'm so sorry! This is my fault."

She turned her head slowly toward me. "I'll hear no more of that nonsense, Father," she replied in a voice so hoarse and faint it was barely audible. "You warned me to leave. 'Tis I who chose to stay and … I who gave that *devil* the alarm code. 'Tis I who should be apologizing." She stopped to catch her breath. "Thank the Lord you and RJ are alive!"

I took her hand in mine and tried to find words that wouldn't come. Finally she said, "I'm glad you came, Father, for I've something to tell you. For a while now, I've been longing to return to my family in Ireland. You know I love you and RJ but …." She pointed to her abdomen. "Now, after all this … it's time. I'm sorry, Father, but I need to return home. You and the lad will be just fine without me."

"No, the lad and I will miss you terribly," I said and kissed her hand, "but I understand."

"Let's not make this any harder than it already is, Father." She reclaimed her hand. "Just remind that Superior General of yours that there are churches in Ireland and souls in need of saving across the pond. I'd love to show you and RJ around my village someday." She pointed to the door. "Now go and get some rest. You look like Satan himself mopped the floor with you."

That night, I prayed late into the evening, asking for God's guidance. My throbbing leg wound and concern about how I would care for RJ, however, made for a restless night's sleep. Around three o'clock in the morning, the full moon streamed its light through my hospital window, ripping me from a fitful slumber. I considered requesting pain medication or a sleeping pill, but instead thought about what Father Demarco had said about reassessing my desires and priorities.

Emily and the priesthood were my desires. But God and RJ were my priorities; these were chiseled in granite. Given the Lord's great love of children and his commands to help the less fortunate, how could I not put RJ's needs ahead of mine?

It was as simple, and as complicated, as that.

I gazed up at the man in the moon and whispered, "You've been up there for eons, so you must have learned something. What should I do now?"

Much like the Almighty, he answered me with silence.

As far back as I could remember, life had happened *to* me. My father's desertion of our family when I was a child had sent me careening into my teenaged rebellion, which resulted in my stint in the Army and a bloody overseas war that had left me with years of guilt and regret.

I sat up in bed and stared out the window. Mr. Moon shined down on me, rock-steady in his indifference. The tides didn't move him. He moved the tides.

And in that moment, in the midst of my frustration and fatigue, I had an epiphany—not the kind I'd always hoped for, but an epiphany nonetheless. Call it a realization, a truth, an awakening, whatever you will. It doesn't matter. I knew what I needed to do.

In the Bible, Jesus commands us to *love* one another. Not the eleventh commandment, although perhaps it should be. Good advice for believers and atheists alike. For me, divine love and human love are inseparable, two sides of the same coin.

Out of love for us, Jesus sacrificed His own life. I too could forgo what I desired for those I loved. The Almighty had placed RJ in my care and Emily into my life, and that was more than I'd ever hoped for. I would honor His gift by loving them both to the best of my ability.

My love of God and my faith were non-negotiable, but as Demarco had said, there were many ways to embrace the sacred. I cherished being a priest and was passionate about my vocation, but it was preventing me from fully embracing the people I loved. If that love forced me to relinquish my role as a priest, I would make the sacrifice for them gladly and find other ways to honor and serve God and my faith.

That was my decision, between my Creator and myself. I hoped and prayed He would understand.

CHAPTER FIFTY FOUR

Wednesday, May 14, 9:00 a.m.

When office hours began in Milwaukee, I telephoned Father Demarco and explained my reasoning and conclusion. I told him I'd be submitting my indult of laicization from the priesthood.

"Not the answer I'd hoped for, Jacob. The religious life is not for the faint of heart, and I certainly understand how difficult and lonely our spiritual journey can be through this secular world. It's your decision to make, of course, but you'd be giving up a great deal. I fear that you'll be left with a profound emptiness if you resign."

Silence passed between us.

"Do you intend to marry then, Jacob?"

"Absolutely, if Emily will have me … and if the Vatican will release me from my vows. Together we could provide RJ with a better childhood than I had growing up."

"I see." Demarco cleared his throat. "Knowing you as well as I do, Jacob, the loss of your ministry saddens me. Not only because I'll be losing you as my investigator and my right hand, but because the Church needs compassionate, caring people like you."

I thought about Pat Lyons, his family life, and his faithful service to the Church as an ordained deacon. Having pulled off a miracle or two against the odds in the past, I rolled the dice.

"Since I was initially ordained as a deacon in seminary, is there any way I could leave the priesthood but remain a deacon? That would at least allow me to have a ministry of service to the church *and* a family with Emily. As a deacon, I could proclaim the Gospel, preach homilies, and assist the priest at the altar. My parishioners already know and trust me. If I was allowed to stay in town as a deacon, the transition at the church and hospital would be seamless, and I could continue to raise RJ where I have support from my friends."

"You never fail to surprise me. I'd say you're the master of thinking outside of the box, but I've come to believe that for you, there is no box." Demarco sighed. "In some ways, your proposal has merit. The Church has a shortage of priests and as a deacon you'd also be able to baptize babies, participate in marriage ceremonies, and counsel families, all while treating the underserved as a doctor at the hospital—except there are two major problems. To my knowledge, no priest has done that in over two thousand years. And to become a deacon with a family, you must be married *before* you're ordained.

He paused. "You know I'd help you in any way I could, Jacob, but you're grasping at straws. Once you leave the clerical state, there's no going back. Even if I unleashed an army of canon lawyers on your behalf and argued that you should have been ordained as a deacon, not as a priest, I doubt the Vatican would accept the premise. No, it would be better if you focused on being the best husband and parent that you can be."

"That much I can promise you. I'll find other ways to serve God and the Church, maybe by helping the homeless and feeding the hungry." I hesitated, then asked, "If the Church will allow, I would at least like to be a Lector and read scripture at Mass, and distribute Communion at the hospital and at the homes of shut-ins as a Lay Eucharistic Minister. Knowing that there might be some resistance after leaving the priesthood, would you be willing to advocate on my behalf?"

He considered the idea. "Although I wanted a priest as my investigator, I believe a creative *lay minister* just might do—so selfishly, yes, I will do what I can on your behalf. God be with you, my son. You'll be in my prayers."

And with that, my world became a little brighter. Hope, even a sliver, is a miraculous thing.

CHAPTER FIFTY FIVE

Wednesday, May 14, 10:00 a.m.

The moment I hung up with Demarco, I telephoned Tree and asked him to do a favor for me.

All he said was, "Navy blue box in the top drawer? I'm on it. Glad you finally came to your senses. Be there in an hour, buddy."

Emily returned that afternoon with RJ and her father. My nephew ran to the hospital bed, crawled up, and gave me a warm embrace.

Irv said, "I visited Colleen this morning. Broke my heart, but she's a strong woman and if anyone can get through this, she can. She, ah, told me about her plans to retire in Ireland when she's better, so ... if there's anything Emily and I can do to help, just ask."

"Thanks, Irv. I'm going to need all the support I can get."

We chatted for a while, sticking to light topics, avoiding any mention of violence, surgery, or hospitals. Finally Irv said, "I have to get back to the snack shop and relieve my friend. I could use some help, RJ. You wanna come? I'll show you how to make milkshakes."

A 100-watt smile lit up my boy's face.

"What flavor do you like, young man?"

"Chocolate."

"Personally, I prefer strawberry." Irv wrinkled his brow as if giving a difficult problem serious consideration. "Maybe we could make one of each. What do you think?"

RJ hopped down from the bed, took Irv's hand, and they headed to the snack shop.

"For a kid," Emily said, "a milkshake may be the perfect medicine. Like chicken soup, it may not cure all that ails you, but it tastes great and it couldn't hurt."

"True." I smiled. "Did you and RJ get any rest, Em?"

She nodded.

"Good, because I have something important to discuss."

She inclined her head to the side and a sheet of auburn hair fell across one eye. She swept it behind her ear, then inched her chair closer to my bed. I told her about my conversations with Bishop Lucci and my Superior General. She raised her eyebrows but didn't respond.

I eased my injured leg over the side of the bed, winced, and sat up. "I've decided to leave the priesthood, Em." I focused on her expression, searching for a reaction. "I want us to be together."

She chewed her lower lip, and her eyes narrowed. A very long silence passed, way to long for comfort.

"Listen, Jake, I love you. You know that," she said in a voice as soft as an angel sighing. "But ... I'm aware of how much the priesthood means to you. I refuse to be the reason you abandon it."

"No, I'm not leaving *because* of you. I'm not running away from the priesthood. I'm running *toward* the family I've always wanted, toward the people I love. I want to have you and RJ fully in my life. I may no longer be able to do the Lord's work as I'd once hoped, but I will find other ways to serve Him."

I tried to stand, but burning pain raced from my thigh down my leg like a wildfire. I eased back down and waited for a reply from her that didn't come.

Now what, genius? I thought. *You've already burned the bridge with Demarco and the Church. What if she says ... no?*

I tried again to stand but failed. "I'd get down on one knee, Em, but ... you know, the bullet wound." I leaned forward and plunged into the bottomless blue of her eyes. "So, Emily Beale ... will you marry me?"

She stood, leaned over, found my face with her hand, and kissed me—long and slow, in a way that left me feeling weightless.

Emily pulled away, then grinned. "Without a doubt, Jake, that is the *lamest* marriage proposal in history. Excuse the pun." She chuckled. "It's a good thing love is as blind as I am."

She sat on the bed next to me. "Fortunately for you, I'm a modern woman and for a chance to have RJ in my life—yes, I'd even *marry* you." Then she punctuated her reply with that killer smile of hers.

She leaned in and kissed me again, deep and hungry this time, the tip of her tongue trailing over my lips as she pulled away. Her perfume lingered, the light floral scent stirring the ghosts of our past and promises of our future.

"But I have one condition, Jake." Her mood became serious. "Guardianship is not enough. As soon as you're able, I want you to hobble that battered body of yours down the aisle so we can marry and the two of us can adopt RJ." Her smile returned. "I can't wait to spend more time with the *younger* man in my life."

"Deal. Any other demands, Your Majesty?"

"A ring would be nice."

I reached into a drawer in the bedside table and handed her a small, blue velvet-covered box. Her expression told me that she had a good idea what was inside. She was wrong.

When she opened the box, removed the ring, and examined it with her fingers, her confidence wavered. It was too lightweight to be an engagement ring and had an engraved heart where a precious stone should have been. I was relieved she couldn't see that the cheap silver-plating had lost its luster and was flaking.

"What ...?" Her confidence collapsed. "I ... I don't understand, Jake."

"It's the promise ring I gave you in high school. The one with our initials inside the heart. Remember? The one you returned when we broke up."

I glanced at the sprinkle of chocolate freckles on her cheek, then ran my hand gently along the arc of her face.

"That ring has traveled with me all these years, Em, as a reminder of paradise lost." I slipped it on her finger. "I meant it then, and I mean it now. I love you, Emily Beale. That ring is my promise that my love for you will never change."

Our kiss this time turned urgent, our embrace desperate. The rush of passion made me lightheaded. For one glorious moment, my hands explored the taper of her waist, the gentle swell of her hips. I was delirious, ecstatic, and wildly adrift in a torrent of emotions.

As our lips parted, I heard the one word in this world that I truly cherished.

"Daddy!" RJ ran to me. "Irv let me make milkshakes and work behind the counter and run the cash register and *everything*. It was soooo cool!"

We broke the happy news of our engagement to Irv and RJ, then spent an hour talking about everything and nothing until a dietician brought my supper tray and they left for dinner in the cafeteria.

I had trouble sleeping that evening, not only because of the excitement about our engagement, but because I couldn't get the events of the past month out of my thoughts: the Night Nurse on the elevator and the trail of evidence guiding us to her murderer, and my misinterpretation of Father Wronka's involvement with Jodi Saroyan leading to a false accusation of pedophilia, then our unlikely alliance resulting in the arrest of Lottie Trumble and Chase Masterson.

When I finally fell asleep, I dreamt I was locked in a cage, watching Giordano torture Colleen while she pleaded for my help. Then images of Snapp's van exploding morphed into the expression on Giordano's face as my baseball bat hit its mark, yanking me back to consciousness, drenched in sweat.

I stared out the window at the moon and pondered what a strange circuitous journey my life had been. Every turn, every fork in the road, had lead me in unexpected directions, and yet I'd arrived at a destination far better than anything I'd ever hoped for—Emily and RJ in my life, *and* new ways to continue serving my faith.

God and His mysterious ways? Serendipity? Destiny? Who can say?

My mind was spinning with a carousel of images and emotions but around four in the morning, I drifted off to sleep. At one point, I was awakened by the soft cooing of a baby … and I swear, when I opened my eyes, the Night Nurse was standing at the foot of my bed, bathed in moonlight. The smell of smoke that had previously accompanied her had been replaced by the scent of lilies. She nuzzled her baby in her arms, smiled down on me, nodded twice … then walked right through the wall.

Or maybe it was just a dream.

Or … maybe not.

CHAPTER FIFTY SIX

Saturday, November 22, 2:00 p.m.

Six months later, on the Saturday before Thanksgiving, Tree stood next to me, a grin on his lips. Dressed in a navy-blue suit and silk tie, the big guy looked almost regal. But RJ stole the show when he marched solemnly down the aisle in his bowtie and boutonnière, lifted a pillow up to Tree, and presented the wedding rings.

As Mendelssohn's "Wedding March" began, RJ walked over to Colleen, who was seated in the front pew, and gave her a hug. Then he skipped back to the nave's entrance and proudly guided Emily and her father down the aisle to the delight of all assembled. Even Father Snapp, seated in the back of the church, smiled.

Stained-glass light from the church windows transformed Emily's white gown and veil into a kaleidoscope of rainbow colors as she joined me at the altar. In that moment, however, she seemed to radiate her own light.

When Emily stopped next to me, RJ walked over to Tree and stood beside him as my *other* best man.

The love of my life smiled up at me, and for a few seconds the world fell away, leaving only the two of us. I took her hand and we turned to face the altar, knowing we would have much to be thankful for this Thanksgiving.

ABOUT THE AUTHOR

© Ed von Hofen

John Vanek is a physician by training, but a writer by passion. While practicing medicine for a quarter century, his interest in writing never waned. Medicine is his life, but mysteries are his drug of choice. He began honing his craft by attending creative writing workshops and college courses. At first writing solely for himself and his family, he was surprised and gratified when his work won contests and was published in a variety of literary journals, anthologies, and magazines.

He now lives happily as an ink-stained-wretch in Florida, where he teaches a poetry workshop for seniors and enjoys swimming, hiking, sunshine, good friends, and red wine. For more information, go to www.JohnVanekAuthor.com